HOMETOWN DETECTIVE

Jennifer Morey

HARLEQUIN® ROMANTIC SUSPENSE

Recycling programs
for this product may
not exist in your area.

ISBN-13: 978-1-335-45644-1

Hometown Detective

Copyright © 2018 by Jennifer Morey

All rights reserved. Except for use in any review, the reproduction or utilization of this work in whole or in part in any form by any electronic, mechanical or other means, now known or hereafter invented, including xerography, photocopying and recording, or in any information storage or retrieval system, is forbidden without the written permission of the publisher, Harlequin Enterprises Limited, 22 Adelaide St. West, 40th Floor, Toronto, Ontario M5H 4E3, Canada.

This is a work of fiction. Names, characters, places and incidents are either the product of the author's imagination or are used fictitiously, and any resemblance to actual persons, living or dead, business establishments, events or locales is entirely coincidental.

This edition published by arrangement with Harlequin Books S.A.

For questions and comments about the quality of this book, please contact us at CustomerService@Harlequin.com.

® and TM are trademarks of Harlequin Enterprises Limited or its corporate affiliates. Trademarks indicated with ® are registered in the United States Patent and Trademark Office, the Canadian Intellectual Property Office and in other countries.

Printed in U.S.A.

Two-time RITA® Award nominee and Golden Quill award-winner **Jennifer Morey** writes single-title contemporary romance and page-turning romantic suspense. She has a geology degree and has managed export programs in compliance with the International Traffic in Arms Regulations (ITAR) for the aerospace industry. She lives at the foot of the Rocky Mountains in Denver, Colorado, and loves to hear from readers through her website, jennifermorey.com, or Facebook.

Books by Jennifer Morey

Harlequin Romantic Suspense

Cold Case Detectives

A Wanted Man
Justice Hunter
Cold Case Recruit
Taming Deputy Harlow
Runaway Heiress
Hometown Detective

The Coltons of Shadow Creek

Mission: Colton Justice

The Coltons of Texas

A Baby for Agent Colton

Ivy Avengers

Front Page Affair
Armed and Famous
One Secret Night
The Eligible Suspect

All McQueen's Men

The Secret Soldier
Heiress Under Fire
Unmasking the Mercenary
Special Ops Affair
Seducing the Accomplice
Seducing the Colonel's Daughter

Visit Jennifer's Author Profile page at Harlequin.com, or jennifermorey.com, for more titles.

For Mom. Wish you were here to see this.

Chapter 1

The bakery owner approached the checkout counter with an anniversary bouquet and Kendra Scott's day brightened. One of her regulars, she knew him by name. She also gave him some of her business, but not because she felt obligated. Denny and his wife made the best pastries she'd ever tasted. A big guy, his lumbering gait made him seem like a teddy bear in an intimidating body. Kendra adored her customers, especially those who showed genuine love for their spouses. She also adored them when they kept her busy or provided much needed distractions over the last few days.

Waiting for Dark Alley Investigations to send a detective was beginning to grate on her. When would someone call? Jasper Roesch had told her he'd assign someone to her case, but so far no one had come. She was anxious to get started on the investigation into her twin sister's murder. She called it murder but the police hadn't. Yet. She'd get them to change their minds. Her twin sister did not commit suicide.

Denny made it to the counter and placed the bouquet down.

"What anniversary is this?" Kendra asked.

"Forty-two." Denny smiled, showing big boxy teeth that somehow matched his jean overalls over a white Henley. At first glance, he'd strike most as a local farmer, but he ran the town bakery with his wife. Kendra seldom met people married as long as them. Or as happy.

"What's your secret?"

Denny chuckled. "Tolerance."

She laughed with him as she finished his transaction, aware of another person in line behind him. "It can't be that simple." No amount of tolerance would have saved her closest encounter with love. She also found that choice of word peculiar. Tolerance could be a negative thing.

Denny sobered. "It's about respect. If you both have respect for each other, there's nothing you can't weather in a marriage. If you can't respect the person you're with, then you shouldn't be with them."

"That's good advice." People like him and his wife were a breath of fresh air. They never deviated from genuine honesty.

"You'll find it someday," Denny said.

She scoffed. "I'm doing just fine on my own. No hurry for that."

"Then you'll get the real deal." Denny took the bouquet. "Have a good night."

"Tell your wife Happy Anniversary for me."

"Will do." He left the counter and the next patron approached.

A short, skinny boy of maybe fifteen put a flowering plant and four Fourth of July ornaments onto the counter. Odd for a kid his age, not to mention the holiday was a couple of months away. She had ornaments for every holiday, all year round.

"Nice choice." She tried to place him but didn't recognize him. "You from around here?"

"My mom went to see a friend. I came in here to blow some time. We live across town."

Chesterville was big enough not to know everyone, but Kendra had gotten to know quite a few in the year she'd been here. She didn't know this kid and didn't believe he'd come into a Christmas shop because he liked the decor.

"Well, thanks for coming in to blow time." She smiled as she tallied up his purchases.

After a while, the boy asked, "You're that lady who called that famous detective agency, aren't you?"

Ah, there it was. The real reason. "Word travels all the way across town, huh?"

"My mom comes this way a lot. She grew up on this side."

She wouldn't get into that. The kid sounded like this side wasn't the better side but he was pretty young. *This side* had the most history in Chesterville, and the town center, which had been maintained wonderfully.

"I did go to Dark Alley Investigations."

"I see that man on TV a lot."

He meant Kadin Tandy. He and his agency frequently made the news. She waited for him to get to what he really wanted to know.

"Do you think your sister was really murdered?"

She could understand how the boy would take interest in a local hiring a private detective agency to look into her sister's suicide. Murder in a small town didn't go unnoticed. But this boy seemed more focused on the fame of DAI, a morbid hero worship. She'd better not encourage him.

She handed him a bag and pushed the plant toward him. "Thanks for coming in today."

The boy took the bag and cradled the plant in one arm. "Do you think I could meet the detective?"

"I don't know who they're going to send." If they sent anyone. She hadn't heard from them.

Seeing a car drive up in front, she said to the boy, "Looks like your mother is all finished."

The boy looked back and then, with one last look at her, reluctantly headed toward the exit.

With the last ring of the storefront door, Kendra clicked on her computer to close out the day. Elegant, upbeat modern classical music still played softly, and now that the sun had set, Christmas tree lights glittered beautifully. Matching bows and ribbons drew the eye. Accessories, bouquets and plants popped multiple colors from shopping counters. Customers could meander through the artful displays. This was her favorite time of day. Evening, all alone in her dream come true. If only her sister was alive to share this. Kendra had moved from Chicago after her death. She felt closer to her here.

Closing down the computer, she left the counter to tidy up and lock the front door. She never tired of seeing the creativity that filled the ample space of her flower shop. Not a typical flower shop, hers specialized in Christmas. She did generate enough business in the off-season to stay profitable, though. Being located in a prime section of Main Street did help.

Nothing in her shop disappointed. Color and texture flowed. Aroma charmed the senses. Music relaxed. A cleaning service kept everything looking fresh and new. She took great pains to maintain flawless presentation.

At one side of the shop, attractive pendant lighting spotlighted small round tables in the coffee and pastry section, a corner wall of shelves filled with books and magazines covering topics ranging from home improvement to gardening added to the inviting coziness. She put books and magazines back in their place, and then headed for the display counters, righting a fallen stuffed bear and turning vases for the best angle. On the other side of the shop, slide-open refrigerators took up most of the wall. Nothing looked out of place in there.

Her best friend in college called her tenacious. Kendra called it ambition. Drive. Maybe even survival.

Winding her way through decorated Christmas trees, she went to the front door and inserted the key to turn the lock. Outside, streetlights lit the sidewalk. No cars drove by at nearly nine-thirty and no one walked the street. The pub at the corner across the street always had someone coming in or out. A man stood near the door, leaning on a lamppost, one black-booted foot crossed over the other. He seemed to be looking at her.

She couldn't see him clearly. Lean rather than noticeably muscular, he towered over others passing on the way to the pub. He had dark, wavy short hair and wore a black short-sleeved golf shirt with light blue jeans. With his face still directed toward her, she had the feeling he wasn't bothered that she saw him.

Apprehension crept over her. Most believed Kaelyn Johnston had committed suicide as the coroner had ruled. No one had questioned that until Kendra had called Dark Alley Investigations. While Kaelyn had died in a small, off-the-map town in Michigan, she had spent her adopted years in Chesterville, West Virginia.

If Kaelyn had been murdered, her killer wouldn't want anyone exposing him, least of all an infamous investigations agency. She always grew nervous when she spotted suspicious strangers. The one across the street didn't approach, only stayed where he was, watching. Maybe she had nothing to worry about. And why would the killer take an interest in her now, after all this time she'd been here? Hiring DAI could provoke a killer, but DAI hadn't taken the case yet.

Leaving the front windows, Kendra let the music, lights and ambience take her away. They didn't take her far enough. She went to the back of the shop, through a wooden door into her office, and sat behind the desk to close out the day. The man watching her disturbed her. He might have nothing to do with her sister's murder, but how would she know that?

She looked down at the notes she'd made over the last several months. Before her sister had died, they had been in contact. Kaelyn had found her after months of searching. They had just begun to get to know each other again, filling in the gap from when they were six. Kendra had loved every phone call and meeting. Kaelyn had always arranged for them to meet in Chesterville. A few times, she'd gone to Chicago to see Kendra. She was thrilled to have some semblance of a family again. But toward the end, Kaelyn had hinted at some darkness. While she had told her many good things about her life, she'd touched on some others that weren't. Her husband abused her. Kaelyn hadn't come out and said the word *abused* but Kendra could read between the lines.

Then Kaelyn had killed herself. Or so everyone thought.

At first, Kendra had believed her sister had committed suicide. The devastation had overwhelmed her. Why would Kaelyn do such a thing? Her sister ending her life didn't make sense. The Kaelyn she'd met hadn't seemed to have reached that point. She'd seemed to have been keeping something troubling from Kendra, but she'd had too much life in her and far too much excitement over reuniting with her twin sister.

Only after her sister's death had she realized Kaelyn had told no one about her. When she'd shown up at the funeral, no one recognized her, not by name or appearance. They were fraternal twins, not identical, so it hadn't been surprising that no one had identified her. What she did find surprising was that she and Kaelyn had been corresponding for months. They'd even talked about the possibility of moving to Chesterville. Kaelyn said she would leave her husband and asked if Kendra would relocate. That had been a big request and Kendra had needed time to think on it. Kaelyn had died before she could agree to the fabulous idea. Kaelyn's parents were in Chesterville. Her daughter had still been in high school so Kaelyn would have taken her with her. Kendra would have a family again. But then Kaelyn had died.

Why had Kaelyn kept her twin a secret from those

in her life? There could be only one explanation. Kaelyn must had intended to use Kendra as an escape route. She would build a new life in Chesterville that didn't include her abusive husband. Plus, if he'd known his wife was talking to her twin, he may have felt threatened enough to stop her from corresponding, especially if he knew Kendra planned to move to Chesterville, where the two of them could see each other much more often.

She'd confirmed her own suspicions when she'd learned Kaelyn's husband *had* been abusing her and Kaelyn's plans to leave weren't just talk. Kaelyn would have moved back to Chesterville. Kendra had no proof, only a certainty that her twin would not have committed suicide.

After learning Kaelyn's daughter, Raelyn, had moved to Chesterville after she'd graduated from college, Kendra had decided to move here. She had felt so robbed after Kaelyn had been taken from her when she'd only just begun to get to know her again. Being close to her daughter was all she had left now. They could make a fragmented family but a family nonetheless.

Raelyn had moved in with her grandmother until she'd gotten her own place. Adoptive grandmother notwithstanding, Raelyn must have come here not only to get away from her horrible father, but to be close to the only family she felt she had.

Kendra had spoken to Raelyn on several occasions, first shortly after Kaelyn's funeral, then when she followed her to Chesterville. The twenty-two-year-old was uncomfortable welcoming her mother's twin. She harbored a lot of anger, Kendra presumed, because by killing herself, Kaelyn left her daughter alone with an abusive dad. Kendra decided to leave her be, telling her to call when she was ready to talk. That had been a year ago. Kendra had lived in Chesterville for two years so far and Kaelyn had been murdered almost five years ago.

Kendra remembered the man outside and decided not to stay too late. Getting her things, she went downstairs and left through the back door. Searching for any sign of someone lingering, she walked down the alley toward her house.

After watching Kendra close her shop, Roman Cooper walked down the street toward the historic hotel where he'd checked in earlier. He planned to meet with Kendra in the morning, write his report and head back to Wyoming. The redheaded beauty moved in her element like a fiery angel. Tall and slender, thick hair left down and natural, she smiled at everyone and spent most of her time ringing in purchases. A zombie apocalypse could be happening all around her but she would go on and continue prospering. Just watching her agitated him enough to light up a smoke. Too bad he'd quit.

He could spot people like her a mile away. Life's bounty fell at their feet. They had charmed, sheltered childhoods, lacked neither money nor imagination, and they only had to reach out and take anything they decided to have. Career. Money. House. Business. Whatever they desired. Nothing bad ever happened to them and they lived in denial that anything ever would. Maybe nothing bad would until the day they died. Roman didn't live that way. He had no illusions

of how awful life could be for some people. Not following a dream—or even knowing what to dream about—
only made it worse. That was the biggest unfairness for
him, not knowing his true calling. Meeting people like
Kendra reminded him of that. She probably lived with
the happy satisfaction that she had found her calling.

Ambition. Failure before success. Yeah, he got all
that. Ambition had gotten him where he was today.
What he could never grasp is how people like Kendra
Scott *knew* what they wanted in life. How did anyone
know that? Did an idea drop into their brain one ran-
dom night or were they born with it already implanted?

Roman wasn't a hopeless pessimist. He could relax
and have a good time with anyone. He just couldn't
live in a cushy bubble that blocked reality.

He passed familiar shops along his way, reminded
again of Kendra's graceful yet wild attractiveness.
Okay, he had to admit her striking beauty did have
something to do with his reluctance to meet her. She
might lasso him into sticking around too long.

Damn Kadin for sending him here. He'd done that
on purpose.

Kendra left Lund's Bakery as she did every Wednesday morning with a box of scones. Stepping out onto
the sidewalk, she collided with someone who had just
appeared in the opening of the bakery. Bouncing backward, she bumped against the still-open door, and with
her hand still gripping the handle, her arm wrenched.

"Ah!"

The man moved back quick enough. Supporting her
arm, he steadied her so that she could free her hand
from the handle.

Holding her fingers, she looked up from legs to hips to impressive chest to the face she'd seen last night. Although he'd been across the street, there was no mistaking his build and the general way he held himself. Tall and imposing, he held an aura of fearless confidence and something darker.

She took two steps back. "You."

Light gray eyes changed from concern to questioning. "Me?"

"I…I saw you outside my…my shop…last night." Maybe she shouldn't reveal that. What if he was a killer?

She took another step back.

Taking note of her reaction, he grew shrewdly alert. "Were you looking for someone?"

Why would he ask her that? "No."

"You're just observant?"

"Who the hell are you?" She'd hardly tell a stranger his impressive build had drawn her attention to him, a peppering of sexy along with a dash of danger.

A half grin almost softened the hardness in his eyes. "Roman Cooper. Dark Alley Investigations. Didn't anyone let you know I was coming?"

No one had called her. Maybe Jasper Roesch thought Roman could introduce himself. He had promised to send someone.

She took in Roman's appearance, rugged but not unkempt. He was quite good-looking in a less than soft way. He was a detective? Although clean and lean, he carried the air of a rebel, a darkly handsome one. No reserved gentleman stood before her. He struck her as the type who let nothing stand in his way. She pictured detectives as more refined, caring more about appearances than their service to humanity.

"Why were you spying on me last night?" she asked.

He hesitated and that gave him away. "It was late."

Why did he lie? "Jasper said he was going to send a detective. I was hoping he'd change his mind and take the case himself."

"He's busy getting married and having a baby right now."

He didn't sound impressed. In fact, he sounded a little condescending, as though marriage should never take priority over a case.

"Did you look into my sister's case?"

"She doesn't have a case," he said. "The coroner's report told me everything I needed to know. I agree with his assessment."

Anger billowed up in a wave. So typical of what she expected in some people! "It is easier to agree with what's already there. What were you going to do? Leave town without talking to me?"

"I would have met with you and you would have received a copy of my report."

"But now that you've conveniently run into me, you don't have to?" She wiped her hands together. "Problem solved?"

"I don't mean to upset you."

"There are other aspects to this case. You can't just read a coroner's report and agree with it. What if the coroner was wrong?"

"He's a good coroner."

"Good coroners can make honest mistakes."

His handsome head bent a little, as though beseeching for understanding. "I have other cases."

He wasn't being rude. He truly believed Kaelyn killed herself. That stung. "There are things you don't know that are important."

Now his brow rose marginally. "What things?"

"Why don't you just admit you don't care enough about my sister's case?"

"Your sister's death does appear to be a suicide. I'm sorry that's difficult for you to hear, but that's my assessment. What things don't I know?"

Her offense eased as she saw him open up to new information. "We talked a lot before her death," Kendra said. "Why do you think the police never questioned me?"

"They didn't need to."

Her ire pricked again, she said, "Kaelyn told no one about me, Mr. Cooper. I went to her funeral and no one knew me. She kept me a secret. Why would she do that?"

He appeared to begin to consider how that might change his initial assessment, but he didn't ask any questions, the biggest one being why she and Kaelyn were separated.

"Don't you see? I was part of Kaelyn's plan to escape her horrible husband. If she could get away without him knowing where she was going, she could be free. She would have run away and come to live near me. I'm sure of it."

Roman studied her a moment, his face unreadable. Then he lightened and asked, "Why don't you tell me more over a drink later?"

Unable to believe he'd suggested that, she gaped at him. Had he just asked her out on a *date*?

He nodded down the street toward the pub. "There. After you close tonight."

Kendra felt her jaw drop open, smart retorts popping to mind but not making their way to her tongue.

"Unless you'd rather I just send you the report?"

Chapter 2

Roman saw Kendra walking toward him on the sidewalk and felt a surge of triumph. He hadn't been sure she'd take the bait and meet him. He didn't think anything she said about her sister's death would change his initial assessment, but the contacts she'd had with her sister and their secretive nature had compelled him to at least follow up. And this wouldn't be a complete waste of time if he shared a nice evening with a beautiful woman. His drive to avenge victims led him to where he was most needed and he had other cases that needed him more than it appeared Kendra needed him, but one night wouldn't harm anything.

As she neared, he took in her form in a wide-leg, Jackie O–looking jumpsuit with a draped neckline, cap sleeves and a leather belt. He could see the hint of movement of her breasts and a slender waistline. She moved gracefully, long legs gliding along. She'd moved similarly in her shop last night, an angel in silhouette.

She stopped right before him. "The only reason I'm here is to talk about Kaelyn's murder."

"And have a drink with me." He held the pub door open for her.

She eyed him suspiciously as she passed.

Pete's Old Ale House teemed with business on this Wednesday evening. Workers celebrated hump day and others participated in a dart tournament. The bartender waved from behind the bar and Roman saw Kendra wave back. The fresh flowers on each round table and booth indicated the owner had a running account with her shop. She probably had a similar relationship with the baker. She must be well-known in town and have a good reputation. Marketing prowess or genuine lover of mankind? He'd met many ambitious women like her and none of them cared more about him than their passion for achievement. Still, something about her drew him in.

He followed her to the only round table left vacant. A group of men dressed in business casual laughed about the day's highlights at the table next to them. Two women leaned forward toward each other at a booth in an intense girl talk. The dart competition made the most noise, cheers from those standing near the throwing point and nearby tables filled with friends and spouses. Regulars sat at the bar, keeping to themselves or engaging in talk with the fellow beside them.

While not a kid place, the pub was clean and well maintained for its age, which must be more than a hundred years. The wood bar with its ornate and swirling trim looked original, but refurbished, same with the trim around the mirrored wall and shelves of booze bottles. The dark brown wood floor, polished and unblemished, must have been replaced. Modern pendant lighting over the bar and larger fixtures over the dining area provided ample illumination without the glare of brightness. Historical photos on the walls finished the aesthetic appeal.

The bartender spoke to the waitress on his way over to their table. She stopped and went to another table instead.

"Your usual?" the bartender asked.

"Hi, Pete. Yes."

"I'll have what she's having," Roman said, continuing to observe the pub and its inhabitants.

The bartender returned with frosty mugs of beer.

"Imported lager," she said, sipping. "Mmm."

"Do you come here because he buys your flowers or for the beer?" he asked.

She smiled, her bright and sunny personality shining through. "Both. Pete's a good guy."

"What about the baker?"

"He and his wife are kindhearted people who love each other. Most of us can only wish we were as lucky."

She seemed so humble for one who had so much. Uncomfortable with the spark that zapped him unexpectedly, Roman tasted the beer. Not bad. A little light, but not bad.

Her cheerful glow remained and she leaned back, drawing his attention to her teasingly concealed breasts. Why was he so attracted to her? He'd met pretty women like her before. What make her so different? If she was a cop or another detective, or anyone who worked in the trenches like him, he might understand these stirrings of desire. But she didn't work in the trenches. She had created a perfect world for herself, even surrounding herself with friends like Pete.

Time to slow down this Cupid's arrow. What better way than to beat her at a game of pool?

Standing, he picked up his beer. "You any good at pool?" He started for the single pool table, neglected on dart tournament night.

Lingering behind a second or two, she at last took her beer and followed. Her slow steps and curious eyes said she suspected his motives. Was this about pool or was this about the two of them?

"I thought we were going to discuss my sister's case." She stopped near him beside the pool table.

He choose a cue stick, ignoring how she kept calling her sister's death a case. He hadn't decided if it was one or not. "I'd like to get to know my new client before we get into death and destruction."

"Does that mean you're going to take the case?"

He had to admit, she had a strong theory that Kaelyn might have intended to run away and live near her secret twin. Kendra hadn't been mentioned anywhere in any reports he'd read.

"Let's play pool." He grinned in a way that often wooed women.

She eyed him warily—she didn't trust easily. He began to pick up on those undercurrents. She wanted to talk about Kaelyn Johnston's death, and he wanted to slow things down. She must know or have some idea that he was attracted to her.

Finally, her cautious nature eased a little and she stepped forward to put coins in the old game table.

Bent over as she inserted the coins, her eyes lifted and he saw a mischievous smile in them.

"I'm really good at this game," she said.

Delighted she'd relented and decided to have some fun, he said with equal flirtation, "Let's find out how good."

He racked the balls while she chose a stick. He liked watching her move, graceful arms and legs and a shapely butt.

Facing him with a stick, she chalked the end and looked at him.

"You break," he said.

"You are so going to lose."

Roman chuckled as he watched her break the balls and sink a solid. Moving around the table for her next shot, she gave him another nice view of her posterior as she made another shot. She sank another solid.

"When Kaelyn and I were six, I remember I was inside playing with dolls and she got mad at me for not wanting to go outside and play on the swing set." She lowered into position for a more complicated shot and sank yet another solid.

He began to wonder if he'd ever get to play.

"She went outside by herself." Kendra studied the table for her next shot. "After a while, I stopped playing dolls because I had this awful feeling. My first thought was of Kaelyn." She poised for another shot and missed this time. Unfazed, she faced him. "I left the bedroom we shared and went to the back door. My mother was out there and lifted Kaelyn. She had blood all over her face. My parents rushed her to the hospital and she had seventeen stitches put in her forehead. She pushed the double swing and it swung back and struck her. I felt so bad after that. If I'd have been with her, she wouldn't have been hurt."

What was the point of this story? He didn't ask.

"I felt that way on and off after we were split up, but I attributed it to my own situation. I felt that way again the day Kaelyn died."

Roman kept his expression carefully blank. She had a bad feeling the day Kaelyn killed herself? Is that why she thought her twin sister had been murdered? He didn't do weird. Maybe he should have stuck with meeting for coffee in the morning, report ready and in hand.

"Except this feeling was different. Instead of worry over Kaelyn being hurt, I felt an element of danger, as though Kaelyn might be in bad trouble. I can't explain it. I only know what I felt, and there can be no coincidence because my twin sister died that day, maybe just shortly after. I felt that way for nearly an hour, and then the feeling sort of…faded. I tried calling and she didn't answer. The next day, I finally reached her adoptive mother, who told me she'd killed herself."

Roman wouldn't comment on what he thought of telepathic twins, or their ability to possess extrasensory perception. He didn't believe in ghosts or the supernatural, but he also didn't disbelieve. She stepped back from the table. "It's your turn."

He chose his shot and aimed, missing by an inch. "Where are you from?"

Instead of answering, she studied him awhile. "Why am I getting this feeling you're trying to make a move on me instead of helping solve Kaelyn's murder?"

He grinned again and this time not to woo her. She'd made him grin with her wit. No man fooled this woman. He felt attraction mushroom to the realm of uncontrollable.

"Your turn."

After a knowing, soft smile, she studied the table, and then went to bend for her shot and made it. "I was born in Chicago."

"Your family moved here after that?"

"No." Pausing for her next shot, she straightened and looked at him. "Our parents were killed in a mass shooting."

He didn't hear that often. Not ever. "That's terrible." Now he knew why she and Kaelyn had been apart.

"We were in a bank when some robbers came in with guns. Kaelyn and I got to the floor like Mother said. Our dad tried to stop the robbers and our mother tried to stop him from stopping the robbers. They were shot."

While he tried to imagine how awful that would be, she made another solid and walked around the table to choose her next move. Did nothing ruffle this woman or was she just calculating?

"That was the beginning of the nightmare," she said.

She might be baiting him to get him to start asking questions, but what she revealed didn't jibe with his first impression of her, the polished, successful entrepreneur who'd made a cushy life for herself.

"What happened?" he indulged her by asking. He also wanted to know.

"We became wards of the state. No one wanted to adopt two children, so we were split up. I didn't know where Kaelyn was taken." She made her shot and sank another solid and faced him, holding her cue stick upright. "When I was twelve, my adoptive father lost his job. A year went by and he still hadn't found anything.

My adoptive mother didn't make enough to support us all and things went downhill from there."

That explanation he hadn't expected. While she had struck him as one of those fortunate types who did with ease anything they set their mind to do, she hadn't had an easy start.

He waited for her to shoot again.

"I went hungry a lot and wore the same clothes to school. By the time I was seventeen, our house had been foreclosed and we were living in a trailer. That's all my adoptive mother could afford." She bent with her stick and aimed. "The day my adoptive father forgot to pick me up after a school event and a strange man tried to get me to get into his car as I walked home was the day I decided I'd had enough. I ran away. I lived with my best friend's older sister until I graduated from high school. My adoptive parents didn't even report me missing."

She hit the ball hard and it crashed into the hole. "Now you know the background of me and my twin sister, how we got separated anyway." She sank all the solids except the eight ball. Roman had all of his striped balls still on the table.

Calling the corner hole, she shot the eight ball there. Then, smiling slightly, she held her cue stick upright. "What about you? Everybody has a story. What's yours? Do you have any tragedies haunting you?"

His childhood had been heaven compared to hers. Heaven compared to most he met. He supposed he should be happy she didn't use her past to segue into her sister's case.

"The only tragedies I've experienced are the ones

victims tell from their graves." He inserted more coins. "I'll break this time."

He racked the balls. As he leaned over and broke, he wondered how Kendra had gone from a runaway to a shop owner. She looked young for her age. Late twenties instead of forty-one, just a couple years younger than him.

He sank two solids. Grinning at her, he moved to his next shot.

She smiled back. "You haven't told me about your childhood."

"Nothing to tell." He made his next shot and sank another ball. "I was an only child of an apothecary and a crime novelist. I grew up in a fantasy world."

"Crime novelist." She tapped her forefinger on her lower lip. "William Cooper... *The* William Cooper? The Australian?"

"You've heard of him?" His father was a popular novelist but not the Stephen King variety.

"Who hasn't heard of him? Wow. You're the son of a celebrity. And Australian. You have a very subtle accent."

"I was basically raised in the States."

"You do have a Rick Grimes kind of look to you," she said.

Great. She thought he looked like the star of *The Walking Dead.* "My dad's not really a celebrity." He made his next shot and missed. "That was your fault."

She laughed lightly. "And your mother is a what? What's an apothecary?"

"She bought an old pharmacy and turned it into an apothecary museum. She studied chemistry in college and developed an odd fascination with herbal medicine."

"That's not so odd. What's odd is they have a son who became a crime detective." A band had begun to play and she started tapping her foot to the beat.

"That's odd?"

"Well…maybe not since your dad is a crime novelist. But your profession isn't as…fascinating as theirs."

"Are you always this blunt?" He didn't dislike that about her.

"Best way to be. I wish everyone treated me the same." Still holding her stick upright, her enchanted expression smoothed and her foot stopped tapping as though something came to her. "Wait a minute. I know that museum. It's here in Chesterville." She sucked in a breath. "Are you *from* here?"

She caught him. They now had a connection. She lived in his hometown. "It's your turn."

"You are?"

"Are you going to rob me of my chance to beat you?"

Laughing, she went to make her move, missing the striped ball. "How is it that you're from here and assigned to my sister's case?"

"There is no case yet. My boss made me come. He did that on purpose."

"So you could see your family? How sweet. A lot of bosses aren't like that."

"I didn't want to go see them." This might venture into the *Too Personal* zone. When he'd lured her out tonight, he had done it with the intention of sharing a night with her before he went back to work in Wyoming or wherever the need took him. He hadn't anticipated getting to know her and she him.

"What? Why not?"

He leaned over the table, aiming his stick.

"You *do* have a tragic story to tell."

"No, I don't. I just didn't feel like seeing them now, that's all." He hit a ball and it plunked into a hole.

"They're your family. Don't they know you're here?"

Standing up, he turned and stepped toward her, stopping close. "I came here to see you." He moved around her to make his next shot, sinking another ball.

"Is it because they're so much larger than you?"

"No. I love my parents and they love me. I had a painfully normal childhood." He dropped another ball.

"What is that?" she asked as though she didn't know.

"Normal. Bedtime stories." He'd had lots of those. "Be home by ten. Eat your vegetables. Don't drink. Don't smoke. Don't do drugs. You can do anything you put your mind to do. Love you and hugs."

"What's so painful about that?"

She didn't get it and he wasn't going to explain. His childhood had been painful because it had been so idyllic. But idyllic hadn't prepared him for the world. All the encouragement to do what his heart told him hadn't opened his mind and soul to awareness of what his heart told him. His heart hadn't told him anything. He'd gone to school to become a crime detective because he'd always been fascinated with his father, his imagination, his success. He'd never achieve that kind of success. He had to be satisfied with what he had.

He continued to drop balls up to the eight. He was going to cream her. Noticing her slanted smile, he sensed her good-sport realization that she was going to lose.

Moving to make the final shot, he stopped close to her again, seeing her sparkling green eyes get all flustered again. "Any last words?"

She breathed a shaky laugh, one born of attraction. He called the hole and won the game.

Wandering over to him, she held her stick in one hand, not having to tip her head back much to look up at his face. He took in her relaxed face that held a hint of flirtation and felt himself responding. "Are you as good at dancing as you are at playing pool?"

"Yes. And I love country music."

Good because he liked the song the band had started playing.

By the eighth or ninth song, Kendra wrapped her arms around Roman as the melody slowed. She couldn't remember having this much fun with anyone. They'd drunk more beer and danced the night away. Last call had been announced and she regretted the night coming to an end. She'd forgotten all about why he'd come to town. She cherished moments like this, when the world's ugliest blows fell away and only celebration lifted her.

She didn't think Roman paid much attention to how or why they'd ended up dancing this close, either. Maybe with whatever kept him from seeing his family he needed a getaway, too. Or maybe this had nothing to do with getaways. Maybe they just liked each other.

She leaned back to see his ruggedly handsome face, so dark and edgy with those light gray eyes that could be a wolf's. His gaze moved down to her mouth, and then slowly rose to her eyes. The beer must be clouding both their judgments.

"All right, folks, time to close up."

Realizing the band had stopped playing and had

begun to pack up their equipment, Kendra stepped back from Roman.

"Why don't you come back to my hotel room with me and convince me why I should start calling this a case?" Roman asked.

"Do you expect me to seduce you into taking it?"

"There's nothing to take yet."

"Stop saying that," she said, unable to repress a soft laugh.

"And no, I don't expect you to seduce me. I'd rather this night not end so soon, that's all." He swung her into a music-free turn and bent her over his arm.

"Me, neither."

Grinning, he lifted her up against him.

"Why is that?" she asked with her mouth close to his.

"Let's not think about it." Moving back, he took her hand and led her from the pub.

With her head fuzzy and light, she stepped outside with him. "For the record, I'm not going to sleep with you."

"Good."

She laughed because she heard what she'd been thinking and feeling, that together they'd enjoyed the evening and wanted to keep the momentum going.

Chapter 3

Maybe they just liked each other?

Kendra rolled her head to the side to see Roman's sleeping face not three inches from hers. She lay in the curve of his arm, with her breast, ribs, hip and leg pressed against him. Thankfully, she still wore her clothes and he his. But how in the world had the night gotten so carried away?

What the hell had she been thinking?

After arriving at the hotel room, Roman had taken care of her, all without infringing on her privacy. She almost liked him. The unpredictability caught her off guard. She hadn't seen their connection coming. And she had completely forgotten he never answered her question about why he didn't want to see his parents.

What kind of man was he? She knew nothing about him personally.

Easing away, she sat up, and then stood from the bed. Tiptoeing to the door, she quietly left the room. Finding a pen and notepad, she scrawled a note, her last-ditch effort to get him to change his mind about investigating Kaelyn's death.

Standing outside Kaelyn's best friend's small two-story Victorian, Roman leaned against the trunk of a tree. He hadn't given in to the nagging compulsion to investigate Kendra's twin sister's death. Yet. He kept telling himself that. Spending last night with her changed the dynamics. The note she'd left, too.

Now he felt something for her. He didn't think he'd ever had so much fun with a woman before. Hanging with her had been like hanging with one of his buddies. Add the bonus of her hot body and he couldn't stay away.

He should have left hours ago. He should be deep into investigating a real murder. Like a magnet, Kendra had kept him right here.

"My sister was murdered," she'd written. "I'm going to talk to Kaelyn's best friend in two hours. With or without you."

Then she'd signed her name, a pretty scrawl.

Since that's where he now stood outside waiting for her, he must have already given in. She'd baited him with that note, probably even planned a visit with the best friend on purpose, to draw him in. He felt the resolve settle in and take hold. Yeah, he wasn't going anywhere. Even if he proved her wrong and Kaelyn's death was suicide, he'd stay until the end. He'd investigate her case.

And yeah, he'd even started thinking of this as a case—but only because of what she'd brought to light about being in contact with her long-lost sister. Why had Kaelyn kept her reuniting with Kendra a secret? He had to find out.

He wished he could smoke.

Really. Why was he doing this?

Because she'd go forward without him. Her note told him that much.

Because in the off chance her sister *had* been murdered, she'd put herself in danger.

Because…

Because he cared.

A few minutes later, Kendra drove up and parked. She saw him before she got out, shock registering before she smiled. She smiled a lot. Her sunny disposition had infected him for sure.

He headed across the street.

"You're going to scare her standing out here like a stalker," she said.

"At least she'll be expecting us."

He experienced a flare of attraction when he noticed she wore another sexy pantsuit.

"What's the matter?" she asked. "You look mad."

Mad? Hungry might be a better word. "Don't make me start smoking again." Passing her, he walked to the house.

"How would I make you smoke again? You smoked?" She eyed him as though he didn't fit the stereotype. "When did you quit?"

"Six months ago. I only want to smoke when I get agitated. You made me stay and take your case."

"At least you're calling it a case now." She winked at him, infecting him more.

Stopping at the door, he rang the bell as he absorbed her beautiful profile, lips still curved smugly.

Blaire Bancroft answered the door. "Kendra." She turned curious eyes to Roman.

"Hi, Blaire. This is Roman Cooper. He's the private detective I hired to look into Kaelyn's death. Would you mind telling him everything you told me?"

So Kendra had planned to trick him into coming here. Of course she would have already talked to her.

"Oh." Her frown told Roman she didn't understand the need. "Sure. Come in."

Before arriving here, Roman had asked an analyst at DAI to look into everyone close to Kaelyn. Blaire and Kaelyn had gone to school together and had both married out of high school. Blaire had stayed in Chesterville. Her husband worked as a mechanic at a local garage and she stayed home with their kids. They'd waited and had them later in their thirties. Kaelyn had left town when her winner of a man dragged her to another town.

Roman entered behind Kendra, and then stood beside her in the small foyer. Blaire's toddler played on an old, faded rug in front of a television in the small living room. The scuffed wood floor needed refinishing. Through a wide archway, the kitchen looked messy. Breakfast dishes remained on the table and the counters needed a scrubbing. Busy mom.

"How are you?" Blaire asked Kendra. "I hear your shop is doing amazing. I've been meaning to stop in." She glanced at the toddler, who threw a stuffed monkey in the air and then sat transfixed by the *Sesame Street* episode. "I hate taking him in public, though."

Kendra laughed a little. "I can see you have your

hands full. We won't take up much of your time. Roman just has a few questions for you."

Roman loved how she unabashedly volunteered him.

"All right. Sorry for the mess. I was just about to start cleaning the kitchen. It took me a while to get *him* to settle down." She thumbed over toward her child.

"How close were you with Kaelyn?" Roman asked, a standard first question.

Blaire glanced at Kendra as though surprised she hadn't told him. "Very. We were best friends through school and after."

"You remained close after school? After you were both married?" That would be important if Kaelyn revealed something no one singled out as significant.

"Yes. We talked on the phone a lot and I saw her when she came back to Chesterville, which she did quite often. Her husband only trusted her to go see her mom." She shook her head with a slight roll to her eyes. "Weird that he'd let her do that but not go out with friends when she was home. Kaelyn must have been able to snow him for once. He must have believed her."

"Tell Roman about how you suspected Kaelyn was having another affair aside from the one she had with Jasper," Kendra said.

Blaire looked from him to her, taking some time to think. "I wasn't really suspicious. One time, she came over and had to leave early. I noticed she seemed anxious. I thought she must have had another fight with her husband, but she said she had another stop to make before she had to get back to her mother's. I asked her where she was going and she wouldn't say. She just changed the subject."

Kaelyn must not have shared the part about the sec-

ond lover with anyone. Roman supposed he should
have sat down with Kendra before coming here and
allowed her to explain all she knew so far. Or make
sure she did. She'd held out on him, probably for this
reason, to get him here and to get him much more curious about the case.

What about Jasper? Kaelyn must have known Jasper could take care of himself. But then, she must have
been having this affair here in Chesterville at the same
time, so why tell him? And if her husband didn't trust
her with anyone but her mother, she must have been
very sneaky to avoid detection.

"When did you last see her?" Roman asked.

"Oh, about two weeks before she died. I spoke with
her the day before, though. She told me Jasper broke
things off and she was pretty upset over that."

"Did she talk about her husband?" Roman asked.

"No, not that time."

"But she did previously," Kendra said, guiding the
direction of the questioning.

"The time before that, when she came to Chesterville, we met for lunch and she had a bruise on her lip,"
Blaire said. "I had already suspected her husband was
knocking her around. She tried to cover the bruise with
makeup but I noticed. I've never seen her so low as she
was then. She talked about wanting to close her eyes
and not wake up so she wouldn't have to go home to
him. She scared me. I didn't want to leave her alone,
but she insisted."

"Don't you think it's possible her husband killed
her?" Kendra asked.

"Oh, I'm sure he would have, eventually."

"Did she ever talk about leaving him?" Roman asked.

"Well, sure. All the time. But it was more like a day-dream. I think she was too scared to try."

"Jasper told her he'd help," Kendra said.

"And he also told her he wouldn't be with her. If she was having an affair with someone else who frightened her as much or more than her husband, she didn't have much to look forward to."

Roman agreed that only supported her suicide. "You think she killed herself?"

"It's what the police think. She wasn't happy. She never talked to me about killing herself but I can see how she'd be driven to that point." She looked harder at Kendra. "Do you really think she was murdered?"

"I think it's a definite possibility," she said. "Whenever I talked to her or when I saw her, she didn't seem like someone who was about to off herself."

"Maybe she didn't want you to worry," Roman said.

He earned a glower from her.

"Thanks for talking to us, Blaire," Kendra said, then turned to him again. "Let's go."

"Did Kaelyn ever mention she was talking with her twin sister?" Roman asked Blaire.

Blaire shook her head. "I was as shocked as everyone else when Kendra came to town."

He could tell his question irritated Kendra. He'd had to ask to confirm what she'd told him.

Out on the street, Kendra headed for her car. "Don't say it."

Roman walked beside her. "I wasn't going to say anything."

She eyed him as he walked next to her.

"I wasn't," he repeated. "In fact, I was going to suggest we call her coworkers."

"What about her sleazy husband?"

"He's in jail. Just found that out this morning. Arrested for embezzlement."

"The streets are cleaner." She reached her car. "Where's your car?"

"I left the rental at the hotel. Took a cab here."

"Get in."

He did. "The husband has a tight alibi the day Kaelyn killed herself."

"Stop saying that. Kaelyn was murdered."

Roman sighed. This was going to be a long day.

"I didn't tell you this yet, but Kaelyn slipped once when we were talking on the phone. She said she met someone in Chesterville and she called him Bear."

"So you knew she was seeing someone."

"No. She said she met someone and she called him Bear. She backpedaled when I questioned her and wouldn't say more."

Kendra contained her frustration after talking with a few of Kaelyn's coworkers. All of them corroborated what the police had surmised. Kaelyn had been unhappy and depressed before her death. Having Roman with her to do the questioning hadn't gotten her anywhere. She felt his doubt oozing through the air between them. The only reason he'd stayed was because of her secret relationship with Kaelyn, and maybe their night together. Would he ever be swayed?

Now they walked along Main Street not far from her shop and the pub. Ahead, a throng of people caught her eye. They'd have to cross the street to get around them. A camera crew lingered among them in front of the courthouse.

"What's going on there?" Roman asked.

"I don't know." Kendra was active in her community but wouldn't call herself up-to-date on everything going on in town.

People had gathered on the steps of the courthouse. What they hoped to see, Kendra couldn't be sure. But then a couple stepped out of the building. The man, tall and muscular with slightly graying dark hair, wore slacks and a vest over a white dress shirt. Not much shorter, with blond hair and a black dress, the woman wore expensive jewels, like Christmas ornaments, and a fitted black business dress with black high heels. Her blond hair was shoulder-length and styled in a perfect, swooping bob.

She stopped with Roman at the crowd of onlookers.

"Who are they?" Kendra asked.

A woman next to her said, "That's Hudson Franklin and his wife, Melody. Hudson is the county prosecutor. He's prosecuting a new case."

Melody waved to the crowd as though acting. Her husband kissed her cheek and she smiled at him, much more genuinely. The two seemed to have real feelings for each other.

Someone broke from the crowd, rushing for Melody and Hudson.

"You sent an innocent man to jail!" the man hollered, feverish to reach them. "All you care about is winning trials!"

Melody's smile vanished and she shrieked, startled and frightened.

Two beefy security guards blocked the stranger just

in time and Hudson swept Melody away, letting the guards flatten the man onto the concrete sidewalk.

From behind the couple, a big, dark blond–haired man rushed forward. "Mother! Are you all right?"

Shaken but safe now that the man had been subdued, the blonde faced the man. "Thank you, Bear. Yes, I'm all right."

As she watched Melody lean away from the man's embrace, Kendra felt a cold chill race through her, prickling her scalp and arms. When Kaelyn had slipped when talking about her second lover, she'd called him *Bear*.

Chapter 4

Raelyn Johnston checked out a customer in line at the gas station counter. This was the only job she could find after college. She didn't want to leave Chesterville. Her grandparents lived here and that was really all she had left of family. Kendra came to mind then. She didn't like thinking about her. Mom hadn't told her a thing about her. Why not? The only explanation was that her mom hadn't been close to her and maybe hadn't wanted to bring her into their lives.

It didn't matter anyway. Raelyn didn't want her aunt in her life. She looked like her mom the way other sisters did but not in a twin way, and just reminded her of the hellhole her mother had left her in when she killed herself.

Raelyn slammed the cash register shut with a fresh wave of anger. She still got so mad over that. How could her mother have done that to her? Living with Dad had been horrible but at least they had had each other. How could her mom have left her in that situation?

The last year living with Dad had been a nightmare. She'd come home from school to cops swarming her house and her mother's body being wheeled out in a black bag. Her dad hadn't even called the school.

A cop had told her that her mother died and the coroner would be in touch to explain how.

After they'd all left, her dad had started drinking and only told her Kaelyn had killed herself by hanging. No hug. No talk over how she'd deal with such a huge loss. He seemed to not care at all. Looking back, she realized he'd drowned whatever sentiment he'd had for her mom in alcohol.

Another patron showed up at the counter. She looked up and saw a tall, beautiful blonde she recognized from the news. It was the prosecutor's wife, Melody Franklin. She put a cold bottle of iced tea on the counter.

Raelyn began checking her out and Melody inserted her credit card into the machine, eyeing Raelyn.

"You're Kaelyn Johnston's daughter, aren't you?" Melody asked.

She recognized her? "Yes."

"I was real sorry when we heard about her death all those years ago."

What was this, Hash Over Her Mom's Suicide Day? She didn't respond.

"She was so well liked in town. No one ever really got to know your dad. He never came with her when she visited."

"My dad was and still is a first-class loser."

"You seem to have turned out all right despite that fact. You're quite lovely."

Raelyn grew uncomfortable with the compliment. She thought she looked okay, but what did *lovely* mean?

"I heard your aunt hired an impressive private investigations firm to look into your mother's death."

What? Raelyn handed Melody her receipt. "What detective agency? Why is she looking into her death?"

Raelyn felt a surge of multiple feelings assail her. Rage. Pain. The sting of tears. She couldn't take this.

"As a possible homicide. You didn't know?"

"My aunt and I haven't spoken much."

"Doesn't she keep in touch with you? I would think she'd want nothing more than to be in touch with her twin sister's daughter."

That was getting too personal. "She does, but I've been too busy."

Melody glanced over the cash register and counter as though she found that difficult to believe. Raelyn only worked at a gas station. How could she possibly be too busy to be in touch with her aunt? Clearly she didn't want to be in touch with her aunt.

"I'm sorry," Melody said. "I didn't mean to pry."

"What agency?" Raelyn asked, borderline snapping.

"It's fairly well-known. Dark Alley Investigations."

"Why does Aunt Kendra think my mother may have been murdered?"

"Good question. That's why I brought it up."

Raelyn would not entertain any thoughts on the matter. She'd had it rough enough without her mother around. She didn't need to start feeding the notion that her mother hadn't abandoned her. Kendra was just reaching. Her mother wasn't murdered. Period. End of story. Time to move on with her life.

Melody took her tea and started to turn. "Have a good day now."

"You, too."

Raelyn saw the next clerk who'd take over at the counter. Her shift was over.

Good. She needed to get out of here and get her mind off Mom. Adam texted her, saying he'd meet her at a local bar near where she worked.

Perfect.

She didn't drink like her dad had, and never would. He'd set a fine example of what not to become. Try as she might not to think about that last year living with him, the memories filled her anyway. Whenever he got drunk, which was every night, he got angry. At first, she'd tolerated it. Without her mom, she'd been so lost and sad. The awfulness had consumed her. She'd come home from school and go to her room and cry every night. Her grades had slumped. Luckily, summer had arrived and she'd had a few months to get past the worst of it.

Dealing with her dad hadn't helped. He yelled at her all the time and made her basically take care of him, cooking and cleaning. She'd hated him for that. She lost her friends because he demanded she be home. Then one night, he'd gotten so mad that she hadn't made dinner yet, she'd lashed out at him and yelled back. He'd smacked her like he had her mom so many times.

She'd packed a bag and left. She went to one of her friends' house. But she couldn't live there for a year so she'd had to go back home.

Her dad had apologized but the violence had returned. She'd barely graduated from high school but made sure she had scholarships for college. Between that and two jobs, she'd paid her own way through school.

She hadn't really had a chance to grieve the loss of her mother. In college she had. But the one thing she never lost was that deep, aching resentment over her mother taking the coward's way and killing herself. Hadn't she thought of her daughter? Why couldn't she have just taken her and left her dad? That had gnawed at her ever since the day her dad emotionlessly told her of the suicide.

For the longest time, she couldn't believe it. She refused. Her mother would never leave her that way. But she had. The coroner had sealed the truth of it when he'd stopped by to tell them. While Raelyn had broken down in tears, her dad had gone to a bottle of whiskey.

Leaving home for college had been one of the happiest days of her life. Now she never wanted to see him again.

Aunt Kendra? She didn't know if she could see her, get to know her. It was just too painful. Now a woman she only knew through the news had told her Aunt Kendra had hired a detective to look into her mother's death.

Raelyn did not welcome the ray of hope trying to butt its way past her control. If her mother had been murdered, that would mean she hadn't intended to abandon her. But what did that really change? Nothing. She'd still lost her mom and that still made her really, really angry.

Chapter 5

"What, exactly, did Kaelyn say to you when she mentioned another lover?" Roman asked Kendra as they headed up to his room at Chesterville's boutique hotel. She still couldn't explain to herself why she'd agreed to come here. Maybe distraction over connecting the prosecutor's son to her sister's mysterious second lover. Yes, that'd do it. She didn't want to be curious about what made Roman avoid his parents. He had such an idyllic childhood from all he'd told her. Was he aloof? Kendra had trouble with secretive people. If anyone had reason to keep secrets, that usually meant they were not very genuine.

The plush elevator stopped at the fourth floor and she walked down the hall with him. "She asked me to meet her here, in Chesterville, on one of her many trips to see her adoptive mother." This town seemed more home to Kaelyn than with her husband, which was probably why Raelyn moved here after her death. Her sister had a much different experience with her family than Kendra had. "I thought it was odd she wanted to meet here. She explained she'd have more time to spend with me in Chesterville. We spent five days here. First we met for lunch, then went shopping, and then I met her mother and father. I stayed there the last three nights and it was like being kids again." She smiled as she felt the same joy she had felt back then.

As Roman opened his hotel room, Kendra recalled playing dolls with her twin. Kaelyn had always been the doer, the one to start things going and to lead the way. Kendra had been more leisurely. She took more time before delving into projects. Not Kaelyn. She dived right in.

"You do have a strong connection to her," Roman said as Kendra passed him on her way into his room. "Even separated all those years, you were still close."

Kendra took in the gray-and-blue decorated living room and small kitchenette. "Yes." She wouldn't try to explain what it was like between her and Kaelyn. Being born at the same time as a sister, growing up with them—even if for a short time offered the ingredients for closeness, but there was more of a connection, an inexplicable one. Had she and Kaelyn bonded in the womb? Had they bonded as babies and toddlers? Who knew?

She put her purse on one of the two chairs in the kitchenette. Through a door she could see a king bed and a bathroom. She faced Roman, who'd gone into the kitchenette to find some glasses.

"When I first met her," Kendra went on, "one of the

things I noticed was her somberness. Kaelyn was not a quiet girl. Everyone grows up but it just seemed a light had been doused in her. She seemed...sad." She hated that memory and threw it off her conscience, watching Roman pour two glasses of red wine. "The last couple of days, she started to perk up and I started to see the old Kaelyn. She laughed loud and talked excitedly about the two of us living in the same town, having families and always being together."

He left the kitchenette and handed her a glass. "Did you ask her about her life in Toledo?"

She met his glowing wolf eyes, momentarily lulled by the ruggedness of his facial features. "Yes. I asked about her husband. What he did. How they met. She answered almost mechanically. She smiled but her eyes didn't sparkle. Then she made a comment that he was a little insecure and he had to approve her friends at home. She said she came to Chesterville a lot because she could be herself here."

"That must have raised some red flags for you."

She nodded, not liking that memory, either. Turning, she walked to the window with a view of a strip mall. There was a nice restaurant there and people had gathered on a latticed patio full of trees and flowers. Early summer in West Virginia. The humidity was most bearable at night. She sipped some wine, hearing Roman sit on the gray sofa. She liked how he didn't invade her space.

"I finally came right out and said to her, *You aren't happy with your husband, are you?*" Kendra faced Roman, not feeling like sitting. "I watched her close her eyes, and then open them with such anguish and despair. She wasn't happy. That's when she told me about Jasper. The transformation in her was amazing. She said that even though she didn't think he was the right man for her, he gave her an idea of the kind of man who was. She loved him for that, for giving her that insight. She told him she wanted to leave her husband. When I asked her why she hadn't already, she wouldn't answer. She kept changing the subject."

"When did she tell you about Bear?" Roman asked, putting his glass of wine onto the coffee table.

Although all of the furniture in the hotel room were probably constructed of inexpensive materials, they made the room look expensive with artful, coordinated colors and textures. Kendra had always been the artsy one compared to Kaelyn.

"Shortly before she died, when I pressed her once more about her husband. I suspected he might be mistreating her. After telling me not to worry, that she planned to move back to Chesterville and I should plan to do the same, she said she thought she already met the man for her, one like Jasper. When I asked her who he was, she got this dreamy look and said, *Bear.* Then she seemed to realize what she'd said and wouldn't tell me more." Kendra had thought Bear a strange name and asked if that was a nickname. Kaelyn had only said yes. "All she said was that she had to be careful and he had to be kept a secret for now."

She watched Roman absorb all she'd just said. He wasn't a hurried man. Who would dare hurry a man who looked like him? His thick, dark wavy hair and stubbly face with angled bone structure gave him a dangerous look. Predatorily dangerous.

"Why didn't you tell Jasper about Bear?" he finally asked.

"I assumed my sister meant she had to keep him a secret from her husband." He thought that was significant? "Or maybe Bear was married. I hoped not, but the thought did cross my mind."

"What if Bear threatened her in some way? If she was attracted to men like her husband, who's to say this other man wasn't just as abusive?"

"Do you think she feared Bear? She didn't seem to fear him. She seemed madly in love with him. If she compared him to someone like Jasper, he must be someone special. Someone good, too."

Again, Roman took his time. Then he lifted his eyes and met hers. "All the more reason to take a closer look at the man."

Just to be sure? To be thorough? Did he think Kaelyn might have been so smitten that she'd missed some important signs?

So he really was going to take the case. He'd indicated as much, but she hadn't been convinced. What had made him change his mind? Her as a woman at first, but now...?

"You never did tell me why you don't want to see your parents." Might as well test him.

He didn't move from the couch, just sat back, legs parted, hands on his thighs. Relaxed. His wolf eyes never left hers.

"It's not that I don't want to go see them. I just don't like facing how much more they've done with their lives than I have."

Kendra moved to the side table, looking up at a cheap abstract in reds and grays. She found his answer peculiar.

"You don't think becoming a successful detective at

one of the world's leading private investigations agencies measures up?"

"My name isn't the one in the news."

She turned to face him, holding her glass over her bent arm. "Unlike your father?"

"Something like that. Growing up with such perfect parents makes me not want to be perfect."

Because he didn't feel he equaled their perfection? He sure seemed to have some kind of identity issue going on. "Solving crimes defines you?"

"It's real."

"You don't think your parents are real?"

"They live an idyllic life, untouched by reality."

He sounded so pessimistic, which went against her way of thinking. Since escaping her adoptive parents, Kendra had made a promise to herself. She'd spend her life striving for happiness, making good choices that didn't bring her the opposite. That meant not welcoming anyone who might threaten her inner peace.

"What's wrong with that?" she asked. "We all have to die someday. What's wrong with living a good, stress-free life?"

"Nothing. That's not what I mean. My father sensationalizes death in his stories. I see the real thing."

She went to the coffee table and sat beside his glass of wine, setting hers down next to it. "What you do is commendable. I don't see why you feel the need to compare yourself to your dad."

"I followed his lead. Not all of us get to pick the life of our dreams. My dad followed his."

And he regretted following in the footsteps of a great man? He'd gone into crime solving to try and capture his father's admiration?

"What would you have done if not for your dad?"

"That's just it. I'm not one of those people who knows. I just do what the cards lay down in front of me. I'm not like you."

"Me?" Where had he gotten the notion she was anything like his father? She'd followed her dreams? She had but not before going through hell to get there.

"You went to college and opened a Christmas shop. You aspired to do that and you did it. Now you live well. Hard times are far behind you."

He had no idea what she'd gone through to get where she was now. And how could he forget she'd been separated from her sister, who died before she could truly reestablish ties? He thought reality didn't touch her. She did her best to keep dark reality far from her door, but what did Roman think Kaelyn's death was? A walk through a pleasant-smelling daisy field?

She'd leave him with something to consider. "The cards led me to my Christmas shop, Roman. I don't know what I'd have done had my parents not been shot to death and my twin sister taken away. Let's not forget the enchanted life I had growing up with addictive and abusive adoptive parents. Is that enough reality for you?" He didn't even flinch, still thinking she lived an enchanted life. Her past didn't matter. It's what she lived now. "Why do I—why does anyone—have to dwell on reality and not seek an easier life?"

Roman moved forward, reaching one hand to her face as he sat on the edge of the couch. "I'm not saying anyone should dwell on reality. I'm saying that's where I live every day, every time I start a new cold case. I don't dwell on it. I live it. I don't live like you... or my parents."

And so he couldn't relate? Is that what he meant? Or did he mean he needed to surround himself with others like him so he wouldn't be reminded of what he'd never have—a life like his parents? Flourishing and enchanted. Full of light-stepping moments and sunny days.

While her beliefs opposed his, his light eyes and the intensity in them that had more to do with attraction than conviction kept her from backing away. She knew as well as he that the two of them did not see eye to eye on life in general, but that ceased to matter.

As though he chose not to think too long on it, he pulled her head closer and kissed her.

The next day, Roman walked with Kendra toward a country club where he'd learned Bear—aka Glenn Franklin—enjoyed a weekly brunch with his parents, Hudson and Melody. He hadn't slept much after Kendra had left. The temptation to have a cigarette hadn't helped. She'd left shortly after he ended the kiss. He'd been surprised he'd had to end it, first of all, and then not surprised when she'd stuttered an excuse and hurried out of the hotel room.

Heat and tension simmered, invisible and without sound. She wore a cheery sundress with a cardigan sweater to ward off the morning chill. The bright colors reminded him of what she needed to live—everything his life could never give her. He'd thought long about that last night. If the two of them ended up together, the grisly nature of his work would drag her down into a black cesspool. She'd have to escape as she did every day to her Christmas shop. She'd live her dream and deny the reality of his world. How many cop or detective shows had he watched where the hero could never stay married?

White blooming dogwoods lined the parking lot and thick, lush bluegrass trimmed along a curving sidewalk stretched to a fence enclosing a pool area. The sun shone in a deep blue sky, mocking Roman with its bright merriment.

"They aren't going to let us in," Kendra said.

Inside the clubhouse, Roman followed Kendra into a small lobby. A young woman stood at a podium, wearing a black skirt with matching suit jacket, with her dark, smooth and shining hair up in an unforgiving bun. She gave them a work-required smile and asked, "Two?"

"We're here to talk to someone," Roman said.

"You aren't a member?"

"We won't be long." Putting his hand under Kendra's elbow, he guided her into the restaurant area.

"Sir, you can't go in there if you aren't a member." The woman followed.

Roman spotted Hudson and Melody Franklin. Melody was dressed as before, this time in a navy scoop neck, knee-length dress, with her stylish hair combed to a sharp-edge, the front tips brushing her collarbone. She tucked the left side behind her diamond-studded ears, her wedding ring big and gaudy. A woman of perhaps sixty, she kept herself in great shape, as did her husband. He wore a dark suit and tie, his salt-and-pepper hair cut short. He read from a menu with reading glasses.

"I don't see Glenn," Kendra said.

"We'll talk to them first." There were three settings on the table and all looked to have been touched. Before the empty chair, a crumpled cloth napkin sat beside a plate and crooked silverware, and the water glass was three-quarters full.

As Roman weaved between tables ahead of Kendra, he spotted Glenn returning from the men's room, his big body taking long strides and the lapels of his silky jacket flapping.

"Mr. and Mrs. Franklin?" Roman queried.

Melody looked up, not appearing surprised someone would approach their table. They were a couple in the public eye. Hudson studied Roman and then Kendra as though trying to identify them. Glenn arrived at the table, briefly eyeing them with annoyed blue eyes before sitting.

"I'm sorry, sir." The hostess stopped near Hudson, looking frightened. "They barged right in."

Hudson held up one hand as though to soothe the girl. "It's all right, Emily." Then he looked up at Roman. "What brings you to our club so urgently?"

"I wouldn't call it urgent so much as a good opportunity to catch you and your son." As the hostess reluctantly turned and headed back toward the entrance, Roman introduced Kendra and identified himself as a private investigator.

"Private investigator?" Melody asked.

"Yes. I hired him to look into the death of my twin sister, Kaelyn Johnston."

"Oh, yes, I remember that," Melody said with eyes expressing sympathy. "That was so long ago."

"I tried for years to get police to look into her death in more detail but no one ever did with any real effort, so I finally decided to get outside help."

"You think she was murdered?"

"Yes. That's why we came to see Glenn."

Glenn looked up from the menu he had picked up, having dismissed them as soon as he sat down.

"I'm sorry…what?"

"Did you know Kaelyn Johnston?"

He glanced from Kendra to Roman. "Why are you asking me?"

"You did know her then?" Roman asked.

"No. I knew of her, though."

"Kaelyn spoke of you, which is why we wanted to talk to you." Roman turned to Kendra, cuing her to interject.

"She called you Bear."

Glenn's eyes shifted toward his parents and then back to Kendra. "She never mentioned a twin sister to me."

"You did know her?" Melody asked, growing concerned, as though the thought of her son lying about knowing Kaelyn offended her.

Glenn ignored her and continued to stare at Kendra.

"She was planning to move back to Chesterville," Kendra said, "to escape her husband. She must have failed in her attempt. Did you know she was coming back here?"

Glenn again said nothing, although he blinked in a telltale way.

"You did have an affair with her," Roman said. "Didn't you?"

Glenn had to see it would be pointless to deny the affair. His lack of response revealed as much.

"My Bear didn't have an affair with anyone." Melody turned to her son. "Did you, Glenn?"

Glenn glanced at his mother, and then lowered his eyes. Again, his lack of response answered for him.

"You didn't." Melody's distress intensified. "What about your wife?"

"I had no intention of leaving her." He looked at Kendra. "I'm sorry. I was going to break things off with your sister, but I didn't get the chance before she…"

"Thank you for not saying 'committed suicide,'" Kendra said.

Melody's mouth still hung open in shock. "Do you have any idea what this could do to our family? Any chance you have of following a successful political career would be ruined if news of this spread." She took a few deep breaths.

Glenn looked solemn. "What happened between me and Kaelyn was unexpected."

"It usually is," Hudson said. "A man doesn't wake up one morning and decide he's going to seek out an affair." With Melody's gasp, he added, "Not that I speak from experience."

"It was a onetime thing, Mother. It won't ever happen again. I promise."

"I remember when she committed suicide." Hudson didn't seem to care what Kendra thought of his choice of words. "I ran into her mother a few weeks after."

"Did you attend her funeral?" Kendra asked. "Her body was transported back here for burial."

"No. I didn't know the family very well."

Melody had slowly begun to emerge from her shock and listened now.

"Did you attend her funeral?" Roman asked Glenn.

Glenn shook his head. "I visited her grave afterward. I had my own private goodbye with her."

He hadn't wanted to risk his wife asking too many questions, apparently.

"Were you here in town when she died?" Roman asked.

Glenn had to think a moment. "I didn't leave town, I know that much. I can't remember what I was doing when she died."

"I do," Melody said. "Hudson and I flew to New York that day to catch a Broadway show. I remember because Hudson told me about running into Kaelyn's mother when we arrived back home. It struck me because I had never heard of anyone killing themselves before."

Glenn nodded with recollection. "I do remember that. The day you flew to New York, I had a cold."

"You were home all day?" Roman asked.

"Yes."

"Can anyone verify that?"

Glenn frowned. "I can't remember if I talked with anyone on the phone. Why?"

"Your wife was home all day?" Roman asked.

"I can't remember."

Roman abandoned that line of questioning for now. "When is the last time you saw her?"

"When she came to town. Maybe a week before that."

"What did you talk about?"

"I can't recall exactly. Nothing unusual. Nothing that would have indicated she intended to kill herself, or that she was in some kind of trouble. I almost told her I wanted to break things off then, but I didn't."

So, he had had a regular secret encounter with Kaelyn a week before she died. He claimed not to remember much, but did he?

"I think that's all we need for now." Roman prepared to leave when Glenn stopped him.

"Why do you doubt it was suicide?" he asked.

"Kaelyn and I were in contact for months before she died," Kendra said. "I think she was going to try to talk me into moving here, maybe come to Chicago first and then the both of us could move together. Every time she spoke of Chesterville, of moving back here, she lit up. And she lit up even more when she talked about the two of us living close and seeing each other often. She was excited, not the sad woman everyone described to me after her death. If she was sad, her husband is the only one who made her that way."

"So you think her husband may have killed her?"

"Perhaps. If not him, then someone else," Kendra said.

"You know for certain she planned to move here?" Glenn asked.

"We discussed it."

"So she may not have planned to move back here."

"It was implied. She seemed to be priming me for the suggestion. When she talked about wanting to live in Chesterville again, she did so as though it was a dream to her, as if she was afraid it would never be."

Glenn fell into thoughtful silence, the menu forgotten.

He seemed genuinely surprised that Kaelyn might have been murdered. Had he tried to hide his affair with her to protect his marriage or did he have other reasons to keep such a secret? He had a weak alibi but appeared to lack motive to murder Kaelyn. Roman wouldn't tell Kendra any of his yet, though. He'd wait until he ruled out foul play. Or confirmed it.

Chapter 6

"Glenn has no alibi." Kendra walked beside Roman on the way to his rental.

"That doesn't mean he's guilty."

He didn't seem innocent. He hadn't recalled what he'd done the day Kaelyn died, but he had when his mother mentioned their trip to New York. Hadn't he cared that Kaelyn had died? Someone who did care wouldn't forget where they were when it happened or when they heard the news.

"He could have a motive."

"The coroner's report said she did die from strangulation and the angle of the rope seems to correlate with how her body was found. But now one thing stands out to me with the report."

The coroner's report could be wrong. Kendra felt

a bolt of hope just as her cell rang. She stopped short when she saw the caller ID.

Raelyn.

"Hello, Raelyn."

"Aunt Kendra?"

She sounded hesitant. Kendra wouldn't say anything to jeopardize her niece reaching out to her. She must have called for a reason.

"How are you?"

There was a lengthier hesitation on the other end. "I heard you hired a private investigator to look into my mother's death."

Her tone and clipped words told Kendra she was upset and had difficulty saying what she had to say, as though she didn't even want to verbalize what troubled her. What troubled her wasn't the investigator. It was the loss of her mother.

"Why don't we meet to talk about this?" She'd rather do that than over the phone.

"Why did you hire a PI?" she demanded.

"How did you find out I did?" The whole town likely knew but maybe she'd found out in a less shocking way. Kendra hadn't told her because Raelyn hadn't wanted to talk to her or see her.

"My grandmother told me." Raelyn must view Kaelyn's adoptive parents as her real grandparents. Kendra liked knowing that.

"I've spoken with her on a few occasions."

"My mother committed suicide." Her tone took on a decidedly sharper note. "Why are you bringing that up all over again? It was hard enough on all of us then."

"Raelyn, that's why I want to talk in person. I've tried before and you weren't comfortable meeting."

"Because you're her *twin*!" She all but sneered the last word.

"I know it came as a shock when you found out about me. I can't explain why your mother kept me a secret. I can only guess it had something to do with your father. She may have seen me as a way out and didn't want him to know. Meet me and we'll talk."

"I don't want to talk to you. I want you to stop causing trouble in town and get rid of that investigator. My mother killed herself. End of story."

"Please, Raelyn. Don't punish me for being your mother's twin. Meet me and I'll explain everything."

"I'm not trying to punish you. I just…"

"I know you hurt. You lost your mother in a horrible way. It's okay, Raelyn."

Her niece didn't say anything, but Kendra sensed a softening.

"I'm not your mother," Kendra said. "I'm your aunt. Let me help you get past what you lost."

"My mother was no loss. She kept us with Dad when she could have taken me away. My life is ruined because of her."

At last, Raelyn was talking to her, but she harbored so much resentment. "She was going to leave him. She talked about her plans before she died. That's why I hired the PI. Meet me and I'll explain everything. We can do something casual like a picnic. Tomorrow. Eleven thirty at Town Center Park."

After a lengthy pause, Raelyn finally said, "Can I bring someone?"

"Of course." Kendra couldn't believe she was finally making a small forward movement with her niece. Raelyn may feel the need to have someone with her as support, but Kendra would take that. "Italian, ham and Swiss or club sandwiches?"

"Club."

"Club it is. I'll get us a picnic table."

"Okay." Her tone had softened even more.

When Kendra ended the call, she stared down at the phone as she basked in delight. Could it be she'd finally have a relationship with her niece? Family.

She had to be careful. Raelyn was in such a fragile state. She didn't like speculating whether her mother hadn't actually killed herself. Kendra reminded her of her mother too much and that also caused her pain.

"You all right?"

She looked up at Roman. She'd almost forgotten he was there. His glowing eyes revealed a glimpse of concern. This man didn't show his emotions much. His doomsday mentality probably dulled his senses to them.

"Fine. Raelyn is going to meet us. Me. I didn't tell her you'd be there."

"I'm no good at picnics."

"All you have to do is eat outside. You'll live. What were you saying before she called? What about the coroner's report stood out?"

"The time of death. Her husband said he found her at eleven in the morning when he woke up. She died almost twenty-four hours before that."

"What struck you about that?"

"Why didn't her husband notice her the night before?"

"He had been drinking. He told paramedics and police he slept late because he'd been drinking the night before."

"Right, but he didn't notice her missing when he got home?"

Kendra believed he had been drinking. "He's a suspect for sure, but the timing seems reasonable to me. Besides, I thought the coroner's report convinced you she wasn't murdered."

"It did, but there might be something significant about the time of death." He opened the car door for her.

Kendra stepped into the open doorway and faced Roman. "You just said her time of death was almost twenty-four hours before she was found."

"Exactly."

"Are you saying she may not have been killed in her house?"

"If she was murdered, whoever killed her had to have made it look like suicide. It's a long shot, but possible."

He thought it was a long shot because of how good the killer would have had to be in setting up the crime scene.

"The killer might have gotten lucky." She sat in the car, excited with this new twist in the investigation. The amount of time that had passed before Kaelyn's body was discovered gave the killer lots of opportunity.

Roman leaned down to bring his head level with hers. "There's one other thing. I didn't find anything in the police report about trace evidence."

None was collected. Her clothes would have been destroyed, so all she and Roman had now were photographs and descriptions of the scene. He still had doubts, and even Kendra agreed the evidence they had pointed to suicide. But she remembered how Kaelyn sounded just before her death—too happy to have taken her own life.

"I think you're onto something with the time of death."

"We're definitely going to look into it."

She met his eyes and saw the determined detective who'd solved many cases and loved doing it. She wondered if he was even aware of how much.

When she began to feel that gaze, simmering in her heart, she turned her head.

Kendra had a charming table ready by the time Roman spotted her niece stepping out of a ten-year-old Ford Escort. He could see and sense Kendra's nervousness. She'd tapped into her artistic reservoir to create a table worthy of a home and patio decor magazine. The day was sunny with a few puffy white clouds, barely a breath of a breeze and on the warm side in the mideighties.

Raelyn's companion was a young man, close in age to her. Roman could see her long red hair from here, and also her goth style of dress. A red-and-black lace skirt swayed as she walked in black ankle boots. Her off-the-shoulder black top exposed a trim belly. Instead of a tattoo, she wore black wristbands. Her friend looked the same, with spiky black hair and piercings on his ear, lip and eyebrow. He wore a short-sleeved black T-shirt with black jeans, shoes and a black silver-studded belt. As they came closer, he saw Raelyn had yet to mark her body with the art that covered her friend's right arm. Roman's first impression was that both suffered from some kind of identity crisis.

"Has she always dressed like that?" he asked.

"No." Kendra sounded disappointed. "Kaelyn sent me a lot of pictures. One more reason why she never would have killed herself. She loved her daughter way too much to do that to her."

Roman refrained from commenting and continued to watch the approaching young couple. Rebellion radiated from the young man, and not the usual kind. This one seemed rougher than the average kid trying to find his or her way early in adulthood. That Raelyn had chosen this kind of person as her boyfriend revealed her insecurities and the lasting effect of losing her mother.

Raelyn wore sunglasses but he'd seen a picture of her green eyes. Her steps slowed and her mouth stayed in a flat line. She must be nervous, as well.

Kendra stepped forward with open arms, going to Raelyn and hugging her briefly. "Thanks for coming."

"This is Adam."

"Hello, Adam." Kendra turned to indicate Roman. "This is the private investigator I hired. I thought he could answer any questions you might have." She led the two closer.

Raelyn took in the blue-and-white checkered runner on the wood picnic table with napkins and silverware beside lighter blue–rimmed paper plates. Three small clay pots filled with dark pink wildflowers were set along the table, mixed with sealable glass jars filled with layered multicolored pebbles—reddish sand on the bottom, lighter earth tones in the middle and light blue on top. Kendra had told him she'd spent the morning putting it all together at her shop.

"Roman Cooper." He stuck out his hand to Adam.

The young man took it for an awkward, weak-gripped shake.

Raelyn eyed him warily.

"Your aunt brought me here to look into your mother's death because she doesn't think your mom killed herself."

"She told me." Raelyn didn't look happy about that.

"I don't have any evidence to refute the suicide, but there are elements about this case that are suspicious."

"Do you think my dad might have killed her?"

"He's someone I'm looking at, but your mother was also seeing two other men."

"I didn't know about Jasper until after she died. She went out when my dad wasn't home. He went to the bar a lot after work so it was easy for her to get away with it. My dad wasn't exactly a bright ray of sunshine. He was a hotheaded jerk."

"What about here in Chesterville?" Roman asked.

"I was with her whenever she came. She went out while she was here, too. I didn't know with whom. I would spend time with Grandmother during those times and I'd spend time with Mom during the day. We usually came here on weekends and my school breaks."

Seeing her face soften with memory, Roman didn't ask her any more questions. He just said, "If your mother was murdered, I'll find her killer."

Raelyn's mouth turned up just a fraction. She still seemed hesitant but more open to the prospect of moving forward.

"I can keep you updated on the progress we make if you want," Kendra said.

"Okay." Raelyn nodded a couple of times, more hesitancy coming out.

"Great." Kendra put her arm around her and steered

her to the picnic table. "How about you tell me how you're doing?"

Adam followed but didn't take a seat. Roman stood beside him.

"Are you working?" Kendra asked Raelyn as the two sat.

"I got a job at a gas station."

"You graduated college with a degree in psychology, right?"

"Yeah."

Adam went to the cooler and lifted the lid, searching for something he must not have found inside. He closed the lid with a thunk.

"What do you plan to do?"

Left unspoken was the suggestion that Raelyn surely couldn't be planning to work at a gas station the rest of her life.

The girl shrugged.

"You can work at my shop if you like."

Raelyn's head straightened as though the suggestion had perked her up. "Doing what?"

"Anything. You can work the cash register or I can teach you how to make floral arrangements. I can teach you the business if you're more like your mother than me." Kendra smiled.

"What do you mean?"

"Your mother had the sharper mind. I was always more artistic."

Roman debated whether Kendra's mind was any less sharp. It took a lot to start your own company and make it successful.

"Do you want me to go grab some beers?" Adam asked as he stood beside Roman.

"No. I don't want any beer." It was the middle of the day. Did the kid have a drinking problem? Roman wouldn't doubt it and hoped Kendra's influence would alter her niece's current path.

Adam stuffed his hands into his pockets and looked around the park as though self-conscious and trying to cover that up.

"I'm gonna go smoke," the young man said. "Wanna join me?"

Roman dismissed all the sarcastic responses that came to mind and said as neutrally as he could, "No, thanks."

He watched Adam walk away, thinking Kendra would make quick work of removing the kid from Raelyn's life. Not that Roman didn't wish the boy well. He hoped he overcame his insecurities; he just didn't want Kendra to have to watch her niece involved in that painful growth. She had her own pain to grow out of, much different—Roman was sure—from whatever had caused Adam's crisis.

"Who was my mom seeing when she came here?" Roman heard Raelyn ask Kendra.

Roman sat across from them as Kendra answered.

"His name is Glenn Franklin. She called him Bear when I talked to her. She kept him secret because he was married, but I know she had strong feelings for him. He's the city prosecutor's son."

Raelyn seemed to take that in for a while before asking, "Did she love him?"

"I think so." Kendra's tone was gentle. She was being careful not to upset Raelyn.

"Why did she marry my dad?"

"I'm glad she did, or you wouldn't have been born."

Kendra bumped her shoulder against Raelyn's playfully. The young woman smiled a tiny bit.

"I think your mom loved him when they first met," Kendra went on. "In the first few years, she was probably happy and the abuse didn't get bad until later."

"Because he beat her." Raelyn's tone decisively changed, deeper and full of anger and resentment.

"Yes, unfortunately."

"Why didn't she take me away from him?" Raelyn asked. "She could have at least tried."

"He probably threatened her," Roman interjected. When Raelyn looked at him, he went on. "I've investigated murder cases involving women who didn't leave because their husband threatened to kill them if they did. You mother was in a damned if she did, damned if she didn't situation. If she left, her husband would try to kill her. If she stayed, her husband would eventually kill her anyway. She never stopped trying. She just had to wait for the right time."

"She could have gone to the cops."

"Without proof they can't do anything," Roman said. This was what she needed to hear from someone who knew the law. "Even if he was arrested, he'd be released on bond in most cases. What would she have done then?"

Kendra put her hand over Raelyn's on the table. "I know your mother was making plans to leave your dad. She asked someone to help her, someone Roman works with."

"But he said no, right?"

"He was going to help her. And she would have taken you and come to live with me."

"Why didn't she as soon as you started talking? Why did she wait?"

"I don't know, Raelyn. She must have been afraid."

"She was a coward! She *killed herself*!"

"She didn't kill herself," Kendra asserted.

Roman disagreed with telling Raelyn that. They didn't know for sure one way or another.

"She might as well have." Raelyn lifted tormented eyes to her aunt. "She left me with that monster! I hate him! I hate him so much!"

The girl felt abandoned. Who wouldn't? Losing your mother at a young age would be hard on anyone.

"Did your dad hurt you?" Kendra asked.

"He yelled a lot. Broke things. Put holes in the walls. He hit me sometimes. He hit my mother a lot more. For a long time, I didn't blame her for leaving, for taking the coward's way out."

"But then you did blame her?" Kendra asked.

Raelyn didn't respond right away, seeming to consider if she'd call how she felt blame. "I got really mad at her. I mean…what was she *thinking*? How could she kill herself and leave me behind? What did she think my life was going to be without her?" Raelyn's voice rose as she talked.

Roman could hear all the pent-up anger coming to the surface. He doubted she'd spoken like this before. Had she told anyone how she felt about her mom dying? Maybe not that she was angry, but what about the loss she'd suffered? Roman didn't think she had anyone. He glanced over at the young man smoking his cigarette. He wasn't in any hurry to get back to their picnic. Not much of a social type.

"What if she didn't kill herself? How will you

feel then?" Kendra had asked Raelyn as Roman observed Adam.

"I'll want to butcher whoever killed her." Raelyn glanced over at Adam. "My life would be so different now if Mom would have taken us away from my dad. I used to dream about living without him, how peaceful life would be with just me and Mom."

Kendra gave her hand a squeeze. "I wish she could have."

Raelyn turned her head to look at Kendra. "I also used to dream about killing him. One night when he was in one of his rages, I took a knife from the kitchen and went to my room. I waited for him to pass out drunk, and then went to his room. I stood over him on the bed, watching him snore. He stunk like booze and gingivitis. I remember thinking, *Should I slit his throat or drive this knife straight into his chest?* The indecision stopped me from doing anything."

"Raelyn," Kendra breathed. "I'm so glad you decided not to do it."

"I was worried about myself the next day. I hated my dad so much for making my mother kill herself and for being such an ass, but killing him would hurt me even more. I'd be the one who went to prison, not him. He's the one who deserves to rot in jail, not me."

"Yes, he does. Any man who causes violence in the home is the one who deserves consequences. It doesn't matter if all they do is throw and break things and be verbally abusive. It's wrong whether they physically hurt you or not."

Raelyn nodded and looked out at the park. "I promised myself that as soon as I graduated from high school, I'd leave home and go to college. I'd never have to see him again as long as I live." She smiled somberly. "I haven't. He tried calling a few times and I changed my number. I never told him where I was living or that I moved to Chesterville. He left me voice messages. Some of them were angry, yelling and calling me names. Others were pleading to call or come see him. He'd say he missed us, me and Mom, but I bet the only thing he missed was having someone to punch and control."

"He's a small man, and I don't mean physically. He's weak-minded and allows his ego to control his thoughts and beliefs. He's not in touch with his spiritual side and isn't smart enough to realize he has a problem."

Raelyn nodded again, turning back to her. "When he wasn't drinking he was actually normal. But I never trusted him enough to let my guard down. I knew in a matter of hours, he'd be drunk again and flying into a stupid rage."

Kendra patted Raelyn's hand and slid hers away to rest on the table. "Well, you don't ever have to see him. He doesn't exist anymore."

Raelyn turned toward the park once again. "I wish my mom was still alive."

"I do, too. So much."

Raelyn sighed in her silent thoughts. Roman watched as Kendra observed her and he felt she also wished she could take her niece's pain away.

Moving her gaze to where Adam took his time smoking, Raelyn seemed to come out of her journey back in time.

"Where did you meet him?" Kendra asked.

"A bar." Raelyn looked away from Adam and Roman heard boredom in her voice.

"Must have been some bar. What's he like?"

Raelyn shrugged. "His dad was a piece of crap like mine. We relate, you know?"

"Maybe. I would think you'd be happier with someone who doesn't remind you of your dad at his worst."

"What, like…I should go for some nerd who'd never understand me?"

Roman saw Adam toss his cigarette butt to the ground and head toward them.

"I wouldn't go for any labels. I'd go for someone who is making something of their life and is healthy and makes you feel good all the time."

"Adam makes me feel good. He brings me flowers when he can afford it. We go out. We hang." She spotted Adam, as well, and watched him walk closer.

"What do you talk about?"

Raelyn shrugged again. "Stuff."

"Your crappy dads…bar nights? Don't you think you deserve more?"

"Why are you ragging on me about Adam?"

"I'm not ragging. I just don't want you to end up with someone your abusive father influenced you into gravitating to. What does Raelyn want? What does Raelyn like in a man? Do you know?"

"Know what?" Adam asked.

Kendra glanced up and back as Adam came to a stop at the table.

"Nothing," Raelyn said, turning her attention to the table. "Where's the food?"

She must suddenly be in a hurry to get this event over with. No more talk of abusive dads and death.

Picking up on the same feeling, Kendra got up and went about preparing their lunch, going slow as though letting the serious talk fade before they all sat down together and had lunch. She kept glancing over at Rae-lyn, smiling when her niece saw her.

It was the beginning of a new relationship. Kendra could feel it. This picnic would be the trigger, the icebreaker.

After sharing a wonderful picnic with Raelyn—she would try to forget her boyfriend was there—Kendra hugged her niece and whispered into her ear, "Come by the shop tomorrow."

Raelyn leaned back with a smile. "I will."

Then Kendra watched her walk away, Adam far ahead and already opening the car door. He obviously couldn't wait to get away from Raelyn's family.

"Charming fellow," Roman said.

She'd noticed his scrutiny of the young man. She'd also noticed how he'd kept his interaction to a minimum, as though he sensed Kendra's need to bond with her niece. Nothing felt better than that, the bonding. Never mind what Roman did to her.

As she began gathering everything from the table, Roman's phone rang. He took it and talked to someone he obviously knew.

"How's Reese? Handling life on flatter ground?" he asked. "Has she dragged you back to her mountains yet?" After a pause, he said, "With a father like Kadin Tandy, that doesn't surprise me."

Roman listened a while longer, responding occasionally but not with enough information for her to decipher what was said. All Kendra could gather was he must be talking to someone at DAI. She finished putting what was left of the food into the cooler.

"Can you get medical records and the coroner's report?" Roman finally asked.

Kendra waited as he finished the call and disconnected.

"Kadin has a daughter?" she asked.

"Yes, Reese. Jamie Knox's new wife. Knox is DAI's head of security. Apparently she likes helping her dad run the agency."

Given Kadin's tragic past and the thing that had driven him to open such an agency, Kendra was happy for him to have discovered he had another daughter.

"He ran a background on Glenn Franklin and your sister's husband, Alex."

She stopped putting trash into a bag to turn toward him.

"Alex was arrested for an assault on a police officer after he was pulled over for drunk driving. Your sister never pressed charges for abuse, but his previous wife did. I doubt Kaelyn ever knew that."

It came as no surprise that Alex had a rap sheet. Kendra gazed off across the sea of green grass and a play area where kids slid down a winding slide and floated back and forth on swings.

How she wished her sister could have escaped her husband. At least she had good and loving parents. That was something Kendra couldn't say about her own childhood and teen years.

"Other than that, he's gone delinquent on credit cards and car loans. Never had a mortgage. Had two previous DUIs before the last that landed him in jail for three years. He was arrested two months ago." Roman went on. "Kaelyn did have a life insurance policy."

Kendra jerked her gaze back to him. "How much?"

"A hundred thousand. Insurance didn't pay because it was suicide and there was a clause stating death wasn't covered by suicide unless the policy had been in place for two years. It has been in place for a year and nine months."

"Ha," she scoffed. "So if he killed her, he didn't get what he wanted."

"Glenn's background is squeaky clean," he said. "Financially, he's sound. No criminal record. Not even a speeding ticket."

"He has rich parents."

"That wouldn't erase a criminal record."

She folded her arms and walked toward him. "So it looks like if anyone killed my sister, it had to be Alex."

"Maybe. Did you know Glenn was married before his current wife?"

"Kaelyn never mentioned it."

"She became sick and died. Rather suddenly, I might add."

"Sick with what?"

"I've got DAI fishing for her medical records and the coroner's report. From what I've been able to glean, she developed a severe case of the flu and had a heart attack."

"You're suspicious?"

"Not yet." He sounded so confident. It gave her a flashing spark. Sexy.

He was only checking every possible lead. Even sexier. He didn't presume guilt or innocence. He remained neutral until all his questions were answered.

"It is peculiar that both his first wife and now his lover died," she said.

"Especially since his first wife was in her early

twenties and was a track star in high school and college."

Too healthy to succumb to a flu bug? What really caused her heart attack?

Maybe Roman was more suspicious than he let on.

Chapter 7

"Adam and I had a fight after we left the park yesterday." Raelyn helped Kendra set up a Memorial Day display near the front entrance. American flag ornaments and everything one would need for a day at the park or backyard barbecue.

Kendra perked up, both from what Raelyn said and also that she felt comfortable enough to say it. "About what?"

"He thinks I shouldn't be around you. Like you're a bad influence."

A bad influence? Kendra had to stop herself from laughing. Instead, she glanced down at Raelyn's black skinny jeans and tight black tank top with four or five necklaces hanging down, the black bands ringing her wrists and all the piercings in her ear and one in her nose.

"Maybe he'd like you to stay where you are and not progress into something more, something better."

She considered that awhile before she said, "He thinks my mom killed herself."

Did she see, then, that this boy, whether intentionally or not, wanted her to stay behind with him?

"And you don't anymore?" she asked.

"I don't want to think she did." She stopped hanging ornaments on the display tree. "I think you're right. It's like he doesn't want me to have anything good happen, like he'd lose that connection we have."

"Both wallowing in misfortune?"

Raelyn thought a moment. "Yeah." She resumed hanging ornaments. "I broke up with him."

Kendra smiled. "Did you?"

"Yes, after he said he didn't like you and Roman, and he didn't want to spend any more time with you."

"How did he take that?"

"He got really mad. He threw his bottle of beer and it broke against the wall and made a mess. I left his house with him yelling at me until I got into my car and drove off." She turned to look at Kendra. "He reminded me of my dad."

"I'm so glad you ended it with him. You're such a beautiful girl and you're so young. You have a college degree. Your whole life is ahead of you. You don't need to settle down with a man yet. That's something everyone should be absolutely sure of before they commit to anything serious. Adam didn't seem right for you when I met him."

Raelyn shook her head. "He was fun for a while, but I'm done with him."

"Add *strong* to my list of accolades."

Raelyn seemed awkward with the compliment. She looked down and sat on the edge of the display window. "What about you? Have you ever been married?"

Kendra hung another ornament. "No. I didn't learn much about what a good family is. I don't remember my parents much. What I do remember is they were good, hardworking people and they loved me and Kaelyn. My adoptive parents were terrible. Like your dad." Kendra had let Roman work in her office and wondered if he could hear this. It was just in the back behind the checkout counter. The soft patter of fingers tapping away on a keyboard drifted out into the store. He was busy doing something.

"Really?"

"Yes. I know exactly what it's like to grow up with awful people."

Raelyn's eyes blinked as she looked up at her and a poignant moment passed. Now Raelyn understood she wasn't alone and in Kendra she had a family member who could relate.

"So you don't want to be with a man?" Raelyn asked as though not wanting to talk further about her dad.

"I wouldn't say that. I like being in charge of my own life. No one can make me unhappy that way."

"Have you ever been with someone who made you unhappy?"

Kendra scoffed with a short breath. "More than one."

"What happened?"

"I met a guy in college and we were a couple for a few years. We lived together after graduation. I caught him cheating on me. About a year after that, I met a guy who seemed nice. We went on a few dates until I discovered he had an arrest record. He told me he graduated from college and had a job, but all that was a lie. He had a high school equivalency and still lived with his parents. He also spent some time in jail. Needless to say, I stopped answering his calls. The third guy I dated who seemed promising started trying to control what I did when we weren't together. That's when I decided to concentrate on me. No more men." At least for a while.

Raelyn looked up at her thoughtfully. "If you meet the right man, you would change your mind."

Picturing herself with a man, living together or married, contemplating whether or not to have kids, Kendra felt sick to her stomach. She could not imagine herself happy that way. What about her freedom? Trusting a man with her life threatened that. She feared what a man might take from her.

"The only thing I'm sure of is I never want to feel the way I did after our parents were killed, and even more so in my foster home and later when they adopted me. I was trapped and always felt in danger and like I had no control over anything." She stopped arranging fake bottles of soda in a bucket cooler and looked at Raelyn. "I might as well have been adrift on a raft in the middle of Lake Michigan, unable to jump off and unable to paddle to shore. Going nowhere, just stuck and scared."

"That's how I felt after mom died, but I still like boys." Raelyn smiled almost sheepishly, as though revealing her youthful attraction to males was a secret she didn't trust many with.

"I didn't say I don't like boys. I just don't want them permanently."

"Unless you find one who doesn't control you." Raelyn looked toward the back office.

"You…" Surely Raelyn didn't mean Roman and her…

She realized the soft tapping had stopped.

"I've seen the way he looks at you. And he doesn't crowd you at all."

Kendra wondered about Roman's past. All she knew about him was he was a detective, had worldly parents and—amazingly and out of character for such a strong, intelligent man—insecurity over his direction in life. Roman might have that insecurity, but she saw none in his interaction with women—with her. He was not shy. He did not lack confidence as a man that way. He did not lack confidence as a detective, either. His baggage with his parents intrigued her all the more. Obviously he needed to measure up and felt he didn't. That said, he had a great amount of respect for his parents. How could he not, growing up so idyllically? Kendra and Kaelyn would have had childhoods like that if their parents hadn't been gunned down.

"You like him."

Jarred from thought, Kendra saw Raelyn's smile and hurriedly finished the display. "Roman is here to help solve your mother's murder, nothing more."

Raelyn looked away but her smile said all that needed to be said. She knew Roman was here for more than that and Kendra welcomed it, albeit deep in her heart.

Deciding to capitalize on this loving moment, Kendra reached over and brushed her niece's red hair back from her face. Then she ran her forefinger down her nose, touching the ring through one nostril and looked at her eyes, rimmed with dark eye shadow and liner and a thick application of mascara. The black lipstick added to the Picasso effect.

"You don't need all that." She gently flicked the nose ring. "Why the dark makeup?"

Raelyn shrugged and averted her eyes.

"You have beautiful green eyes, just like your mother's."

"And yours." Raelyn flashed a brief smile.

Kendra's and Kaelyn's eyes had been very similar. "You don't need so much makeup." She touched the black bands around her wrist. Or that. "Do you know how pretty you are?"

"Aunt Kendra," she protested.

But Kendra wasn't finished. She went to a shelf not far from the window and found a vanity mirror, one that stood daintily on a small pedestal and swiveled between a normal and magnified side. Taking it over to Raelyn, she sat beside her and held the mirror so they could see both their faces. Their eyes looked strikingly similar, almost hauntingly, which gave Kendra a momentary pang of loss. But that quickly vanished as she gazed at her pretty niece. "I bet if you wore less makeup you'd see how pretty you are. So would everyone else. And your clothes don't have to make such a dark statement. Are there any other styles that catch your eye?"

Raelyn moved away and stood, and Kendra could see she'd pushed too hard, too soon.

Her niece rounded on her. "Are you saying you think I'm a slob?"

Putting the mirror down, Kendra stood. "No. The opposite."

Raelyn spread her arms out and looked down at herself. "What's the matter with the way I look?"

It's a stamp, Kendra wanted to say. "It...makes you seem harder than you are. Tough."

"I am tough."

"Yes, you are, but not in a hoodlum kind of way."

"Now you're saying I'm a *druggie*?" Raelyn's voice rose with insult and anger.

"No." This was quickly going down the drain. Kendra didn't claim to be an expert on kids or young adults. She only called things the way she saw them. Now she'd upset her niece.

"Maybe I shouldn't have come here." Raelyn snatched up her purse and started for the door.

"Raelyn, wait." Kendra followed her to the door, which Raelyn swung open hard.

"Leave me alone!"

"Wait." Kendra stood in the open doorway, watching her niece march down the sidewalk toward her car.

"Give her time to cool off."

Kendra jumped with Roman's voice so close behind her. She hadn't heard him approach.

Turning and letting the door close, she first had a breathless look at his handsome face, and then said, "What are you, a cat burglar? Do you always sneak up on people?"

"It's the shoes."

She looked down at the black leather shoes. "Stealth shoes?"

He just grinned.

"I was going to offer to take her shopping," she said.

"That might have set her off more."

She may have assumed Kendra intended to change

her wardrobe. Although that may have been partly true, she meant no insult. "I'm only trying to help."

"Don't force her. You planted a seed. Let it take root awhile. She'll come around."

"How do you know so much about kids her age?" Did he have kids of his own? A flash of alarm zapped her. She didn't know if she could handle that. And then she wondered why she thought she'd have to. Was she anticipating them starting something?

"I was with a woman who had a daughter. She was a teenager when I knew her." He went to one of two chairs Kendra had set up as a seating area in front of one of the Christmas trees to promote sales.

He sat, his big body taking up the delicate chair.

Kendra sat on the chair next to him. "You must have been with them awhile." Otherwise he wouldn't have learned so much insight into the minds of young women.

"Yeah. About six years."

"Were you married?"

He shook his head. "I was never convinced she was the one."

"Why not?" Kendra felt starved for information about him. She wanted to know everything and couldn't explain why.

"I met her at a farmers market. I was with another girl and she was with another man. We bumped into each other in a chili peppers tent. The people we were with were in other tents. We talked awhile and hit it off. I gave her my card. About a week later, I broke up with my girlfriend and about a month later I received a call from her. She seemed so down-to-earth at first."

He must have discovered the woman hadn't been so down-to-earth after all.

"Her daughter never liked me," he said. "But I learned how to handle her. We sort of had a tolerant relationship. She liked to tease me. She kept calling me Harry because she said I had the same dry and boring personality as Harry Bosch." Roman chuckled. "I never thought Bosch was dry and boring."

"Dry sense of humor, maybe. Not boring." And neither was Roman. "Did you end the relationship or did she?"

"I did. She was the chief executive officer for a tech company. She worked a lot."

"That was a bad thing? She sounds successful."

"She was, and that was most important to her. I don't think she ever really had strong feelings for me. She liked that I worked a lot, too. I think she thought we made a good couple because of that, like I fit into her world."

"Problem was she didn't fit into yours?"

He shook his head. "Her world was too fabricated."

Right, because he lived in reality. Depressed reality. Reminded of how different they were, how he clashed with her positive nature, she curbed her curiosity. Why get to know him, why let herself start to like him too much, when they would eventually fizzle out and go their separate ways?

"She had everything," he went on. "Money. Career. A smart kid. Nice house. Perfect friends. I just felt like I was acting a role in her life just like everyone else around her. She wasn't real."

"Are you sure her success didn't threaten you?"

"Threaten me? Yes, I'm sure it didn't."

She believed him. Nothing threatened a man like him.
"I was...disillusioned."

She believed that, too, but not in the same light as
he probably meant. "Disillusioned about yourself, most
likely."

He didn't respond at first and she watched him think
it over. Then he finally said, "Her success didn't bother
me. It was her icy facade. She had to act emotion.
Friendships. Kissing. Making love. All an act to keep
her world perfectly in balance."

"You'd rather take a roller coaster?"

"The rockier the better."

Because then it would feel real to him.

"The only time I saw her without her guard was
when she was with her daughter, just the two of them.
I was envious, and I knew she'd never be that way
with me."

That almost sounded normal. She wouldn't have
wanted to stay in a relationship with someone who had
to act out their love, either. Kendra caught sight of the
clay clock next to the front window. It was almost time
to open the shop.

"I heard you talking about your experiences," Roman said.

"I thought you might have."

"A cheater, a liar and a control freak, huh?"

"Yes." She nodded, looking down at her feet. Today,
she'd worn a summer dress and sandals. Last night,
she'd painted her toenails dark pink to match the pink
flowers on her yellow dress.

"The cheater and the liar are predictable, but the
control freak?"

She raised her head. "What about him?"

"How did he try to control you?"

"He expected me to spend evenings and weekends with him."

"Isn't that what couples do?"

"I spent time with him. I just didn't want to spend as much as he demanded."

"He demanded?"

Kendra thought back and couldn't identify any time when her boyfriend had actually *demanded* they spend more time together. He always made the suggestion and she had to decline.

"Was he really trying to control you or did he just like you a lot?" Roman asked.

Her boyfriend had liked her and she remembered feeling like he liked her more than she liked him.

"Are you going to stay single your whole life?"

Why was he asking? "No." But even as she answered, inside she felt conflict, that same sick feeling she always had when she imagined getting married and having kids. "I don't know. I don't want to think about it now."

"When are you going to think about it? You aren't in your twenties anymore."

She might be too old to have kids already. But she had the gift of good genes. Her mother had looked far younger than her years, too.

"How old do you think I am?" Kendra asked, fingering the coaster holder on the table between them. A small, slender glass vase with two fresh, red carnations partially blocked her view of him. She moved it aside.

"I already know you're forty-one."

Of course, he had checked her out before he'd come

to Chesterville. "Well, then it's not fair I don't know your age." She slid the vase back.

He grinned. "Forty-three."

His face transformed into rugged gorgeousness. Kendra had to stare, unable to stop absorbing the light in his eyes and lines crinkling in just the right places.

"Do you ever feel like you're missing out by not having kids?" he asked. "I'm not asking to drill you. I've often wondered the same about me."

She felt the flare of commonality that he shared this life circumstance. "You feel you're missing out?"

"That's just it. I don't know."

The sense of camaraderie intensified. How could she feel so connected to him when they were so different? "I don't, either. I don't think I ever wanted to have kids. I never had that urge, you know?"

"Yeah." He nodded a couple of times.

"All I do know is I never wanted to be poor or addicted to drugs and alcohol."

He chuckled. "You succeeded in far more than that."

She'd done all right for herself, but now that they talked about this, she did have some lonely moments.

"You've made a perfect life for yourself. Nothing can touch you."

She had the feeling he wasn't being complimentary. "Anything can happen."

"You're prepared for that?"

"For what? Total annihilation?" He sure had an apocalyptic view of the world. "I hope to live happy and healthy for as long as possible. Why shoot an arrow through that by preparing for the worst? I'd much rather prepare for the best."

"I could live with nothing just as easily as I could

live with everything. All I'm saying is people weather life's curveballs better when they're prepared for them, rather than living in a dreamworld that will only shatter in the end."

He needed a giant dose of positive thinking. "What's your favorite movie?"

His brow crinkled a bit. She'd caught him by surprise with that question. He leaned forward, forearms on his knees, fingers entwined. "I don't really have one. Who doesn't love *Fargo*?"

Boy, she had sunk that dart right into the bull's-eye. "Dark comedies. Just what I thought. You're far too cynical, you know that? I prefer happy endings where the dog never dies."

He grinned again and she realized he was enjoying this. He sat back against the chair again. "But dogs *do* die in real life."

"Yes, but I don't have to dwell on that."

"No, but you should be able to watch movies that include a dog dying."

"That's like saying it's okay to desensitize, that it's okay to watch the news and not feel a thing when a reporter announces a shooter walked into a school and killed a half a dozen."

"That's not what I'm saying. I've been solving murders for two decades and I still feel every one of them."

But he was prepared to deal with them. Isn't that why he was such a good detective? He had to see how flawed his thinking was, though. Didn't he? Just because some—probably most—didn't plan ahead for disaster didn't mean they were incapable of surviving.

"Take me to your mother's apothecary museum." His warped thinking was a product of his difficulty measuring up to his parents. She was sure of it now. Why not thrust him right into the fray?

"What? No."

She stood up. "I can open late today. Come on. We can walk there from here." She went to the back to get her purse, finding her keys and returning to the front, where Roman stood. He seemed to be trying to calm his agitation, mouth tight, eyes wider than before.

Ignoring him, she unlocked the front door and held it open for him. He stood still a moment longer, but then breathed a soft laugh and left the shop. She locked the door and started walking.

"I know what you're doing," he said as they walked.

"I've never been to an apothecary museum."

He chuckled. "You've never met my mother, either."

Chapter 8

The Chesterville Apothecary Museum was in the old-est part of town. Built in the late 1700s, the redbrick Federal-style architecture had charming accents of the era. Brick-trimmed arcaded windows symmetrically lined the first and second stories. The double front door was particularly eye-catching, with one larger brick arch over two doors, each topped with smaller arched windows and a decorative circle filling the gap above. Ducking from the sudden driving rain, Kendra followed Roman inside.

Shaking her hair and stomping her feet on the commercial-grade rug, the smell of old wood and faint scent of perfumes mingled with damp air. She also heard voices coming from the upper level, a woman giving a few visitors a tour. She spoke with enthusiasm and the vibrancy of a strong, happy woman. Roman's mother. As she listened, Kendra stole the free moments to take in this fascinating place.

The apothecary seemed to be set up exactly as it had been when it closed its doors for the last time as a shop. Dark- and light-colored granite mortars and pestles decorated the countertop along the left side. Long ago, herbs would have been ground into pastes and powders that way. White shelves with labeled wooden drawers might still hold herbs.

Thunder rumbled outside, vibrating the walls.

Kendra ran her gaze to the back wall, where beautiful delftware jars lined another shelf. An oil painting of an apothecary shop hung on one side of the shelf, patrons assembled before a counter and a man a few steps up on a ladder, leaning toward shelves full of jars. On the other side hung a portrait of George Washington.

She stepped farther into the shop, vaguely aware of Roman doing the same, although he was far less enchanted than her.

The wood floors creaked as she stepped but gleamed with recent renovation. White crown molding and trim around doors and floor was thick and delicately carved. The dark slate countertop running the length of the left side of the museum contrasted with white cabinets and shelves. On the right, another counter and shelves stretched—this counter a display case enclosed in glass. It contained open books and some infographics on the history of the museum and its time as an apothecary shop. As she read about the generations of families who ran the shop, lightning flashed and thunder followed almost immediately. She glanced through the window as rain fogged the air, making visibility poor. Roman stood before one of the windows, watching the storm.

She took a moment to admire his backside—trim, fit butt in faded jeans and a black spring jacket. Droplets of water still clung to his thick black hair. A sliver of the column of his neck was exposed between the edge of his hair and the collar of his jacket.

When he began to turn, she averted her head and resumed reading. Another rumble of thunder and she looked up at the wooden drawers filling the shelf behind the display counter, then moved back to inspect the labeled white cabinets beneath the counters, pleasantly surprised to see this apothecary must have also sold more than herbal medicine. Some of the cabinets were marked as surgical and dental instruments, as well as essentials like soap and other toiletries. In the corners near the entrance, farm and garden equipment was displayed and more paintings filled the walls— a couple sitting on a park bench, a bundle of fruit, a portrait of a doctor and a landscape of an herb garden.

She went to the counter containing the mortars and pestles and read some of the labels on the wooden drawers. Valerian root. Mandrake root. Cannabis tincture.

"Dragon's blood?" She read the next one that caught her eye.

"You'll have to ask my mother."

Only then did she realize Roman had gone to the back of the shop, checking out the guest book on the counter there.

The voices grew louder, coming down the stairs. The visitors sounded pleased and happily excited to have received such an unusual glimpse into the past.

A tall, slender woman with dark hair cut short and smart appeared from the doorway to a narrow stairway adjacent to the rear counter. She wore rectangular glasses with flowers on the sides. She wore a cream-colored pantsuit with a flowing kimono and flat shoes. Her jewelry was minimal, a solitaire wedding ring, diamond earrings and a long silver necklace with a leafy pendant. Although likely in her early sixties, she was a strikingly beautiful woman with smooth skin and attractive wrinkles around her stunning blue eyes.

Three visitors, a smiling older couple and a forty-something woman talked a little longer with Roman's mother, who caught sight of Roman and brightened. She finished with the visitors, taking payment when they chose some souvenirs while thunder continued to roll through the clouds outside. At last the visitors left, all talking at the same time.

"Roman." The woman walked to him with arms outstretched.

Roman hugged her. "Mother."

"You didn't tell me you were coming." She leaned back to inspect her tall son. "You look older. That job of yours is ravaging you."

Kendra loved her already. She didn't hold back. She spoke true.

Roman didn't appear to like her bluntness. He moved back and without inflection said, "This is Kendra Scott. I'm looking into her sister's death. Kaelyn Johnston. You probably heard about that."

The woman turned to Kendra as she put together the pieces. "Oh, yes. I know her mother. The poor girl. And her mother." The woman shook her head in sympathy. "She was devastated over the loss. She and Kaelyn were very close. Kaelyn visited often. I'd see her accompany her mother to community events. Her mother was quite active in town, a good role model for her daughter."

"My mother knows everyone," Roman said.

The woman sent her son an admonishing look. "You would, too, if you weren't so antisocial."

"I'm not antisocial. I'm just not as social as you and Dad. Few can keep up with you." Again, he turned to Kendra. "They might as well be voted Chesterville's Most Popular."

The woman laughed and said to Kendra, "I'm Abby Cooper."

"Nice to meet you." Kendra smiled.

"She's quite attractive, Roman. Are the two of you…"

"No, Mother," Roman interrupted.

But Abby wouldn't be deterred. "Are you seeing anyone right now?"

"No, Mother," he repeated, his tone warning not to go where he must know she was headed.

"Are you seeing anyone?" Abby asked Kendra.

Kendra laughed softly, charmed by the woman. "No. Not at the moment."

"She might be a little young for you."

"She's two years younger than me."

"Oh my. Well, you have good genes in your family."

Kendra didn't say *so do you*, but she thought it.

"You…" Something seemed to dawn on Abby. "I remember hearing about you. You're Kaelyn's twin sister, separated at a young age after your parents died."

"That's me. I'm beginning to see why you're so popular in town." The woman remembered everyone and everything she heard. She had a genuine interest in people.

Abby laughed again, her bright and positive spirit shining through. How on Earth could Roman have ended up so different?

"What brings you by?" Abby wagged her finger in front of Roman. "Shame on you for not calling."

"I would have. Kendra wanted to see your museum, so we walked here from her Christmas shop."

"Oh, of course. I know who you are now. I've heard of your shop and have been meaning to stop in. I haven't seen you around town, though. How is it that I've missed you?"

"Yes, how did you?" Roman asked, teasing.

"I've been to a few festivals and run the usual errands. I suppose we just haven't run into each other yet."

"Maybe not. And you aren't active on any committees like Kaelyn's mother was."

"No. I only enjoy what the committees do for the town."

Abby still smiled. "I like her," she said to her son.

"Kendra was wondering what dragon's blood is," Roman said, changing the subject. Apparently his mother played matchmaker.

"It's a resin obtained from a variety of plants." She moved to the counter with the mortars and pestles. "Croton is one, but was also used as a laxative."

Kendra saw the drawer labeled Croton.

"Dracaena is another. One example of a dracaena is a lucky bamboo plant, but it can be used for many other things ranging from antiviral to eczema." She pointed to another drawer. "Daemonorops produces a red resin called dragon's blood, but was also used as an anticoagulant. Rotang and Pterocarpus are two others.

Pterocarpus produces a reddish wood called Padauk, which is used for skin parasites or fungal infections."

"Fascinating."

"What's fascinating is my son came to see me with a lovely woman. You both have to come over for dinner tonight. Your father will never forgive you if he finds out you came to town on business and didn't stop by to see him."

"Dinner it is, then." Roman did not sound enthused.

"You know you want to. Stop resisting." Abby looked at Kendra. "He thinks he followed his father's footsteps like he had to impress him and feels he hasn't." She took a step closer to her son and pinched his cheek. "You're fine just the way you are."

"Mom, I know." He drew away from her hand.

"Yes, you think you do. A mother knows her son." Dropping her hand, she turned to Kendra again. "He was a rebellious kid, always trying to get our attention. I was amazed he graduated from high school with good grades. His college degree was a real bonus." She looked adoringly at Roman. "Looks like your dad and I did all right." She laughed breezily.

Despite what she said, which could be construed as not very flattering, Roman's mother clearly loved her son. Kendra felt the sting of memory, what little she had left of her own mother. Bandaging a scrape. Reading bedtime stories. Telling her the Barbie doll could be anything she wanted, a doctor or a lawyer or an artist. She had encouraged in creative ways and never talked down to her and Kaelyn. Kendra had never forgotten feeling loved. It was the only time in her life she'd ever felt that way.

* * *

Roman told Kendra his parents lived in the same house he'd grown up in, and as he drove up the stately driveway, her breath caught when she saw the beautiful house. Earth-toned, rough-face stone made an eye-catching English manor–style exterior. Two gables and dormers on the second level broke up what had to be several thousand feet of living space. He parked on the circular driveway. She got out and walked with him to the low front porch, covered with two seating areas, one on each side of a mahogany door bordered by a transom window above and two sidelight panels.

Roman opened the door and called, "We're here."

A connoisseur of interior design, she stopped to take in the foyer. White lap siding covered the walls, knotty wood the ceiling and slate tile the floor. A shell bowl was on a steel-and-white-ceramic-topped console table. Two paintings of starfish and seashells hung above.

"In here!" his mother called.

Kendra sniffed the air. "I smell spaghetti sauce."

"My mother likes to make spaghetti pie for new guests. It's her casual dish."

"I love spaghetti." She followed him into a living room with blue accents and big windows and a huge abstract painting of a girl in blue shorts leaning back on a tire swing, more blue washing the background in the sky.

A seating area was visible on one side of a partial wall and a kitchen island that could fit four on the other. Entering the kitchen, she spotted Abby and William Cooper standing at the stove along the partial wall. Steam billowed up from mildly boiling water. William held a spoonful of sauce up, ready for a taste. A tall man with gray hair and glasses, he looked up and saw them. He put the spoon onto a spoon dish and smiled.

Kendra made a quick round of inspecting the kitchen. Medium brown cabinets had brushed silver pulls. They rose to the trim of twelve-foot ceilings above gray stone counters. A table and seating area with a coffee table she'd seen from the living room was a different twist on dining. More social.

"We're just about ready to get this in the oven," Abby said.

Roman pulled out a stool for her at the island counter. "Something to drink?"

Seeing Abby and William each had a glass of wine, she said, "What they're having."

Abby took the boiling water to the sink and drained the noodles while William got out a shallow casserole dish.

Roman retrieved two wineglasses from the cabinet above a wine cooler. The bottle of red was already out on the counter. He poured them both a glass and brought them to the island. As he handed her the glass, she met his eyes. Their hands brushed in the transfer, warming the moment.

Kendra saw William notice as he poured the sauce into the casserole dish. Luckily, Abby appeared with the noodles and his attention had to go elsewhere.

"That'll take about thirty minutes." Abby straightened after putting the dish into the oven, and then wiped her hands on a towel. "Let's go in here." She walked to the dining table, which had been set for four.

Roman pulled out a chair for Kendra. She found the gesture odd, given his lack of desire to be here. Maybe he didn't mind his parents drawing the wrong conclusion about them.

He sat next to her, his mom across from him and his dad across from her. His mother wore a very slight smile but her eyes smiled for her. She approved of them as a couple.

"How close are you to solving Kaelyn's murder, son?" William asked.

"I just started. I've got another case I'm working, too."

Kendra set her glass down and turned to him, not having expected him to work other cases while he was here. She wasn't sure she liked that. What if his attention was drawn too far off her sister? Or did he still need convincing that she had, in fact, been murdered?

"What's that one?" his mother asked.

"A doctor in Montana was murdered in his practice. His receptionist found him. He had a partner who recently lost his license because he carried on a sexual relationship with one of his patients. The victim's daughter told me her father was the one who exposed him. I started checking the partner out. He had an alibi, but I noticed he withdrew ten thousand from his bank account the day before the murder. During questioning, he denied any involvement."

"But you still suspected him?" William asked.

Kendra thought he must love talking about these cases with his son. Did they give him ideas for his stories?

"Yes, but his alibi checked out. He wasn't the one who killed the victim. A witness said they saw a red SUV leaving the crime scene. They couldn't get a good description of the driver. It took me a while but after searching through bank video surveillance, I found one of a red SUV matching the description of the witness. Another video showed a man making a deposit that I later found out was for ten thousand."

"That was enough to make an arrest?" William asked.

"No, but the SUV was a rental and DNA on one of the knobs matched the man's. He must have been sweating and wiped his skin before touching the knob. There was no DNA recovered from the crime scene. We also had a boot print in the victim's blood. I'm waiting on testing, but I'm sure we have our guy. He'll talk soon."

"Do you have to travel to Montana?" Kendra asked.

"No. The rest I can handle remotely."

She was glad he was close to wrapping that up. "Is that the case you nearly turned me down for to solve?"

He met her eyes. "But I didn't turn you down."

"No. Something did keep you here, didn't it?" She didn't mean to flirt; it just came out that way, a natural response to his gorgeous eyes, with their manly glow and answering attraction.

"Yes, something did."

"You were going to refuse to investigate her case?" Abby asked.

"I didn't think there was enough to show motive. But Kendra told me how she and her sister talked and how excited Kaelyn was to spend time together and that she had plans to move back to Chesterville."

"And *that's* what changed your mind?" Abby glanced at Kendra.

"Yes."

"I don't know, Roman. She's awfully pretty. Are you sure you didn't have other ideas?"

"He did," Kendra said. "He coerced me to go out on a date with him."

"That wasn't a date."

"Admit it. You used my case to get me to meet you."

Roman sat back with a sexy grin. Kendra felt a rush of heat, so loving how unabashed he was about being caught going after her—as a woman and not a new case.

"Well...maybe a little."

Kendra swatted his bicep, all in play, and felt the hardness of muscle. "That was the only reason. You didn't believe I had a case."

"Not at first, no. And I did enjoy our pool game."

She had enjoyed it, too.

"This is a delightful surprise," Abby said. "Roman works so much we were beginning to think he'd never find himself a girlfriend."

"Oh, we aren't...like that...yet."

Roman met her eyes again and she couldn't turn away. They weren't like that yet, but they could be. She felt him think the same. What scared her is she might feel too much.

Clearing her throat, uncomfortable, she faced Abby and William. Abby made no attempt to hide her approval. She oozed joy in seeing her son attracted to a woman. William was a bit harder to read. He watched and wore a slight smile but that could just as easily be the delicious wine.

"Tell me how you got into writing," Kendra said, desperate to change the subject.

William drew in a deep breath and slowly let it out.

"A lot of readers ask me that question. I don't know what made me write those first pages. I was always drawn to it. I was also an avid reader myself, and I loved English. But if there was one triggering event that drove me to pursue a career, I'd have to say it was my father being convicted of murdering my mother when I was fifteen."

The unexpectedness of the revelation struck Kendra. She felt her head flinch backward ever so slightly. "Oh my...I'm so sorry."

"Kendra's parents were killed in a mass shooting," Roman said.

"Yes, we knew about that. Kaelyn's mother told us. So tragic. She never mentioned Kaelyn had a twin, though, or why the two of you were split up."

"Kaelyn must not have been ready to tell anyone. Like I've told Roman, I believe she intended to use me as her escape. She may have planned to come live with me for a while, before she could make it back to Chesterville."

Abby nodded as she mulled this all over. "That makes sense."

"How old were you?" William asked.

"When my parents were killed? Young. Six."

Abby grimaced in sympathy.

"I was older but I still had to go to a foster home," William said. "I know what it's like to lose your parents to murder. Mass shooting. Domestic violence. Doesn't matter how it happens. It's all murder. I'd be fooling myself if I said it had nothing to do with what led me to writing. I think I like catching the killers." He smiled and glanced at Roman. "Something my son here is good at in real life."

"I've read some of your books," Kendra said. "You're really good. Not just the stories, the writing. You put the reader right in the scene. Like that one book, where the woman went missing and the husband claimed she ran off without taking things a person who was planning to leave for good wouldn't leave behind. I felt like I really knew the victim and it was all through the eyes of the detective. I loved the detective, too. He had such a dry sense of humor." She laughed a little, back in the story. "Are you like that?"

William chuckled. "No. People always ask me if I write based on real experiences. Stories wouldn't be entertaining if they were based only on the experiences and the personality of the writer."

"They aren't real," Roman said, an edge to his tone.

"Thank God for that," his mother chimed in. "Why did you become a detective if it makes you so morose?"

Roman didn't answer and Kendra could see why he perceived his parents didn't think he measured up. But they did. They just knocked him for his pessimistic attitude.

"Well, I think you must be a very smart man, if your writing is any indication," Kendra said.

"I doubt many leave Harvard who aren't smart," Roman said, sounding teasing. "My dad has lived a charmed life."

"So has your mother, it seems," Kendra said. As his mother and father smiled with his teasing, she realized they had no idea how much of an Eeyore their son had become.

"Yes, a real *Hocus Pocus* character."

Abby laughed, clearly loving the analogy. She

looked adoringly at her son, a look Roman missed as he turned to his father.

What was he thinking right now? Did he realize how much he idolized his parents? Was he jealous? Not maliciously. Kendra suspected he truly longed to generate the same hero worship as they did in others. And she bet he didn't realize he already did. How could he miss the significance of working for Dark Alley Investigations? He didn't get there by being an average detective.

Kendra felt herself gravitating closer to him. Her desire to know more of his inner workings intensified. She held back, though. Whenever she felt this way before, she always ended up either suppressed or heartbroken.

Chapter 9

"Are you sure about this?"

Roman didn't glance back at Kendra, who had arrested his senses when she came out of her house dressed like a cat burglar. All in black, tight jeans, black T-shirt that stretched over her breasts and a fitted leather jacket that left her rear exposed. Sexy as hell. He'd drooled for a good sixty seconds and had to stare at her awhile after she sat in the passenger seat before driving away from the curb. He planned to break into Alex Johnston's storage unit and she'd insisted on accompanying him.

He heard and felt the click of the lock as he picked it. The night was cloudless, quiet and cool. Bush crickets chanted their tune, sounding like they were saying *Katy did... Katy didn't.*

"Yes."

"But if we find anything, it won't be admitted as evidence."

He lifted the overhead door. "Only if we take it with us." Anything they found he'd photograph and leave. Nobody had to know he'd either taken them or been in this unit.

"I'd never get a warrant without enough cause and we don't have enough cause. Yet. I hope to find something to go on in here."

"Something that will give us cause."

"Yes." He switched on the light on his hat and turned to Kendra to activate hers. That brought him up close and personal with her. The light showed him the soft, pretty lines of her face and her green eyes looking up at him, emitting the same heat he felt kindling inside him.

"Don't look at me like that right now," he said.

"Like what?"

"Like you want me to kiss you."

"Then stop looking at me like you want to kiss me."

He chuckled and went to work, glad they didn't have time to fool around even if he decided to take it to that level.

Alex didn't have much. He must have gotten rid of lots of his things before going to prison, or maybe his criminal lifestyle had gradually diminished his belongings. Boxes stacked on the right side and furniture the left. A narrow row had been left down the middle. Whoever had packed the storage unit had been meticulously organized, which told Roman Alex hadn't been the one to pack it. Criminals weren't typically patient and organized unless they were the Bernie Madoff or Ted Bundy variety. Alex was more along the lines of a petty criminal. He stole when he needed money. He assaulted when he wanted his way.

The furniture would tell them nothing, so he started on the first box. Kendra went to work on another. They were labeled, which made quick work of going through them. A good thing since he'd broken into the storage unit.

"Office," Kendra said.

Seeing her struggle to heft the box off the top of several others, he went to her. Standing behind her, he lifted the box. She went still, and then so did he, realizing how close he stood. His body pressed to hers, especially in the act of lifting the box and moving for more leverage.

Ducking under his arm, Kendra moved to his side, rubbing her arm and unable to look directly at him. He put the box down and sat on the other side with her. She opened the box, seeming glad to have something to do. He watched her dig through the contents of the box. She took out a stack of carbon copy checks, held together with a fat rubber band. Next came an old calculator, one of those big ones—ten keys with the paper roll.

Roman saw how her red hair fell in shiny strands along her face. What a face. She had smooth, olive-colored skin and a pretty, sloping nose. With her lips slightly parted, he imagined her breath warm on his mouth as he came in for a kiss.

The fantasy turned into a real possibility when she looked up. He barely registered that she held a cell phone. He felt the connection between them, hot and electrified.

Leaning toward her, he put one hand on the concrete floor and reached for her with the other. Sliding his fingers into her hair until he cupped the back of her head, he moved closer, until he touched her mouth with his. Just a taste. He pressed gently, smelled her, felt her warm breath as he had longed to. She moved her lips and he gave in, kissing her deeper.

He couldn't believe he'd done this, didn't understand what had driven him. Her beauty, but more. What about her drew him so irresistibly? She was nothing like the kind of woman he envisioned for himself. Another detective would be more suitable, not the dreamer who ran a Christmas shop.

With that dose of reality, he withdrew. Her eyes opened slowly, drugged with passion. He must look the same. It took all his willpower not to give in to the clamoring desire to lay her flat on the hard, cold concrete and take this to the next level.

He let out his held breath and released her. She breathed fast and looked stunned, staring at him and testing his control.

Now would be a time when he'd leave the storage unit and have a smoke. Instead, he forced himself to dig into the box. Finding the cord that went with the cell phone, and then checking the box for anything else that might be promising. There was nothing, so he took the phone from Kendra and stood.

Outside, he waited for her to join him at his rental. At last she did, finally coming out of the trance he'd put her in. He'd put himself in a trance kissing her. Had he ever felt a kiss so strongly before? Damn.

Kendra was still wrapped in the buzz of that kiss when Roman took her to his hotel suite. He plugged in the cell phone. They'd have to wait to see what it contained. He busied himself on his laptop, which he'd hooked up to three monitors that took up most of the space of the desk. He sat on the chair, facing her, his head above the tops of the monitors, the bedroom behind him.

She went into the kitchenette and took out a bottle of water from the refrigerator, then passed the table to go into the living room. Sitting on the sofa, she picked up the remote and turned on the television. She wasn't much of a TV watcher, but she needed the distraction right now. Roman seemed so unaffected by their kiss. Why had he done it? She had been about to tell him she'd found a cell phone and the next thing she knew she was transported to fairyland.

"It's charged enough," Roman said.

Kendra stood and went to stand beside him, careful to keep plenty of distance between them and still see the screen of the phone.

He navigated through the call log.

Kendra quickly saw this wasn't Alex's phone. "This was Kaelyn's phone. There are a lot of calls to her adoptive mother."

Roman glanced up at her, and then checked the text messages. Nothing in the call log or the texts indicated anything unusual at first glance. The last call had been placed the morning of her death and there were a few incoming calls, none of the numbers recognizable. The last text had been the day before to a coworker, saying she wouldn't be in the next day.

Had she made plans for the day? Why did she notify her work she wouldn't be in? To kill herself?

No.

Kendra refused to believe that. "Alex kept her phone?"

"Maybe he didn't realize he had it," Roman said.

He navigated to the photo album.

Kendra felt a pang of loss as she saw her sister's last photos. Many were of her adoptive mom and dad and some selfies around Chesterville. A day of shopping. Dinner. Church. Hanging out at her adoptive mom and dad's house.

Then a video clip. The image was black. Roman pressed Play and Kaelyn's frightened voice began.

"He hit me again." The video clip brightened and showed Kaelyn's face, a cut on her lip. Kendra had to turn her back. It was too hard to see.

"I hate him so much," Kaelyn said. "I can't wait to get away from here. He threatened to kill me if I tried to leave him, so I have to be careful." Kendra glanced sharply at Roman as Kaelyn continued. "He suspects nothing and I want to keep it that way. Kendra doesn't know it yet, but she's going to save my life. We talked about moving to Chesterville yesterday. She seems open to the idea. She'd have to quit her job but she's smart and resourceful. She can get something going in Chesterville. I'm sure of it."

Hearing the desperate hope in her sister's tone, Kendra began to choke up with emotion.

She heard Kaelyn suck in a sharp breath. "He's coming."

The video ended.

Slowly, Kaelyn turned. Roman looked up at her.

"Sorry," he said.

"That proves I was right," she said.

"This is powerful evidence. It's dated a week before

she was killed and clearly shows she had plans to leave him and move to Chesterville. Nobody who planned to kill themselves would talk like that."

"Thank you." Now he was wholly and completely on her side. He had no more doubts that Kaelyn had not committed suicide. "What now?"

"Tomorrow morning we return this to the box and go talk to Alex."

"In prison?"

"Yes."

That should be interesting.

"Let's go over the police report again. I'll arrange to also get copies of her home phone records."

Good. They'd be busy the rest of the night. Too busy for any more kissing.

The Harris Correctional Facility was old and gray and bleak. Couple that with darkening skies and the distant sound of thunder and the place could be in a ghost story. Roman held the door for her and they entered. By the time they left, it would be raining. Kendra had arranged for one of her employees to cover for her at her shop.

After a lengthy check-in, a guard led them to a room where Alex had been taken to wait for them. It was an open room with a few tables taken by other inmates with visitors. In an orange jumpsuit, Alex was cuffed to the table and saw them enter. Around six feet tall, he had silvering blond hair and buggy blue eyes. Not overweight but chunky at the middle.

"Who are you?" he asked as they reached the table.

Roman pulled out a chair for her and she sat as he took the seat next to her.

"Guard said you were some kind of detective," Alex said to Roman. "You here to get me out of here?"

"No. This is Kaelyn's twin sister, Kendra."

Alex turned to her for a brief, uninterested inspection. "Yeah, I heard Kaelyn had a sister. She never told me about her."

"I see from the police reports that you were out drinking with some friends the night Kaelyn died?" Roman asked.

"I stopped after work."

He worked construction and his boss had confirmed he'd arrived early in the morning and worked a ten-hour day. The bar where he'd spent the evening had also confirmed he'd paid his tab at two in the morning.

"When did you find Kaelyn?"

"Late the next morning. I didn't see her when I got home."

"You didn't care enough about her to look," Kendra couldn't stop herself from saying.

"I cared about her," he shot back indignantly. "I had too much to drink. I slept hard."

"Enough to threaten to kill her if she ever left you?" Kendra countered. She felt like gouging his eyes out with an ice pick.

"I never did that," he sneered. He looked around for the guard.

"What if we said we have proof that you did?" Roman asked.

"Like what?" He seemed confident they'd find nothing.

"You threatened her more than once, didn't you?" Roman asked. "We know you beat her."

After a long pause, Alex finally said, "We had a few fights, but I loved Kaelyn."

"I bet you did," Kendra said. "Like a sociopath *loves* his victims?"

"Kendra." Roman put his hand over hers.

"I did love her...and not like a sociopath. Why are you here if you already know I had an alibi the day Kaelyn killed herself?"

"She didn't kill herself," Roman said. "She had plans to move back to Chesterville. She was going to leave you."

"What? No, she wasn't."

"She and I talked about moving closer together. We hadn't solidified any plans yet, but it would have happened. That's why she never told anyone about me. That was her way out."

Alex stared at her. "You think I killed her?"

"You threatened to kill her. Did you hire someone to do it for you and make it look like a suicide?"

Alex scoffed. "I wouldn't have needed anyone else to off her if that's what I wanted. I didn't kill my wife."

Kendra held her tongue still. Roman didn't say anything either and the message was clear for Alex, whose brow lowered over his eyes.

"I didn't kill my wife," he repeated.

"You didn't," Roman said, "but who did?"

"That's your job, isn't it, Detective?"

Was he taunting them or did he really think Roman should do his job and catch Kaelyn's killer? He hadn't lost his temper when Kendra had shot her retorts. Maybe jail had taught him to control it. Or maybe he controlled it to hide his guilt.

"In case you feel like talking." Roman handed the man his business card.

Alex took it as Roman stood and offered his hand to Kendra. She thought he didn't do it on purpose. She gave him her hand and stood with him.

"This was a waste of time," he said as they headed for the exit. "He'd never admit to killing Kaelyn or arranging for her to be killed, but I hoped he'd slip up somewhere."

He hadn't. Career criminals learned how to deceive to avoid prosecution. Alex didn't have a long sentence right now but if he were convicted of murder, he'd never get out.

As they were escorted to the next door, Roman let go of her hand. She'd enjoyed the brief contact but probably best to avoid much more of that.

"Do you think he's telling the truth?" she asked.

"About not killing her? Yes."

He did? Could he read people that well? "But did he pay someone to off her?"

"Exactly."

At the exit, she saw the torrential downpour and remembered she hadn't brought a jacket or an umbrella.

"You wait here."

He was really treating her like a lady. She almost stopped him out of fear of what it would do to her heart, but he had already pushed open the door and jogged out into the parking lot. She watched as he disappeared among the vehicles. Thunder rumbled. She could hear the patter of rain through the glass, some rainwater splashing up to distort her view.

Roman's rental appeared and she went through the door, running to the passenger side. She opened the door and all but dived inside, slamming the door shut. Even that brief amount of time had gotten her drenched. She looked over at Roman. His black hair was dripping and his clothes were soaked through.

She smiled first before a laugh broke free. He chuckled with her and drove from the lot.

Back at his hotel room, Roman buried himself in the police reports. He'd gone over all the photos and everything written about Kaelyn's death. Something had always bothered him about the way her body had been found. She hung from the main bathroom light fixture, a stool below turned over. Alex must have gone to the master bedroom and hadn't gone into the main bathroom—if he was telling the truth.

Hearing Kendra shift on the chair she'd chosen when he'd brought her here, he looked up. She'd curled up with a book and every once in a while looked out the window at the rain. The storm wasn't moving fast. Her appreciation for such a simple thing went against his initial impression of her as an ambitious go-getter who'd set up a cushy life for herself. When he began to think he had her figured wrong, he felt unease chase through him. She had come from a rough upbringing and made a life for herself. He had to respect that. She could have turned to crime instead of fighting to get away from a lifestyle that bred that kind of living. Instead, she'd made the right choices.

He had no illusions about how harsh reality could be, but that probably wasn't the only issue he had with women who never experienced a bad day in their lives. In fact, he wondered if his relationship with the CEO had more to do with his reluctance to give romance another try. His work made finding and maintaining a real relationship difficult. If all he could have was something fake like what he'd already had, then he'd rather not get involved. He dated now and then, long enough to satisfy needs, but he'd never considered getting serious again.

Maybe his penchant for all things real boiled down to that. He wanted and needed something real with a woman. What if he could have that with Kendra?

She didn't seem the trusting kind. She'd been burned before. Knowing the hours he'd have to work, would she ever be able to trust him? That seemed like a mess he'd be better off avoiding.

Just then, she looked from the window to him. That same spark warmed the energy between them.

"Find anything?" she asked.

Yes. Stay focused on the investigation. "Other than the fact that I don't think your sister died where she was found?"

Instantly, Kendra uncurled her legs and stood to come to him. He quickly minimized the photo he'd had up on one of his screens.

She stood so she could see his computer screens. "Why?"

"The photos are gruesome, but I've studied them for a while now. At first glance the marks on her neck appear to match like the coroner reported, but if I look closer, I don't think they do." He picked up his pen and on his notepad, drew a crude neck with a rope line. Then he shaded an area below and along the side of the neck. "There are red marks that fall below the rope. The tension makes the rope tighten on an angle if someone hangs themselves. But the marks are more horizontal, as if someone strangled her from behind."

"Wouldn't her movements as she hung herself cause those?"

"Maybe, but they seem more severe than I'd expect if the marks were caused by the rope rubbing as she hung herself."

"Okay...that's good. What do we do with that?"

"We talk to the coroner." He checked his computer for the time. "It'll have to wait until morning."

Kendra straightened, looking wary and stiffer than when she'd first approached.

"Also, I don't like where the stool is lying," he went on, knowing the cause of her discomfort was anticipation of the time they'd spend alone together. Or maybe she didn't want to go home.

"What about it?"

"It's right under her feet. If I was going to kill myself by hanging, I'd kick the stool out of the way. The photos look like the stool was placed there, not kicked over."

"Placed right under her feet."

"Yes."

"That's brilliant, Roman. We have enough to get a warrant and recover the phone now."

"Possibly. Let's convince the coroner first."

"Okay."

"In the meantime, what do you want to do? Are you going home tonight?"

With that question she grew even warier. He hadn't meant it the way it sounded.

"Um...yes, I was planning on going home at some point. I suppose now is as good a time as any. You've found something we can go on and we can't talk to the coroner until tomorrow."

She was babbling.

"Unless you want to play some more pool and have dinner?" As soon as he asked, he wondered why. What was he doing to himself by letting his attraction get carried away?

She hesitated as though considering saying yes. Excitement revved him up for a few seconds, but then her eyes lowered and lifted as though she was coming to her senses.

"I'll be back for the call with the coroner tomorrow morning."

Disappointment rushed forth before relief. Any more personal time with her and he might let nature take control.

Chapter 10

Kendra told herself she didn't dress up for Roman. She liked putting outfits together, that's all. The white, sleeveless sundress fit to her waist, and then flowed to her calves. She also wore handmade, blue-stone-accented necklace, bracelet and earrings. Her sandals were higher than she normally wore. The reward came when Roman first saw her. He opened the hotel room door after she knocked and his eyes caught sight of her dress and roamed all over her, lingering on the scooped neckline.

"Come in." He stood aside.

Kendra walked past him, smelling his aftershave and a man fresh out of the shower. He wore light blue jeans and a navy blue short-sleeved button-up, exposing strong, lightly haired arms. She dumped her purse on the small table and saw he had files and a notepad cluttering the desk, his cell phone on top of the latter.

"He should be calling in a few minutes," Roman said. "Would you like some coffee?"

"I had some on the way over."

"Everything all right at your shop?"

She didn't have a big staff and she rarely missed a day, something he must have picked up on. "My manager and Raelyn are opening my shop for me today. Raelyn is learning fast."

"That's nice. Is she working full-time now?"

"Just about."

This felt like small talk. The way she'd left last night must have sent the message she'd intended. She didn't want to be involved with him personally. The attraction still burned, however. She liked to tell herself his pessimistic outlook on life made them a bad match, but her heart felt differently. He wasn't as pessimistic as he tried to convince everyone. If he could figure out how to overcome that, she couldn't think of a single thing about him she wouldn't like, or love. That's what frightened her most—the degree of her attraction. It had developed its own energy, an unstoppable one. Why her feelings threatened her she'd love to know.

She kept going back to that time he'd said his relationship with the woman who had the child hadn't worked because it hadn't been real. Maybe that's what threatened her. The intensity of their attraction had the makings of something real and she'd already thought she had that before and ended up completely wrong. She didn't trust herself any more than she trusted men. Could she make a decision she could rely on? If she chose to get involved with Roman, would that be good for her or would she end up in another painful situation?

Pulling a chair from the table over to the opposite

side of the desk, she sat and busied herself with moving a pen and the notepad, tidying them up. Unnecessary but better than engaging with him while they waited.

After a few minutes, he asked, "You okay?"

She looked up as he passed her to take the seat across from her. "Yes."

"You seem…quiet today."

"Am I normally a chatterbox?" She went with humor to skirt that question, toying with the pen on the desk.

He leaned back, studying her like the detective he was. "Why did you leave last night?"

"Instead of playing pool and having dinner?"

"Everyone has to eat."

"It was getting late."

"That sounds like an excuse. I didn't mean to ask you out on a date. But I suppose I did. Are you uncomfortable with that?"

Was he seriously contemplating taking this to a much more personal level? "Are…are you asking me to date you?"

"One date. It's not like we have to commit to each other. It's too soon for that, isn't it? We're both obviously attracted to each other. Why not see where it goes?"

She couldn't believe he was suggesting this. She appreciated his directness, and his lack of fear in confronting the feelings they had, but did she want to date him? "I…" She had no words. She felt so undecided. Yes, she was attracted to him, but should she put her heart out for him? "I thought I was too sheltered for you. Not…real."

"When I first met you, I thought you were like my last girlfriend, but you're different than her."

Should she be insulted? Did he stereotype that much? She put her elbow on the desk, still holding the pen. "You thought I'd act my way through a relationship with you?"

"I'm always careful. I try very hard to avoid getting myself into another relationship like my last one. No one gets hurt that way."

Now he thought she was different and wanted to give her a try? He was rotten at making a girl feel special. Well, at least when it came to his baggage. "What has you so afraid of falling in love?"

His head sort of flinched with the unexpectedness of her question. "I'm not afraid. Just cautious."

"Afraid."

"I just think the odds are against most people and I try to be as sure as possible when I start seeing someone. The early stages are the most important. No one is too invested if it doesn't work out."

She lowered her hand to the desk, letting go of the pen. "Early stages don't need all that precaution. No one gets hurt whether you dive right in or wait to learn more about the person. Isn't that what first dates are all about?"

He grinned a little, not from discomfort. He might actually be enjoying this. "I guess we didn't need a first date."

"We're already at the next stage?" she teased.

"Two or three, maybe." Reaching across the desk, he ran his finger over the back of her hand, soft and sensual and with a playful light in his eyes.

Tingles spread all the way up her arm and touched her heart like sparks from a fairy's wand. She had to force herself not to fall for him too much. He was probably only teasing anyway.

Wouldn't they have already had sex by now if they were that far along? "I think you're afraid you won't be enough for the woman you fall in love with." It came back to how he saw his parents and how he always compared himself to them. They were such good people and they were both so successful.

"If I found something real with a woman, I wouldn't be afraid to marry her."

Okay, she did believe that, but he still had this hang-up over his self-worth. Or maybe it wasn't self-worth. Maybe it was more of a self-discovery thing. He had to be able to look in the mirror and see a man who was, indeed, the son of two interesting and dynamic people and he was equally interesting and dynamic. He might see himself as successful, just not sure he'd followed his heart. Feeling less fascinating than his parents didn't make him insecure. It only made him, well, pessimistic.

She couldn't look away from his eyes, a window into a man who was not afraid of anything. Having a glimpse of that power changed how she saw him. She knew him better than before this talk. That chilled her and got her heart going faster at the same time.

His cell rang and he pressed the answer button and then speaker.

"Cooper."

"Detective Cooper. Doctor Mortenson."

"Thanks for calling, Doctor."

"Sorry for the delay in calling. You said in your email that you have some questions on the Johnston death?"

"Yes. I read the report you sent Dark Alley Investigations."

"I was surprised an agency like that took an interest in this case. That was pretty straightforward as far as I'm concerned."

Kendra looked up from the phone at Roman. She didn't think the report was all that straightforward and was pretty sure Roman would agree.

"I can see why you'd think that," Roman said. "When I first saw the report I was ready to tell Kendra I agreed, but then she told me Kaelyn had plans to move back to Chesterville and was in the process of convincing her twin sister to join her. People who are planning to kill themselves don't make plans like that for the future. That's what made me take another look at the file."

"It's normal for a sibling to want closure."

Kendra wanted more than closure. She wanted Kaelyn's killer caught and put behind bars.

"If you look at the photos, you can see ligature marks that might suggest strangulation from a different angle." Roman went through a lengthy explanation and waited for the doctor to look at the photos on his end of the call. "There's also the time of death that bothers me. Did you check for lividity during your exam?"

What was lividity? Kendra waited to see what Roman would say.

"That was a while ago," the doctor said. "I'd have to look at my notes again."

Kendra looked up at Roman. Did the doctor seem reluctant to talk?

"There's no mention of it in your report."

"Then I may not have made any notes because I was sure the cause was suicide."

"I'm not challenging your competence," Roman assured the man. "Many others would have drawn the same conclusion."

The doctor said nothing in response.

"It's hard to say for sure from the photos," Roman continued, "but to me it looks like lividity formed on the right side of her body. I don't see any lividity at her feet, like I'd expect if a body had been hanging for so long. In fact, lividity doesn't change after twelve hours, so even if the body was moved, the pattern of discoloration would appear the same."

How could he have missed something like that? Wouldn't a coroner check for signs the body had been moved? Maybe not if he was sure of the cause of death.

"Have you spoken with the police about this?" The doctor sounded much more concerned now.

"I wanted to talk to you first."

"I suggest you do talk to them. Much of my examination is based on my discussions with them when the body is brought in. If there are now reasons to believe the Johnston girl was murdered, we should exhume her body."

"She was cremated. The photos are all we have."

The doctor made a disgruntled sound. "Then your best path forward is with the police."

"Thank you for your time, Doctor."

"Good luck."

Roman looked at Kendra after he disconnected.

"You didn't tell me about the discolorations. The lividity as you called it," she said.

"I just noticed it last night. I had nothing else to do since you wouldn't go out with me."

She let his good-natured poking go for now. "You think her body was moved."

"I *know* it was."

The police weren't any more help than the coroner had been. Everyone who handled her case, from the first responders to the police and detectives and finally the coroner, all seemed to assume right away that Kaelyn had killed herself. All of her friends had told of a depressed woman. No one had questioned her mother. Roman, like Kendra, had found that particularly unusual. Her mother had been notified of her death, that's all.

Now knowing without a shred of doubt that Kaelyn had been killed took this case to a new level. He felt driven more than ever to solve her murder. He realized he felt this way every time he ran a case.

He'd spent hours looking at the kind of rope used in Kaelyn's hanging. It was thick and the search warrant for Alex's storage unit confirmed he'd had some. The search had also produced bank statements and receipts they'd had express shipped to them at the hotel. The warrant had also allowed into evidence Kaelyn's cell phone, which proved she'd not only been in contact with her secret twin sister, she'd also been abused and was planning to run away.

Right now, he pored over the bank statements around the time Kaelyn was killed. Kendra sat on the floor with receipts surrounding her, organizing them into piles. He spotted a withdrawal dated the day before Kaelyn had died. She'd taken a thousand from the checking account, all but draining it.

"I found something," he said.

Kendra stood and leaned beside him to look over the bank statement. "Withdrawal." Then she pointed to another entry. "She also purchased gas that day."

Roman noticed another gas purchase in West Virginia. "She drove to Chesterville."

Stunned, he turned with her and their eyes met as the significance sank in. Had Kaelyn been killed in Chesterville or had she driven home first?

"What happened to her car?" Kaelyn asked.

"Let's find out." He made a call to a detective who'd helped gather the information he needed. The detective didn't know about Kaelyn's car and nothing had been mentioned about it in the reports.

Next, he called the prison to arrange for a call with Alex. Thirty minutes later, they had him on the phone.

"We only had one car. I rode with the guys to work every day," he said.

"Was the car at your house when you found Kaelyn?" Roman asked.

"It was in the garage. Why?"

"Did you know Kaelyn drove to Chesterville the day before you found her?" Roman asked.

"She was home. She didn't drive anywhere."

"No, she drove to Chesterville." She had been found at home but she had to have been taken there already dead.

"No. I didn't know that. Why did she drive all the way there, and then turn around and drive back?"

Roman didn't answer. Was he telling the truth?

"I did notice she got into a fender bender. I was

going to get on her about it. That's when I found her hanging."

"What kind of fender bender?" Roman asked, excited. This could be a big lead.

"The whole side looked like she drove against a concrete divider or something."

Or another car had driven her off the road?

"Did you tell police that?"

"Yes. They asked about the cut and bruise on her forehead. I told them it must have happened when she wrecked the car."

"Did they follow up on the accident?"

"What would be the point? She was dead. I told the police I thought she might have taken too many of her antidepressant pills and got into a wreck. Hell, the wreck might have made her even more depressed and that's what sent her over the edge."

"Where is the car now?" Roman asked.

"My brother is keeping it on his farm. I got the fender repaired."

Yes. They could find proof Kaelyn's body had been in the car postmortem. He'd get a hold of local police and have the vehicle taken in to be searched for trace evidence.

"You would describe her as a depressed person?" Kendra asked.

"She was never happy around me."

"Who would be happy living with someone who beat them?" Kendra asked. Did men like him not understand that?

Roman held up his hand to stop any further retaliation. He sympathized with her, but she was being too emotional.

"I know I wasn't the ideal husband, but I did love her. I think about her every day. Mostly I wish things could have been different for us."

In that he wished he hadn't beaten her? Some men couldn't control their temper and realized afterward what they did was wrong.

"So, no one knows where or how she was in this car accident?" Roman asked.

"I guess not."

After ending that call, Kendra got a hold of Kaelyn's adoptive mother and asked her when she last saw Kaelyn.

"A week before."

That corroborated Glenn's statement.

"Did she tell you she was coming back?" Roman asked.

"No. Why?"

"She drove to Chesterville the day she died," Kendra said.

"She…that's not possible. She would have told me."

"Not if she was trying to escape her husband," Roman said.

"She would have told me," the woman insisted.

"She didn't tell me, either," Kendra said. Not that she would have had any reason to. They had just begun to get close again and Kaelyn had intended to talk her into moving with her to Chesterville. She just hadn't had the chance.

"We have copies of her bank statements and one of them shows she purchased gas just outside Chesterville the day she died," Roman said. "Maybe something happened to make her decide last minute to drive here."

"I'm telling you, Kaelyn would have told me if she was coming to see me."

Roman met Kendra's eyes again.

"Maybe she wasn't coming to see you," he said.

After ending that call—having to calm the woman down—Roman jotted down some of his thoughts.

"Who could she have decided to come see last minute?"

"Glenn?"

"He didn't tell us she was coming."

"Of course he didn't." Why had she driven to Chesterville and not told anyone? Had she planned to see her lover, and then stay? Alex didn't seem to know she'd left that day. Or why.

Glenn could have known she was coming and driven her off the road before she made it to town. But why…?

Chapter 11

Kendra went with Roman to a café over lunchtime, where they would find Glenn. He was a partner at a local law firm and his secretary had told them he'd be here having lunch with his wife. The café had small town charm with only about ten round tables covered in white linen with tiny, slender vases containing single blue carnations that matched the valances over French casement windows in the front. Kendra spotted the dark blond–haired Glenn sitting with a petite woman dressed in a floral short-sleeved dress. Her blond hair was shoulder-length and she wore stylish rectangular glasses. She held her fork daintily over her plate, chewing politely as she listened to her husband, who seemed more interested in hearing himself than whether his wife was interested.

"Does his wife know he was having an affair?" Kendra asked in a low voice as they approached.

"I don't know. We'll be tactful."

They reached the table, Glenn stopping talking as he saw them, his blue eyes going chilly.

"Glenn, how are you today?" Roman asked.

"What do you want?" He glanced at his wife. "This is my wife, Vikki."

He seemed to introduce her to make sure they understood if they'd come to talk to them about Kaelyn, they could do some harm.

Roman gave a nod and Kendra said, "I'm Kendra Scott and this is Roman Cooper."

"Oh," Vikki said. "You're that detective looking into that woman's death." She turned to Kendra. "You're her twin sister, right?"

"Yes."

"You think she was murdered?"

"We know she was," Roman said. "In fact, we just learned she was on her way to Chesterville the day she died."

Vikki seemed to freeze up a moment. The news that Kaelyn had been murdered came as a shock to her. Kendra wanted to question her as to why but thought that might lead into her husband's infidelity.

"How does that convince you she was killed?" Glenn asked. "I thought she committed suicide."

Roman turned to him. "We have evidence that her body was moved. She didn't hang herself, and the time of death puts her here when she was killed."

Vikki put her hand to her chest and looked across the table at her husband. He sat staring up at Roman. Kendra couldn't tell if he was worried or not.

"You wouldn't happen to know of anyone who may have seen or spoken with her that day?" Roman asked.

"No," Glenn said.

Kendra saw how Vikki lowered her head, and then looked away. She fingered the knife beside her salad bowl. Nervous.

"Are you sure?" she asked, watching Vikki.

"Yes, we're sure," Glenn said in a sterner tone.

Roman put a card on the table. "In case something comes to mind."

Glenn looked up and the two men's gazes met in silent understanding.

Kendra leaned over and slid the card closer to Vikki. "Give us a call if you think of anything."

With Glenn's deepening frown, Roman stepped back and Kendra followed him out of the café.

"She knows something," she said when they reached the sidewalk. "Did you see how nervous she got when you asked if they knew of anyone who may have seen or spoken with Kaelyn?"

"They were both fidgety," Roman said.

"How are we going to get them to talk?"

"We'll have Glenn brought in for questioning."

Glenn wouldn't talk. "What about Vikki?"

"She'll call us."

Kendra stopped outside the restaurant. "How do you know?"

"I could just tell. She won't be able to keep whatever she knows to herself and she doesn't want her husband to know. She'll call."

He was an amazing detective. He was amazing in other ways, but she'd rather not let her daydreaming go too far right now.

Thirty minutes later, Vikki did exactly as Roman had predicted. She called to request a private meeting.

Kendra waited with Roman in the lobby of the hotel and spotted her come through the front door, still in the floral dress.

She glanced around as though worried she'd be recognized. Unless a worker knew her, the guests weren't permanent residents.

"Thanks for seeing me." She moved to stand beside a plant as though it would conceal her. "Glenn doesn't know."

"Know what?" Roman asked.

After a long sigh, Vikki adjusted her purse strap, and then said, "Kaelyn called me the day before you said she was on her way to Chesterville."

Kendra barely smothered a gasp. They hadn't yet checked the phone records for that time frame.

"She said she needed to meet with me in person. She had a warning for me. She wouldn't say over the phone, but she told me not to trust my husband."

Kendra flashed a glance at Roman.

"I didn't believe her. I told her not to bother coming to Chesterville. I already knew my husband was fooling around. I didn't know with whom, but after she called, I suspected it was her and maybe she was trying to alienate me from Glenn. I confronted him. He swore to me that he wasn't involved with her anymore and that he would be faithful from then on. We went to marriage counseling. It took me a while, but I finally forgave him. I wouldn't say our marriage is what it once was, but it's good enough to stay for the kids."

"Why do you think Kaelyn wanted to warn you?" Roman asked.

"Like I said, she wouldn't say over the phone, and

after I heard she committed suicide, I thought she decided not to try and split up me and Glenn."

"And he's been good to you ever since?" Kendra asked.

She nodded. "Yes. He comes home right after work and at a decent time, and I don't see any strange phone numbers in his call log."

"Glenn doesn't know Kaelyn contacted you before her death?" Roman asked.

Vikki shook her head. "And now I don't know what to do. If Kaelyn was killed on her way to see me, then whatever she had to say to me must have been important. She must have discovered something when she was seeing Glenn."

And that something had gotten her killed.

Over the next few days, a DAI team helped obtain Kaelyn's phone records, and Roman had spent another day going through those around the time of her death. He confirmed what he already suspected. Vikki had told the truth. Kaelyn had phoned her from her home line. She'd also phoned Glenn's mobile number. She must have been on her way to Chesterville by then. He'd lied about not speaking with her prior to her death.

Now, on a rainy morning, he and Kendra listened to him lie all over again to police. The phone records and new evidence proving the body had been moved had ramped up the investigation. Detectives in Toledo were working with detectives in Chesterville, who also worked with Roman. They treated him like part of the team and everyone had one common goal—to catch Kaelyn's killer. When Roman found new information he'd agreed to share, the team of other detectives had agreed to do the same. Roman would continue to work alone, as was his preference and the main reason he'd gone to work for DAI.

Who had masterminded the crime? It had taken a lot of premeditation to run someone off the road, kill them by strangulation, put them in the trunk, drive them back to their home and stage a suicide. Whoever had committed the murder had a big motive to keep a secret. What was the secret? The killer had known Kaelyn was driving to Chesterville. Alex hadn't known. Her mother hadn't known. Glenn and Vikki had both spoken with her just prior to her death. One of them had to have either leaked the information to the killer or one of them had done the killing. Vikki could be putting on a show to cover her guilt. Had she killed Kaelyn in a rage after learning her husband had been sleeping with her? Or had Glenn killed Kaelyn to keep her from delivering her warning? Or had they both worked together? Maybe he'd misinterpreted their nervousness.

"We obtained copies of your phone records and found that Kaelyn called you the day before she was killed," the detective said. "You spoke for five minutes."

Glenn stared at the man without flinching. "I don't recall talking to her that close to her death."

"But you did talk to her."

Glenn said nothing.

"Did you leave your house the morning of Kaelyn's murder?" the detective asked.

"No. As I said before, I was sick that day."

"Can anyone confirm that?"

"I've already told you all of this. My wife might be able to. I don't remember if she was home that day."

"Did Kaelyn discover anything about you that might have threatened you?"

Glenn scoffed as though he thought that a ridiculous question. Why would he tell the detective anything like that?

"Remember whatever you say will go on record," the detective said.

Glenn's condescension faded. "No."

"What about your wife? Would she have any reason to want to kill Kaelyn? Jealousy over your affair, perhaps?"

With that, Glenn sobered further and contemplated his answer before he said, "No. Vikki isn't capable of killing anyone. She was forgiving, more forgiving than I expected."

People who bottled up their emotions could hide a darker side that was, in fact, capable of killing.

"Do you know of anyone else who might want to harm Kaelyn?"

Glenn shook his head. "No."

"Did she ever talk to you about anything unusual, anything that she might have been afraid of?"

"No."

With no evidence to prove Glenn murdered Kaelyn, the detective had to let him go.

"Well, he stuck to his original story," Kendra said, disappointment dripping from her tone.

"Didn't talk to Kaelyn. Doesn't remember talking to her," he said.

The detective who'd questioned Glenn entered the observation room. Six-four with dark hair and blue eyes, he had a Michael Fassbender look going for him. And his name was Calum.

"He knows we're onto him," Calum said.

"I want to see what he does now," Roman said.

The other detective nodded. "Let's coordinate a surveillance plan. Meanwhile, we'll keep chasing leads as they come along." He looked at Kendra. "I'm sorry for your loss."

"Thank you." Kendra smiled as though liking that she'd just discovered he was a perfect gentleman.

The spurt of jealousy that followed flustered Roman.

Chapter 12

Now that this was officially a homicide investigation, Roman could get information from doctors on Glenn's first wife's death. A few more days passed before he had all the information he needed. Deidra had gone to see the doctor the week before complaining of flu-like symptoms. Then she'd been rushed to the hospital with the heart attack. The hospital hadn't had the capability to perform a blood test that would have identified poisoning. They had only her physical symptoms, and because Deidra had been found to have an irregular heartbeat along with a heart murmur during her autopsy, they hadn't looked any further.

Deidra's death had been ruled natural.

But Roman would bet her family had some reservations over that. Her father was a retired army colonel and her mother was a retired nurse, which fit Glenn's family heritage and likely satisfied his parents enough for them to approve his marrying her. Deidra went to college for a law degree but didn't practice as an attorney. She had died seven years ago. He had been married to Vikki for six years. Kaelyn had been younger than Vikki, which may have accounted for at least some of Glenn's attraction to her.

On another rainy morning, Roman stepped up behind Kendra onto th e porch of Bob and Regina Saunders's two-story Colonial. He had phoned ahead to arrange this meeting, so when a gray-haired man with black-rimmed glasses opened the door, he smiled and shook his and Kendra's hand. This must be Bob.

"Come in."

Roman entered behind Kendra as thunder rumbled and the sound of rain pattering to the ground intensified.

"Looks like we're in for a gully washer," Bob said.

Kendra stomped her damp feet and removed her rain jacket. Roman removed his jacket, as well, and Bob took them and hung them on hooks above a vintage bench. Trimmed in dark, half-walled paneling, the boxed-in entry had wood floors and a staircase on the left. A small vintage wood table held a vase of flowers next to the bench.

"Regina is waiting in the living room. She made some tea and scones."

"You have a lovely home," Kendra said.

"Thank you."

They seemed like wholesome people, happy to be part of a community and to live in the home they had built together. Roman wouldn't say homebodies, but he had the impression they enjoyed just being at home.

Down a narrow hall, Roman followed Kendra into

a living room where part of the kitchen was visible but still separated by a wall. The living room had a very English look to it, with more dark paneling and wing-back chairs and an arching sofa. Bookshelves on one wall and a brick fireplace cozied the room.

Regina stood from one of the chairs, wearing jeans and a long-sleeved T-shirt and a pair of tennis shoes. Bob had on jeans, as well, and a black Henley. The two had gray hair, both cut short, and both wore black-rimmed glasses. Neither was overweight, healthy and happy aside from the somberness Roman saw in both of their eyes. Both smiled with straight teeth, but their expressions didn't brighten. They carried their loss heavily.

"Please, have a seat." Regina indicated the seating area, and then the tea and scones.

Kendra sat on the pretty sofa and Roman sat beside her, ever aware of her closeness.

Bob took the chair beside the one his wife had vacated.

Regina indicated the tea and scones. "Tea?"

"I'd love something warm on this rainy day," Kendra said.

Regina put a tea bag into a flowery teacup and lifted a matching teakettle to pour hot water.

"None for me," Roman said.

Regina poured a cup for herself and Bob, and then, after placing Kendra's in front of her, put the other two on the table between the chairs and took a seat.

"Help yourself to the scones. They are quite delicious."

"Regina's favorite place to vacation is London," Bob said with a fond smile at his wife. She responded with equal warmth but there was still that element of dull-ness lingering in their eyes.

"We were glad to learn someone other than us thinks our daughter didn't die of natural causes," Regina said.

"We're exploring the possibility," Roman said. He didn't want to bring their hopes up only to shatter them later.

"We've often wondered if someone poisoned her," Bob said.

"That's one area we plan to explore," Roman said.

"We've read that arsenic can cause flu-like symp-toms," Regina said.

"So can antifreeze," Roman responded, seeing the anger and pain cloud both their eyes.

"We never really liked Glenn." Bob crossed one leg over the other. "He was always so pompous, just like his parents. Deidra had a law degree but she didn't want to litigate. Glenn always belittled her for that, as though he thought she wasn't capable. Deidra wanted to help people, not fight in court. She was active in charities and worked as general counsel for Habitat for Humanity. She was a good person and extremely health-conscious."

"She didn't smoke or drink alcohol," Regina said. "She jogged every day."

"No heart disease runs in our family, either," Bob added. "But police could find no motive. Deidra's life insurance was typical and had been in place ever since they married. Besides that, Glenn already had money. His parents had a trust fund for him. He had no rea-son to kill her."

"None that anyone can see," Roman said. "What

can you tell us about Glenn?" Other than the fact they didn't like him because he was pompous.

"His father is a city prosecutor."

Roman nodded, already knowing that.

"Hudson's got a tough reputation. Criminals who go up against him don't leave free if he's on the case."

Did he send innocent people to jail? What prosecutor didn't? "What about personal details. How's his marriage to Melody?"

"Several years back, there was a scandal involving him and the mayor's wife. It was rumored he had an affair with her. Nearly ended his marriage. But his wife, Melody, likes money and Hudson comes from a long line of it. She forgave him eventually."

"No one found out for sure?" Kendra asked. "It was just a rumor?"

"No one ever saw them together other than in public, and neither would admit to it."

"Did you know Glenn was having an affair with Kaelyn?" Kendra asked.

"No. We weren't involved in Glenn's life after Deidra died," Bob said, "but I suppose I'm not surprised. Glenn never struck me as a gentleman, much less an honorable one. He cares about money and reputation the way his parents do."

"What about the mayor's son, honey?" Regina said. "When he was arrested for drugs?"

"Ah. He was arrested and released and he never went to court. Some say Hudson dropped the charges as a favor to his mistress."

"We saw someone accuse him of only caring about winning," Kendra said. "Right on the courthouse steps. Are you suggesting he's crooked?"

If all he did was fix a drug charge then he wasn't highly corrupt, but it certainly showed capability.

"Seems that way to me."

Bob told them a little more about the Franklins from what he'd seen at family functions. Elaborate parties. Holidays. Town events like the annual Bluegrass Festival and political fund-raisers. Nothing that raised Roman's antenna.

He thanked them, and he and Kendra left.

"Do you think there's more to that drug charge Hudson dropped?" Kendra asked when they were outside.

"Let's go find out."

Just then, a car drove by and someone in the back seat with the window down threw something at them. Before he hooked Kendra around her waist and dived with her to the grassy front lawn of the Saunderses' house, Roman registered a dark blue Toyota Camry and the ski mask the thrower wore. Something hard shattered the driver's side window of Roman's rental car. The thrower's car's tires screeched as it swerved around the corner down the street.

Roman looked down at Kendra, her eyes round with fear and ready for a flight for life. "Are you all right?" He'd tackled her pretty hard.

She nodded.

Then he grew aware of every part of her underneath him. No time for that now. Despite the awakening it caused him, he stood. "Come on!" He took her hand and pulled her up with him.

Kendra ran to the passenger side of his rental and he raced into a U-turn to chase after whoever had thrown the object. He sat on shattered window glass. Kendra held up a rock that had something fastened to it with a thick rubber band—a piece of paper.

He drove into the turn at the street corner. The other car was nowhere in sight. He searched side streets as he passed and saw no dark blue Toyota.

"'Back off or die,'" Kendra said, having removed the rubber band and read the paper.

Someone had written the warning in black Magic Marker.

"Don't handle it anymore. We'll have Calum run some forensics on it."

Kendra dropped it back to the floorboard, where she'd picked it up.

Calum dug out the file on the drug dealer Hudson let go. After reading the case, the prosecution hadn't had much evidence. All they'd had was possession and the defendant claimed it wasn't his.

"Can we hack into Hudson's accounts?" Roman asked.

Across from him at the conference room table in the Chesterville Police Department, Cal looked up and over the top of his laptop at Roman. "I can't, but you can."

Roman grinned. "I'll pretend I didn't just hear you say that."

"Say what?" Kendra entered carrying three coffees. It was almost eleven at night. The rain had stopped but it was still damp outside and she wore a long black jacket with black boots and pale blue jeans. Every time he saw her, she made him want only to stare at her beauty. That red hair was up in a ponytail and her green eyes smiled from him to Cal.

"Roman's got a lead."

Roman saw how Kendra eyed him, having picked up on Cal's joking tone. She put down the coffee.

"You're an angel." Cal took his cup and sipped. "Where did you find her?"

"She found me." He met Kendra's eyes as she sat with her cup and put her feet up on the table, leaning back, looking tired but intrigued by his choice of words.

"I had a relationship with a coworker once. It didn't last."

What had prompted him to say something like that? He watched Cal look from her to him with a knowing glint.

"We don't work together. She's my client," Roman said.

"You're working with her on her case."

"I'm right here," Kendra said as they continued to talk as though she wasn't.

"What's your deal with women you work with?" Roman asked. He'd become something of a pal with the man and he sensed he must have had a bad experience with a woman he worked with.

"No deal. I just have a policy not to get intimately involved with them."

Roman could tell there was something troubling to Cal about the woman he'd had a relationship with on the job. He claimed he had no issue with that, but Roman bet he did, maybe a big one.

"Do you have a girlfriend right now?" Kendra asked.

"I did."

"Let me guess…it didn't last?"

"Nope. I started a new case and basically wasn't home for two weeks. I couldn't see her. She got sick of that and told me *see ya later.*"

Roman understood the challenges of balancing a personal life with detective work. Not only did he require something real with a woman, he had the added difficulty of finding someone who would be able to go long hours and days between seeing him and spending family time together.

He glanced at Kendra, whose eyes drooped even with her coffee. He couldn't help wondering if she'd be the kind of woman who could handle a relationship like that. She ran a successful business so maybe she could. But then that same doubt entered his thoughts. Her world was too perfect. She'd come home to him and his dark world, one filled with murder every day. Would that dim her cheery light? How could it not? He didn't think she'd be happy with a guy like him. She might be fooled into thinking she was at first, with all this hot passion they had going for them, but eventually the everyday grind would infiltrate the spritely bubble.

She yawned and he grew flustered that even watching her do that turned him on.

"Let's pick this up tomorrow." Roman shut down his computer. "I'll get a team of investigators on the Franklins. They'll be able to find out things you and I can't with the resources here."

"Great. I get to go home to my lonely house and you get to go home with that." Cal looked at Kendra. "I mean that as a compliment."

"I'm too tired to be insulted. Besides, I have my own lonely house to go home to. Roman has his lonely hotel room." She stood up.

Reminded of the rock, Roman didn't think her going to her lonely house was such a good idea.

"Until we get forensics back on that rock, maybe you two should consider staying together."

Roman almost grinned again, it was so uncanny that Cal was the one to bring that up. "He does have a point."

Kendra sort of froze and stared at Roman.

"We can go by your house so you can pick up a few things. I also have a pullout bed in the room. I can sleep there and you can have the bedroom."

"I won't call myself a matchmaker yet." Smiling, Cal stood as Roman packed up his computer.

"You must need a good night's sleep," Roman teased as he went to the door, Kendra still quiet. She may not have decided to stay with him, but he'd make sure she did.

The next day, Kendra had to stop by her shop and Roman had to get back to work with Cal. Not that she minded. She needed a break from him. Last night had been all right. It had been so late that she'd focused only on packing a few things. The worst had been having him in her house—alone—and then the drive to the hotel room. She'd gone straight to the bedroom and closed the door. She was so tired she'd fallen asleep almost instantly.

This morning had been awkward. She'd showered, and then let him shower. In the hotel room, both smelling fresh and clean, she'd had this strange feeling of domestication, getting ready for the day together. They'd shared breakfast in the hotel restaurant and she'd discovered he was a healthy eater like her. She'd ordered a grapefruit with a side of cottage cheese, and he'd ordered the same, only he'd added a ham and egg muffin without cheese.

The news had been on and covered a story about a child who'd survived cancer.

"There's something wrong with a god who allows kids to suffer like that," she had said.

"Unless there's a reason for everything," Roman had answered. "The kid survived and is healthy now."

She liked his view, which was open and respectful of every kind of religion, including agnostic. She let the rest of their conversation replay in her mind.

"Do you think you will ever want kids?" he had asked next, bringing the awkwardness back. Why did he bring that up again?

"Why do you ask?"

He paid for their breakfast and said, "That news story made me think of it."

"I suppose so, if it were to happen, I think I'd embrace it. What about you?"

"I think kids are great, but I doubt I'll ever find a woman to have them with."

There was his pessimism again. "What are you, a fortune-teller?"

"No. My lifestyle isn't conducive for having kids. Yours doesn't seem that way, either."

He could have a point there. She stood up. "Why are you so negative all the time?" Without waiting for his answer, she turned and headed for the door.

"I'm not negative all the time," he'd said when they left the restaurant.

Stopping, she faced him, not understanding why he tripped her trigger so much. "Yes you are. You don't have a single good thing to say about falling in love."

"I would be happy to fall in love. I just know the odds are not in most people's favor in finding it."

"I agree it's not easy to find, but if you are patient and don't hook up with the first partner who comes along, then the odds aren't so dismal. Certainly not as dismal as you see it."

"You think you're going to fall in love?" he challenged. "For real?"

She scoffed in frustration. "You and your *reality*. I dare you to spend an entire day thinking nothing but positive thoughts about your future with love."

"You dare me?" He'd actually grinned. She was fuming on the inside with aggravation and he had enjoyed the teasing.

"Yes."

"Okay. My first positive thought is of you and I sleeping together and loving it. Hitting it off. And I mean, really hitting it off. That rare kind of chemistry I've so far only heard about. The rarest. The *real* thing."

He'd so startled her with the words he's said that she had felt flushed. She'd warmed everywhere and imagined kissing right then. Kissing, and then rushing back up to his room to make his dream come true.

After several seconds, she recovered and said, "But you don't believe that will happen."

And then it was his turn to be rendered speechless.

He'd dropped her off here at her store. She could still hear his new rental running as he waited for her to get inside. She could also still hear his rich voice saying, "I'll pick you up for lunch." He didn't want to leave her alone long. She wouldn't be alone here. She had a clerk who'd be here any minute and Raelyn said she'd stop by this morning.

She unlocked the door and looked back. He held up his hand and she waved back. A flutter tickled her stomach. He was so handsome. And a good man. She would do well snagging a man like him.

She entered her shop berating herself for even considering that. She'd do well with a man who didn't believe in love? Not quite. Love was the single most important thing to her. She needed a family someday. She'd been vague when he'd asked that question about having kids. She did want kids, but she hadn't felt comfortable revealing that to him.

Her clerk arrived and she welcomed the busy task of opening the store. Raelyn arrived shortly thereafter. She walked briskly, with such energy, for a moment Kendra imagined her twin sister coming to see her. Kaelyn had had that kind of energy. Raelyn's hair had the same red sheen and floated light as air as she moved.

She entered and her face lit up when she spotted Kendra, whose heart did a lurch of love for her niece. That was the first smile she'd seen Raelyn give her. Before now, the sight of her brought Raelyn pain.

"Hey, Aunt Kendra. What's happening?"

She was in orange shorts and a matching multicolored tank top and sandals, conservative compared to what she'd worn previously. Was she coming out of her dark phase? Today's forecast was a lot warmer than it had been, so she could just be trying to stay cool. Kendra could hope, though.

"You ready to get to work?"

"Yes." She leaned in for a quick hug, and then went to the checkout counter, where she began getting the register ready. "Anything going on in your investigation?"

She asked almost hesitantly, as though dreading to learn all her hope had been for naught.

"Yes. A lot. Are you okay to hear it all?" Kendra moved so she could better see Raelyn's lowered face.

Raelyn's pretty green eyes lifted as she glanced at her. "Yes."

"We know for certain now that your mother was murdered."

Resting her hands on the register, Raelyn took a moment before she raised her head.

"She was on her way to Chesterville when she was killed. Her body was moved and staged to look like a suicide. She was close to Chesterville when she must have been run off the road. We don't know who did it or why yet, but we know she was murdered."

"You never doubted it," Raelyn said.

Kendra could see where this was headed. "Don't blame yourself for believing your mother killed herself. You didn't know she was talking to me or the things she said to me, the plans she was making for her future—for both of you. Where she went, you were going with her."

"Then why did she go to Chesterville without me?"

"She didn't come here to stay. She came here to warn her lover's wife about something. That's what we need to find out. Why did your mother drive to Chesterville with the intention of meeting with Glenn's wife—or Bear's, as she called him? And why all the secrets? There are still many unanswered questions, but the case has definitely been moving forward. We now have the support of the CPD."

"Wow. That's amazing."

Kendra could see she still wasn't past her doubt over

her mother's state of mind. "Raelyn, your mother would not want you to feel bad."

"I should have known." Her tone sharpened. "My mother was strong. The only time she wasn't was when my dad beat her. She was afraid for me and her. That's why she didn't leave."

"She would have left. She would have taken you with her. But something happened to stop her and we don't think it was your dad. We think it has something to do with her lover, Bear. Glenn Franklin. Your mother didn't tell you to protect you."

"She was so full of love and life." Raelyn's eyes teared up. "My bastard of a dad didn't appreciate her. He was threatened by her integrity."

"I've thought the same thing." Kendra took Raelyn into her arms. "Cry if you need to but never have bad feelings about your thoughts after she died."

"That's easier said than done."

Kendra rubbed her back. "Now that you know she didn't leave you and take the coward's way out, you can mourn. You haven't done that yet. You haven't really mourned, so give yourself some time, okay?"

Raelyn sniffled and nodded as she said, "Okay."

Leaning back, Kendra had to fight not to cry with her. She wiped her cheeks with her thumb. "Let's go buy some inventory."

They went to the back to the small office area. The shop clerk could run the front. Kendra pulled up another chair at the antique desk and went to her favorite vendor's website. Antique chests were a popular selling item. She'd add in some handmade jewelry and let Raelyn pick some out.

"Aunt Kendra?"

"Yes?"

"If I can't have my mom, I'm glad I have you."

Oh, that burst a sunbeam straight through her heart. "Not as glad as I am to have you." She kissed her cheek.

Chapter 13

Roman asked Cal to start the disinterment process to exhume Deidra Franklin's body. They made their case center on the evidence that Glenn's lover didn't commit suicide, that her body had been moved and her case was now being investigated as a homicide. Kaelyn had warned Glenn's wife about her husband and was killed before being able to talk to her. They further argued Deidra Franklin was a healthy young woman who may have learned something about Glenn and he may have been forced to silence her for good. Kaelyn may not have told Vikki she had an affair with Glenn. More likely, she, like Deidra, could have discovered something much more deadly. Both women could have been murdered for the same reason. Cal requested the disinterment of Deidra's remains to either rule out or confirm poisoning. Both he and Cal expected the court to agree they had enough to justify a necessity.

Now a day later, he sat with Cal and Kendra in the conference room at the CPD. He watched Kendra studying Deidra's autopsy report. She'd already asked a lot of questions. She also read her sister's again.

Just past her, he spotted a man walking toward the conference room. Except his steps weren't normal, like he'd come for a casual visit. No, these were long and hard strides. Glenn Franklin's brow hung low and stormy, and the lapels of his suit jacket and hem of matching pants flapped with the angry pace.

Word must have gotten around they planned to disinter Deidra's body.

A police officer chased after him.

"Incoming," Roman quipped.

Cal looked up just as Glenn reached the office door. He held up his hand and waved off the police officer.

Kendra abandoned the files, closing them to look up at Glenn as he passed the table.

"Exhuming my first wife's body?" Glenn roared, stopping at the corner of Cal's desk. "What on this green earth possessed you to do that? And by what right?"

"Everything was done legally, I assure you," Cal said.

"You think she was murdered? What the hell is going on?"

"Maybe you could tell us."

Glenn's face reddened and his jaw clenched. "If you're implying I had anything to do with her death—"

"We're not implying anything. We're making sure she actually did die of natural causes."

"She got sick and died. Why can't you leave her to rest in peace?" He leaned down and slapped his palm on a stack of files on the desk. "Do you have any idea what this is doing to me and my family?"

Cal just looked up at him.

Roman felt the same detachment. "Do you care whether she was murdered or not?"

Glenn's face reddened more. Steam may as well stream out of his ears as he straightened. "Have you ever lost anyone you loved, Detective Cooper?"

"No, but just about every day, I see what losing someone to murder does to people who have. I would expect you, as someone who loved his first wife, to be nothing but supportive of our efforts."

Some of his fury eased as he must have realized how his outburst appeared. "I loved my wife. It nearly killed me when she died. It took me a long time to get past losing her. Finding out her body is being removed from the ground is upsetting."

"We're sorry for that," Cal said. "Unfortunately, it's necessary. We'll have her back in the ground as soon as we can."

Glenn calmed further. "Why do you think she was murdered? Why do you need her body?"

"We think she may have been poisoned," Roman said, watching Glenn closely for a reaction.

He seemed genuinely taken aback. "Poisoned?"

"We also think there may be a link between Kaelyn's murder and your first wife's," Cal said.

Roman wasn't sure he would have revealed that information. Maybe Cal didn't think it mattered. Would Glenn, knowing how much they had uncovered about Deidra's death, change how he behaved? Would he make a run for it? Would he confess?

"I don't understand." With his brow still hovering

low, Glenn rubbed his forehead, seeming to have difficulty absorbing this new information. "Poisoned," he repeated, stepping to a chair at the conference room table and sitting as though he needed to.

Glenn appeared genuinely surprised to learn this. Either that or he was a good actor. Why get so angry over exhuming his previous wife's body? He had to have known since a court ordered that an investigation into her death had begun.

Then he regained his aplomb. "Why do you think there's a link?"

Roman hoped Cal wouldn't reveal too much about that.

"Did you notice anything different about Deidra prior to her death?" Cal asked.

"Like what? No." Glenn seemed to gather himself even more now. "I was working a lot, so maybe she was different but I didn't notice."

"Did she mention anything to you?" Roman asked. "Maybe bring up a name or talk about someone who resented her? An argument?"

Again, Glenn shook his head.

"What did she do the last two days of her life?" Cal asked.

"She went shopping the day before." He fell silent as he thought some more. "She and my mother had lunch like they always do. They have a favorite restaurant. They usually went once a week."

"They were close?" Kendra asked.

"Yes. They became good friends. Deidra liked nice things like my mother. They had that in common."

They were both materialistic. Like-minded people would get along. Glenn seemed to have picked two women who fit into this lifestyle and his parents approved. They'd welcomed both into their circle.

"My family has always been close-knit," Glenn went on. "We spend a lot of time together. That's how Deidra became such good friends with my mother. My parents are pretty social anyway. They have a large network of friends and acquaintances."

"What about Deidra? Did she have any friends of her own?" Roman asked.

"Oh yeah. She had lots of friends. Most of them were both of our friends, but she kept in touch with her college roommate and one of her high school friends."

"When was she last in contact with them?" Cal asked.

Glenn hesitated a moment. Was he trying to remember or was he reluctant to provide them that information? "It had been a while. They talked every few months or so, rarely got together in person."

"Any bank or credit card statement during that time would help us retrace her activities," Roman said while Cal finished writing down the names.

Glenn nodded. "Sure. All right. I'll send you those and anything else I can find. I'm not sure I still have copies anymore."

"Do the best you can." If they had to, they'd get a search warrant, and they would if Deidra was poisoned. Roman would make sure of that.

"When will her body be exhumed?"

"I believe it's planned for the day after tomorrow," Cal said. "You can be there if you like."

After a few seconds, Glenn shook his head. "I already buried her once. I'd rather not bury her a second time."

"Thank you, Mr. Franklin," Cal said. "You've been a big help."

Roman bet that was the last thing Glenn figured on doing today. He hadn't come to help them. He'd come to express his displeasure over Deidra's disinterment.

Glenn got up from his chair.

"If I could ask a few more questions?" Kendra stood from her chair and moved in front of the door.

"Sure," Glenn said.

He was cooperating very well for a man who didn't want his wife's body exhumed. Did he want his wife avenged if she was killed or was he covering his own hide?

"Why was Kaelyn on her way to Chesterville?" Kendra asked.

"I don't know. The last time I talked to her, she didn't have any plans to come here. At least, she didn't tell me of any."

"Why do *you* think she might have driven here?"

"Probably to see her mom. That's why she always came to Chesterville. That and to get away from her crazy husband."

Roman wondered why Kaelyn didn't tell anyone why she was coming to Chesterville. Had she feared Alex would come after her? Most likely she had. Maybe she also didn't want to bring that kind of drama to her hometown, to her parents' doorstep. Too bad she hadn't. Maybe she'd still be alive. Maybe it wouldn't have mattered. She'd discovered something and it had nothing to do with her abusive husband.

"She wasn't coming here just to see her mother," Roman said.

Glenn's head slowly lifted and he looked right at

Roman. Roman couldn't tell what he might be thinking but he sensed some belligerence.

"Well, she wasn't coming to see me."

"Was she going to see Vikki?" Cal asked.

"Vikki? Why Vikki?"

Cal didn't answer and Roman was glad. Let the man
wonder why they might think Kaelyn had been on her
way to see his current wife.

Roman accompanied Kendra to her shop the next
morning and she struggled with heightened awareness
of his presence. She couldn't afford to be away from her
business for too long, and with the threat of someone
attacking them, she had little choice other than to bring
him. Raelyn was a fast learner, but she wasn't ready
to run the store by herself and Kendra didn't like the
idea of allowing one of her clerks to do it. Still early,
Kendra finished prepping the shop for opening and
had time to spare. She felt fidgety without anything
to do but look at Roman. He sat at her antique desk,
doing something on her computer. She went to the office door and leaned against the door frame. Sunlight
streaming in from the back window hit his dark hair
and made him squint slightly, creasing the skin at the
corners and making his eyes sparkle. He wore dark
blue jeans with a short-sleeved white button-up. More
than once she'd stopped and ogled his muscular arms
and the sight of him in the sunlight.

Magnetism brought her closer. She sat on the edge
of her desk. "Doing detective work?"

He looked from her butt on up to her face. "Reading about Petra."

Not working? His interest in such an ancient historic site surprised her and allured him to her even more than she already was with him. "Are you planning your next vacation?"

"I might go there someday."

He liked to travel. She didn't know why but she wouldn't have thought a man like him would enjoy things like that. He absorbed himself in his work.

"Where have you been?" she asked.

"Rome. Yucatán. Cotswolds."

His deep voice with all his love of the mentioned places enriched the sound and made her heart do a peculiar little lurch. He liked historic places. Aside from selling Christmas ornaments, some of her favorite pieces she collected for her shop were antiques. "You travel a lot. Cotswolds." She looked heavenward. "I've wanted to go there for such a long time."

Pushing back the chair, he stood, and she caught the amused glint in his gorgeous eyes. "When I'm not working, that's what I do."

"You travel to historic places?" She'd always wanted to travel like that but not alone. Roman was much different. He must enjoy being alone, or not mind it. She didn't mind being alone, but vacations were different. It was always nicer to share the fun.

"Sometimes I wish I would have majored in history in college." He moved a step closer.

He loved history but would he have been happy working in that capacity? Vacationing to historic places and learning about history and earning a living with it were poles apart.

"You seem surprised," he said in her silence.

"That you like history or that you don't realize DAI was your calling in life and not anything else?"

Now he was the one surprised. She could see she'd made him ponder what life would have been like without DAI.

"I don't just *like* history. When I discover new things I feel the way my dad probably feels when he writes."

It made him feel good. Interests did that to people. That didn't mean it was his calling in life. The whole point of leisure time was to relax and enjoy.

"If you had gone into some profession relating to history, whether it's a curator at a museum or a school or university professor, you would have missed out on your career as a detective. And think of all those vacations you took that wouldn't have meant as much if you worked every day in history."

"Seeing those places live isn't the same as learning about them from a book or a television program."

"No, but it still wouldn't have been as special." He confounded her. "Why can't you see how valuable you are as a detective?"

"I do. I help a lot of people overcome loss. I'm good at solving crimes. It's just…such a…morbid profession."

So he didn't like the grimness of it. "What a relief you don't get off on murder." She didn't know any other way to respond other than with teasing. When he sent her a sarcastic look, she said, "What do you feel when you're working a case, when you get to that point when you know you're going to solve it and the victim will be vindicated and the family set on their path to moving on?"

"Great. Pumped up."

"Don't you think that's how you're supposed to feel when you're doing what you were meant to do?" She pointed her finger at his chest, his hard, broad chest.

He started to grin. "I like it when you get sassy."

"I'm not getting sassy. I'm just trying to make you understand that you're already doing what you were called to do."

He looked down at her awhile, still seeming to enjoy this talk. "Like you? Were you called to open a Christmas shop?"

Kendra put her hands on the desk on each side of her hips and stretched a little. No one had ever asked her that and she had never thought it over. Reminded of her rough childhood and teen years, she knew that was the only thing that had driven her to open a shop like hers.

"I don't think I was called to do anything," she finally said. "I wanted cheer in my life. What's more cheerful than Christmas?"

He moved a step closer and his nearness stirred her senses.

"I like your version better than mine."

He'd rather not believe he was meant to be the elite detective he was? That sounded like denial to her, and learning she'd fallen into her work the same way he believed he'd fallen into his somehow made him connect to her, as though he'd discovered something he hadn't expected about her, something he liked. Kendra felt the prick of warning that he connected for the wrong reason. He needed to connect with himself before he could connect with anyone else.

His gray eyes had warmed and she didn't want to look away. When he trailed his finger over her mouth, the warning fled and in its place came delightful fire.

"What are you doing?" she asked, fighting for control.

"I'm going to kiss you." His hand slid into her hair and tipped her head back.

Now? He was going to kiss her right now? Her breath hitched and the fire roared hotter with anticipation. He drew out the moment as though intentionally arousing her first.

At last, he lowered his mouth to hers and began with a soft touch that gradually built into something much more demanding. She slid her hands up his chest and then down his biceps, satisfying a mounting desire.

She parted her lips and he gave her more. He moved over her mouth and they devoured each other. Then he broke away and kissed her neck, sucking her skin. She felt his heated breath and his hands going down her back to her butt. Scooting her to the edge of the desk, he pressed against her and kissed her again.

This quickly escalated beyond control. Kendra wouldn't have stopped him even if she could. Even as the thought came, his warm kiss chased any doubt away.

Going on instinct, she let go and gave in to temptation. She pulled his shirt up. She longed to see his bare chest. He broke away long enough to finish taking it off.

"Are you sure about this?" he asked.

"Absolutely not." She found his mouth again for more kissing, feeling his deep chuckle vibrate against her skin.

"Me, neither." He tugged at the buttons of her shirt. She'd worn a skirt today so that would give him easy access. "It feels right, though."

"Yes." It felt so right.

She leaned back to help him with her shirt and he

went to the office door and shut it. She tossed her shirt to the floor on top of his. He came back to her and stood still for a few seconds looking at her breasts.

"I knew they were beautiful," he said.

She had on a lacy bra that he reached forward to unclasp, giving her a fleeting sense of vulnerability. She felt resistance building—that maybe this was a mistake—but Roman bent to take one of her nipples into his mouth. She was gone then.

He undid his jeans and she couldn't wait to find out if all this hot attraction meant the sex would be mind-blowing.

She slid off her underwear and he pushed the hem of her skirt up. From there she stopped thinking. She only felt. She tipped her head back to the unbearable pleasure. He made quick, hard work of it, catapulting them both to an incredible plane of pure ecstasy.

When coherency returned, she gradually felt the vulnerability build again, this time without passion to stave it off. While Roman fastened his jeans, she slipped her underwear back on and finished dressing with her back to him.

He stepped closer and planted a soft kiss to her neck, melting her and easing a rising panic attack. She'd never felt more loss of control in her life, and it terrified her.

Facing him, she saw his eyes soft in the aftermath, no more hardness of the reality that made him so pessimistic. She saw the man he tried hard to bury, a man who craved to live the way others did, others he mocked for living on a cloud of what he'd labelled denial, but was really a cloud of happiness. People should steal every moment of happiness they could in this life.

Life was scary, but no one had to live under its dark spell all the time.

"I'm late opening up." She went to the door, opened it, and saw two customers waiting at the door. Smoothing her hair and fighting to gather herself, she forged ahead. A busy day at work was exactly what she needed right now.

Kendra finally gave up trying to sleep and got up off the bed. She hadn't invited Roman in here to sleep and he hadn't asked. After their quickie yesterday morning, they hadn't spoken much to each other. She'd indeed had a busy day at the shop and he'd worked in her office. The drive back to the hotel had been awkward to say the least.

She thought about how good they were together all day and the thoughts didn't stop when she turned off the bedroom light. She'd tingled a few times, but mostly she was in awe. She couldn't believe such a wonder had happened to her. She had never felt like that with any man. No man had turned her on so much that she'd come apart so fast. He set her on fire. How was that possible? She didn't feel she could trust him emotionally and that hadn't mattered in the heat of the moment. How did he see her as a woman? Things went too far too fast for her, and she sensed he felt the same.

They'd conversed about what to have for dinner, ate dinner, and then she'd run off to the bedroom. She sensed his tension as much as she felt hers. He probably didn't know what to make of what happened any more than she did. Had he ever had an experience like that with a woman?

Dressing in sweatpants and a sleeveless shirt, she

left the bedroom. Out in the living room, she saw Roman sleeping with the covers at his waist, revealing that chest she had the pleasure of touching.

She needed to take a walk or something. The hotel had a bar and it wasn't late enough for them to be closed. She could go down and get a cold soda or some tea. She wouldn't leave the building. That could be dangerous. Slipping into some sandals, she took her wallet and a room key, and left the room. In the hall, she headed for the elevators. Another door opened behind her. She glanced back and saw a man leave the room next to Roman's. She thought twice about going into the elevator. Was it coincidental this man had come from the room right next to the one she'd just left?

Reaching the elevators, she pressed the button and pretended to wait. The man appeared next to her. She covertly checked him out. Around six feet, short clipped medium brown hair under a baseball cap. Dark eyes. He wore a sweatshirt and black jeans. Heavy-duty boots. He looked ready for combat.

When she looked up, he turned his head. Smothering her alarm, she smiled a little and nodded once in greeting. He didn't return any gesture.

She feigned looking into her purse. Finding the room key Roman had given her, she held on to it and said, "Darn it," then moved behind the man and started back down the hall.

A glance back confirmed that he followed, face set with evil intent.

With a shriek, she bolted into a run, lifting the card key out of her purse. At Roman's hotel door, she pounded and yelled "Roman!" as she inserted the card.

The man reached her as the green light blinked on.

She pushed the door open as the man grabbed her by the arm and brought her back up against him. He held a gun to her head.

Kendra dropped her purse but still held on to the card key, squeezing her eyes shut for a second, fighting stark fear.

"You aren't going to get another warning," the man said.

Roman's room door opened and he appeared, shirtless and barefoot and in jeans. He held his own weapon, a big black pistol aimed at the man's head.

He stepped out into the hall. "Let her go before I drop you."

"Go back to Wyoming or somebody's going to get hurt," the man said.

The man began backing down the hall. Would he force her to go with him? Kendra stared at Roman, wishing she could will him to rescue her, make this man let her go.

"Who hired you?" Roman asked, following.

"Stay where you are."

"Who hired you?" Roman repeated.

The man scoffed, as though thinking, *as if I'd tell you.* "I was sent to deliver a warning, that's all. Next time, you won't see me coming. Stop your investigation."

"Or you're going to start shooting at us?" Roman mocked, moving forward again. "I've been threatened by guys like you before, and I'm the one who's still standing."

"You don't know who you're dealing with. Listen to me. This is your last warning."

Kendra saw they were almost to the elevators.

"I am listening. Now you listen to me. Tell whoever

hired you I hope they're ready to go to prison, because that's where I'm going to send them."

The man stopped at the door to the stairs.

"Overconfidence will get you killed, mister. I've done what I came to do. You've been warned." With that, the man shoved Kendra hard. She fell into Roman.

"Are you all right?" he asked.

"Yes."

He set her aside and ran for the stairwell. Kendra followed cautiously. She saw him leap down the stairs after the man. She stepped down, peering over the railing. She heard footsteps running down the stairs but didn't see anything.

Then gunshots reverberated in the open space and against the cold concrete walls. Who shot at whom? Concern for Roman made her run down to the next level, then the next. Finally, on the main level, she caught sight of Roman bursting through a side door. She carefully inched up to the door and peered outside. Roman ran across the parking lot, chasing the other man.

He disappeared out of the range of the lights. Three more shots rang out, and then silence followed. Kendra went to the side door and waited.

A few minutes later, Roman appeared under the parking lot lights again. He jogged toward her, looking around and behind him. He slowed as he reached her.

"He got away," he said, barely winded. "I would have kept chasing him but I didn't want to leave you alone."

She ran her hand over her forehead, noticing her hand trembling.

Roman took her hand and held it in both of his. "What were you doing outside the room?"

"I couldn't sleep."

"So you decided to go for a walk?" His tone grew edgier.

"No. I was going to get a soda."

"Why couldn't you sleep?"

She looked down at his bare chest, and then back up at his face, which smoothed as he understood. "It took me a while to fall asleep, too." He moved back, still holding her hand. "Come on. Let's go back to the room." He glanced around them before walking with her to the hotel entrance.

They went into the lobby, where the sound of sirens preceded a police car, and then two more. Police officers scurried out of their vehicles and entered the lobby. Roman and Kendra stepped onto an elevator.

"He came out of the room right next to ours," she said.

An officer's head turned sharply toward her. "We need to get in there."

On their floor, they walked down the hall. Her purse still lay where she dropped it. She picked it up and inserted the card key into the room door.

Roman found his phone and Kendra waited while he called Cal. Cal would inform police what had happened and make arrangements for them to let him and Kendra into the room next to theirs.

Kendra went with him into the hall, where police stood with a hotel manager, who opened the stranger's room for them.

"Detective Cooper?" one of the cops asked.

"Yes."

"Officer Wellman. You can go on in."

"Thanks." He entered ahead of Kendra, his gun now in a hip holster.

Kendra saw nothing in the room except surveillance equipment, a laptop and some kind of device.

"What is that?"

"It's used to pick up sounds. He's been listening to us."

They hadn't spoken about the case in the room since before they'd begun the disinterment process. Was the stranger trying to keep Kaelyn's murder from being solved or Deidra's?

Or both...?

Chapter 14

In order to catch the mayor's wife alone, Kendra and Roman followed her to her hair salon and waited until she finished before intercepting her in the parking lot. An older version of Melody, she dressed in an expensive, olive-colored pantsuit and held her matching purse at her elbow, forearm up and hand bent down. Her dark hair was stiff and perfectly styled. Dark red lipstick ruined otherwise fine skin for a woman in her late sixties and big sunglasses hid eyes Kendra had seen were gray and lined with heavy makeup.

Today, the rain had abated to give them a break with clear blue skies and warmer weather. Kendra had opted for a blue spaghetti-strap sundress and sandals. Roman wore tan pants with a black short-sleeved button-up. He'd shaved this morning but a faint stubble had formed by late afternoon.

She and Roman stepped into her path. She stopped, looked from one to the other, and then seemed flustered. Her mouth opened as though she'd say something but then nothing came out.

"We didn't mean to startle you," Roman said, introducing Kendra and himself. "We just want to ask you some questions about your affair with Hudson Franklin."

The woman's mouth opened briefly, and then she tried to move around Kendra, who blocked her way.

"I didn't have an affair." She again tried to go around, but Kendra stopped her.

"Did Hudson do you a favor when he got your son's drug arrest reduced?" Roman asked.

"I don't have any idea what you're talking about."

"Your son was arrested for drug possession, was he not?"

"Yes, but it wasn't a large enough amount to put him in jail."

"What did your husband do for him?" Roman asked. "What did he owe Hudson in return?"

"I don't have to answer these questions. Out of my way!"

This time Kendra allowed her to pass, but followed her along with Roman to her parked Lincoln.

"We could get the police involved. We have enough evidence to include this in our investigation. If you provide false information, that could be held against you."

The woman stopped with an indignant huff at her car. "All right. I did have an affair with Hudson. We began as friends. He and my husband were friends until he found out about us. My husband told Hudson if he didn't help our son, he'd go public with the affair. Hudson didn't want it getting out."

Why was it so important that the affair be kept secret? It had already leaked out in gossip. Melody had known. More likely there had been something else at play, something the mayor hadn't told his wife.

"Are Hudson and your husband good friends?"

"My husband and I have known the Franklins for many years. We used to be closer."

The affair had caused a rift. "Did they do any other favors for each other?"

"I don't know what you mean by favors. When they were friends, they did what most friends do. Spent time together."

Roman remembered the man who'd rushed Hudson and Melody Franklin outside the courthouse. He'd ranted about someone being innocent. There had also been a camera crew there. Given Hudson's tough prosecutor reputation, an outburst like that might not be alarming.

"Do you know if Hudson ever took any kind of payments for favors similar to the one he did for the mayor?" Roman asked.

The woman drew her head back. "No."

"Are you and Melody friends?"

The woman scoffed. "What do you think?"

"You must have been at one point."

"Yes, I suppose we were. I grew tired of Melody's superiority complex. She's no better than I am, but she sure tried to keep me a level beneath her."

"Did she ever talk to you about Hudson's favors?"

"We didn't talk about their work, not ever. And I don't know why you think Hudson did favors for anyone. He puts criminals behind bars where they belong."

"Like your son?" Kendra put in.

She had a way of placing her barbs in one-liners. That particular trait amused Roman. Maybe because it showed she didn't sugarcoat the truth.

But the mayor's wife clearly took offense. "Who are you to call my son a criminal?"

"He was arrested for drugs." Kendra sounded matter-of-fact.

The other woman huffed and pivoted to open her car door.

They'd get nothing more out of her. The mayor obviously never told his wife anything about his work—or the *favors* he elicited for his gain.

Roman took out his phone and searched for news coverage on the day the man had lashed out at Hudson. He found an article describing how a local had been charged and convicted of murder. On the surface, it appeared no one else could have committed the crime. He found the name of the convict and searched for his family. With a name like Barfknecht, the man who'd lashed out at Hudson wasn't difficult to find. That was their next stop.

Phillip Barfknecht worked at the Chesterville Amusement Park. Kendra walked with Roman past the antique car and paddleboat rides. The park also had a carrousel, Scrambler, Tilt-A-Whirl, Wave Swinger, bumper cars and a waterslide. She could see the Ferris wheel turning in the distance, and smelled cotton candy and popcorn. Kids screamed and laugher filled the air along with the up-and-down roar of an old wood roller coaster. The sunny day had grown long in shadows with barely a breeze, and blossoming trees providing shade here and there.

Reaching the Wave Swinger, Kendra spotted Barfknecht starting a ride. Staying outside the chained-in line of people, They stopped before the fence where Barfknecht stood on the other side. Roman started talking to him, getting through the usual introductions.

"We're here to talk to you about Prosecutor Franklin," Kendra said.

Barfknecht's face glowered, brows lowering and mouth tightening briefly. "That no-good louse? What do you want to talk to me about him for?"

"We think he may be involved in some corrupt practices and wondered if you could help us," Roman said.

Barfknecht's face smoothed and he appeared surprised.

"We saw you outside the courthouse a while back. You weren't very happy with him," Kendra added.

The man glanced at the moving ride as though checking to be sure all was well. Kids screamed and laughed. The first few people in line watched and probably listened to the three of them talking.

Barfknecht faced them again. "He sent my son to prison and he's innocent."

"The evidence didn't seem to indicate that," Roman said.

"My son drove the car and didn't know what his friend was doing until he came out of the alley with a bloody flashlight."

Kendra had read the report Roman had shared with her describing the crime. A man had been murdered in an alley. His wallet had been stolen. A witness placed Brock Barfknecht near the alley where the murder occurred and others had confirmed seeing him in the passenger seat of the car driving away. No one could identify the driver.

"Who is his friend?" Roman asked.

"Percy Gordon. He was the one walking to the car with the flashlight."

"Your son also knew the man who was killed?" Roman asked, clearly ignoring the father's insistence that his son was innocent.

"Knew him and got into a bar fight with him over a girl a few nights prior. But my son said Percy had a bigger reason to kill him. He was after him for money. The man didn't pay for some drugs that added up to a significant amount. The jury didn't believe that. There was no evidence of any drugs. No one could place Brock in the car. But Brock saw Percy give drugs to the man killed about a week prior. Jury didn't believe him because that crooked prosecutor made sure Percy was never implicated."

"What about the murder weapon?" Roman asked.

"The victim was killed from blunt force trauma to the head and Brock's flashlight was found in his car with blood on it that matched the victim's."

"Percy's prints had to be on it, but it never came up in court."

"Only Brock's prints were on it?"

"That don't mean my son is the killer."

Police had showed up at Brock's home just a few minutes after he'd arrived. He likely hadn't had time to get rid of the murder weapon, or enough time to think he needed to.

"We're not here to prove whether or not your son is innocent, Mr. Barfknecht. However, we do agree

Franklin could be corrupt. Can you tell us what you know about that?"

"I found out Franklin plays golf with Percy Gordon's father and Gordon bought him a trip to the Canary Islands the week after the trial. Don't you think that's odd?"

Had Percy's father bribed Franklin to keep his son from being implicated in the crime? Judging from all she'd read, Kendra was pretty certain Brock had been the one to commit the crime, but this was the second incident that suggested Hudson Franklin was violating some serious ethics laws. Bribery. Corruption. In her book, that would be enough motive to make an unscrupulous man murder anyone who found out.

"Yeah." Roman nodded twice. "That is odd."

"You think you can prove he's a fraud?" Barfknecht asked. "My son should be released from prison."

"I'm sorry about your son, Mr. Barfknecht," Roman said. "If Hudson is guilty of corruption, I'll expose him."

Kendra noticed how Roman avoided addressing him on his son's innocence.

Barfknecht nodded his understanding. Whatever fight he had for his son was going to have to be his issue.

The ride ended and Barfknecht had to go to work.

Ready to go, Kendra thanked him for his time and Roman followed her away from the ride.

They started walking back toward the parking lot.

"Wanna go on a few rides?" Roman asked with a spark of playful enthusiasm.

Kendra turned a quick glance at Roman. He must not want to leave the amusement park just yet. Was he satisfying a youthful whim or was he being romantic? She had to be sure.

"Are you asking me out on a date again?" she asked.

"We're already in an amusement park. Didn't you ever like them?"

"Of course. When I was a kid."

"You can't stop being a kid when there are rides just steps away."

She smiled and laughed a little. "Okay. How about that roller coaster that looks like it could crumble at any turn?"

"Naw. It has to be the Ferris wheel."

"Why the Ferris wheel?"

"I want to talk to you about us."

"And you want to do it on a Ferris wheel?"

"Yeah, I want to *do it* on the Ferris wheel."

Kendra stopped short and he did the same with a mischievous grin. She'd never seen him like this before, so full of light. "Was that humor I just heard?"

"You're the one who said *do it*." He chuckled. "Come on." He took her hand and, after buying tickets, took her to the Ferris wheel line.

"I'm not so sure about this," Kendra said. He'd sobered since his quip earlier. "Why do you want to talk to me on a Ferris wheel?"

"Because you can't walk away from me if we're sixty feet in the air and locked in our seats."

He thought she'd run away? What was he going to say that would make her do that? Was he sorry they'd had sex?

They reached the front of the line and it was their turn to sit in a cart. He let her get in first and then sat beside her, his big body close and doing things to her she'd like to ignore.

The Ferris wheel moved to allow more people to board.

Roman stretched his arm across the back of the cart and gazed off across the amusement park and beyond. Only then did she notice the setting sun. Would sunsets ever not be romantic? Was it the colors, the dark horizon against a painted sky or the onset of night?

The Ferris wheel moved again.

Roman seemed content to watch the sky, although Kendra wondered if he was gathering his thoughts.

"That sunset reminds me of a fishing trip with my dad," he said.

Fishing was not what she expected. She watched the sunset as the Ferris wheel rose up some more.

"We didn't do a lot together because he was always in his office writing, but the time we did spend together was like that. Sitting in a boat, drinking lemonade my mom made, four rods in the water. He'd tell me stories about growing up, about his parents and when he was a kid. His dad never did anything with him and he wanted to make sure he wasn't the same. He wasn't. My dad was always there, always home, never violent, never lost his temper, but all we did together was fish. I don't remember him ever asking me what I wanted to do with my life."

She enjoyed the tone of his voice and the visual he gave her. "Maybe he wanted to let you figure it out on your own."

"My mom was the same way. They were great parents, but she was every bit as ambitious and social as my father. They took me to all my sporting events and after school this and that. My mom was a master scheduler."

The Ferris wheel had begun to move continuously now, taking the sunset away until they came up on the other side again. All his talk about being a kid with his parents triggered a memory of her own, one of few she had.

"One night, my dad came home from work with news he got a big promotion. My mom was so happy for him. I can see her face and how his lit up in response. She made a nice dinner and we talked about taking a trip to Disney World. After dinner, my dad played with me and Kaelyn. I can still hear us all laughing." She turned her head away with the next memory—being taken away after being told her parents had died.

"It's tragic, what happened to you when you were young," Roman said.

She watched the sunset until it disappeared again.

"And I can see how that, and being raised the way you were, would affect your relationships as an adult."

She turned to him. Is this what he'd meant to talk to her about?

"You don't trust anyone, do you?"

"I tried to, once." She'd been betrayed. Who wouldn't be cautious after that?

"Do you ever think you can let your guard down again?" he asked.

That was the question he'd sequestered her to ask. She had to pause, to give herself time. She needed to be honest now. She sensed his need for honesty. This all stemmed from their night together. He was fishing to see if it was real.

She met his eyes so he could see them as she answered at last. "I don't know."

The Ferris wheel came to a stop and began letting people off.

She leaned forward for one last look at the sunset. "These rides are always too short, aren't they?"

She felt him continue to observe her.

"Thanks for being straight with me."

She didn't ask if he'd ever figure out he was meant to be a detective. He had to do that on his own.

A metallic ping sent her on alert. She looked up at the bar holding the cart as another ping sounded against the front of the cart.

"Get down!" Roman leaned over her, lying on top of her as more pings hit the cart.

Someone was shooting at them!

The cart moved. No one had noticed but them. The shots were silenced.

Roman lifted his head to search the ground. He ducked as another bullet hit metal. The cart moved higher. The cart in front of them now blocked the direction of gunfire.

Taking out his pistol, Roman crouched low and looked at the ground. He must not see anyone. The cart moved again, letting more people off. Kendra sat up, staying low like Roman. They were on the back side of the Ferris wheel now, two carts away from getting off the ride. They would be in the line of fire again as soon as the cart in front of them emptied.

Roman spotted a figure standing on the other side of the iron gate surrounding the ride. Wearing a hooded sweatshirt and sunglasses, the person's identity was concealed. Where had he stood when he fired at them on the Ferris wheel? He must have hidden somewhere, and then approached the iron fence around the ride.

The people in front of them got out of their cart. Roman aimed his gun as the hooded figure raised his. Roman fired first. As screams spread through the crowd, the hooded figure ran. People ducked and bolted out of line to escape the gunfire. The ride operator leaped behind his ticket pedestal.

Roman climbed out of the cart and ran toward the iron fence. Reaching it, he catapulted over and chased after the disappearing figure.

Shaky, Kendra climbed out of the cart as the ride operator stood and moved out from behind the pedestal.

"Are you all right, ma'am?" he asked.

She nodded and ran through the exit among the terrified onlookers who'd dared to remain. She ran past a few other rides, not hearing any more gunfire. At the entrance to the amusement park, she stopped and searched the parking area, a large gravel lot where people walked and cars drove at low speeds. Nothing in what she saw indicated anyone had run through here with guns. She turned back toward the park and walked in the direction she'd come from. At the second passageway between rides, she spotted Roman under a picnic canopy. The gunman scattered people from their tables and made grillers pause above smoking burgers and brats.

She ran forward, skirting the tent and alarmed onlookers. On the other side, she saw Roman jumping up onto a Dumpster, and then swinging over a stone fence. Grabbing a chair from a table, she put it down at the fence, climbed on and then jumped for the top of the fence. Pulling herself up, she swung one leg onto the ledge and then the other, hanging down on the other side and then letting go.

Searching around, she heard a creek running through a thick line of trees. A bike trail wound along the amusement park fence and curved to a bridge. She ran for that and crossed the creek. The trail led along a strip mall and into a neighborhood.

Hearing gunfire, she veered off the bike path and onto a grassy area between that and the pavement behind the strip mall. Reaching the end of the building, she peered around the corner and saw Roman.

Gun held up, he peeked out from his corner to the front of the building, and then fired. The other man fired back, and then the gunfire stopped. Had they run out of bullets?

Roman disappeared from the shelter of the building.

Kendra went to the place he'd vacated and saw him gaining on the gunman. He caught up to him at a parked car. The two collided, Roman tackling the man and crashing into the car. The man rammed his elbow back into Roman and managed to turn before Roman punched him. The man swung back and Roman held up his forearm to block the blow and at the same time went into a side flip and used his feet to kick the man's head. The man went down to his knees and then rolled out of the way of another kick. He jumped to his feet and ran.

Roman chased after him and Kendra left the building to follow. The man vanished in a tree-lined alley in the neighborhood. Kendra's sandals crunched over the one-lane dirt and gravel road, and she was careful to avoid tripping in the many potholes. A dog rushed the fence of a backyard, barking viciously and startling her. She veered to the other side of the alley.

The man Roman chased did an acrobatic side swing over a low chain-link fence. Roman used a dead tree stump to jump over. The man running was small and wiry, and could turn and pivot tightly. He avoided patio furniture and ran to the side of the house. Jumping another fence, he ran into the street, where a car was parked and running. The small man got into the passenger seat and the car sped away.

Kendra opened the gate in the low chain-link fence and walked cautiously to the front yard of the house. Down the street, Roman stopped running after the car.

It was hard to tell from this distance, but Kendra didn't think there was a license plate on the car. Tires squealed as the car spun into a turn and went out of sight.

Roman started walking toward her.

Stopping in the street, she watched his long, strong strides and the slight bend of his head. Wide shoulders swayed and muscular arms swung in a masculine swagger.

As he neared, she saw him look down her blue sundress and back up to her face as though admiring her the same way she admired him.

"He got away," he said as he came to a stop.

"I saw that," she said. "No plates, either."

"There was an In Transit sign in the rear window."

"Clever. Did you get a look at the driver?"

He shook his head.

"Awfully bold to be shooting at us in such a public place." His eyes squinted as he looked behind him.

She glanced around with him. "Kind of desperate."

"We're getting close." He took her hand. "Let's get out of here."

She trotted to keep up. "Where are we going?"

"Back to work."

As opposed to riding a Ferris wheel talking about love?

Chapter 15

Cal brought Chinese food to Roman's hotel room and the three of them sat at the small kitchen table to discuss the case. Roman had already briefed him on what they had uncovered so far. The Barfknechts. Perry Gordon and the trip to the Canary Islands.

Roman opened a file on his laptop and turned it so they could all see the screen. "Brock Barfknecht wasn't falsely convicted. All the evidence points to him."

"Even though we can understand why his father would insist his son is innocent," Kendra added. She still wore that sexy blue spaghetti-strap sundress. Roman was beginning to get uncomfortable in his tan pants and black short-sleeved button-up. Women didn't sweat like men did.

"Right, but Mr. Barfknecht gave us some pretty insightful information on the Gordons." Roman clicked

through the files and opened several financial transactions made by Hudson. "And then we found this."

Kendra leaned closer to see the screen and Cal remained seated. "We've uncovered two instances of
bribery, one involving the Gordons and the other the
mayor. But Perry Gordon was arrested prior to his involvement with the murder and let go. Hudson appears
to have been bribed in other cases, as well. He owns
a boat, but there is no record of him ever purchasing
one. Same goes for a BMW parked in his four-car garage." Roman pointed to a deposit. "This deposit isn't
in association with any legitimate income."

"It's twenty thousand," Kendra said.

Roman clicked to another bank statement. "Look at
the date for this ten-thousand-dollar deposit."

Cal leaned forward now. "It coincides with Perry
Gordon's prior arrest on drug charges. They were
dropped to misdemeanor." He opened his laptop and
turned it so all could see. "I reviewed all his cases. That
twenty-grand deposit was made before a trial involving a man who worked under the mayor. He headed
up education and community development. He was
arrested for a DUI and the charge was mysteriously
dropped. He never saw a judge."

"Hudson and the mayor have a history," Kendra
said. "A scandalous one."

"I bet if we presented all of this to the mayor he'd
talk," Roman said.

"Let's not play that hand until we're ready to make
arrests," Cal said.

Roman had to agree. They still needed Deidra's
body exhumed, and Kaelyn's car and the rock that was
thrown into Roman's rental were still being processed.

"Hudson has to know we've got enough on him to put him away. What do you think he intends to do? Will he run?"

"I'll get a car on him," Cal said.

"The more heat we put on him, the more dangerous he could be," Roman said.

Leaning back, Kendra thoughtfully put curled fingers to her mouth. After a time, she lowered her hand and looked at Roman. The green beauty of her eyes sparked a reaction in him.

"Kaelyn must have discovered Hudson's corruption," she said.

"Not necessarily," Cal interjected. "I think she discovered Deidra was poisoned and Deidra is the one who learned of his corruption."

Roman ticked through the timing and concurred. "Hudson's been taking bribes for years. Deidra must have caught him when he first started."

"When he was sloppy," Cal added.

Something still didn't add up. Kaelyn called Vikki with a warning. She wouldn't have done that if she hadn't known Deidra was killed.

"Kaelyn called Vikki to warn her about Glenn, not Hudson," Roman said.

The other two were silent for a few seconds, thinking through what he had said.

Then Kendra asked, "Do you think Glenn is protecting his father?"

By killing off anyone who discovers his corruption? "That's possible." Not only possible, it made the most sense. "The gunman at the carnival wasn't Glenn."

"He or Hudson could have hired someone," Cal responded. "They have the money."

"And the connections," Kendra added.

"Glenn and Hudson are working together?" Cal suggested.

Roman wasn't sure if they were working together. Glenn seemed to be trying to be honest, as though he didn't want to believe his father was corrupt or that he was capable of murder.

"Kaelyn may not have known about Hudson, but if she discovered Deidra was poisoned and he found out, he'd have reason to kill her."

"How would she have discovered Deidra was poisoned?"

"Hudson must have put the poison in something she ingests on a regular basis. His being there wouldn't be suspicious. He's Glenn's father. He could have easily done it."

"And somehow Kaelyn found out."

"She found the poison," Cal said. "Maybe she confronted Glenn about it and he told his father."

"Or he confronted his father," Roman interjected. "And if his father denied it, he would have believed him because he wouldn't want to believe his father killed his first wife." He stood from the chair, feeling stiff.

"It's not Glenn. It's Hudson?" Cal tapped his fingers on the table.

Kendra raked her fingers through her thick red hair, making Roman want to touch it, too.

He walked to the windows, having to pass the unmade sofa bed on the way.

"Kaelyn might have used another email address to communicate with me. Has anyone checked that account?"

"The account on her computer was checked," Cal

said. "We didn't know she had other accounts. We looked but didn't find any in her browsing history."

"She would have kept that wiped clean out of fear Alex would find out she was talking to me."

"I'll get some people on that," Roman said.

"Must be nice to have that freedom." Cal got up and went into the kitchenette.

"If you worked for DAI, you could have that same freedom."

Pausing in the act of pouring coffee, Cal looked at Roman. "I like my job."

"You just said you don't have any freedom. DAI is always looking for good detectives. Kadin is expanding the business, opening satellite offices all over the United States. You wouldn't have to move. Besides, Chesterville seems to have its dose of corruption and murder."

Kendra glanced at him sharply. "This is a nice town."

"My parents wouldn't live here if it wasn't. But even the most charming towns have crime and scandal."

Kendra yawned and eyed the unmade sofa bed. "Are we finished?"

"I'd like to go through some more files," Cal said, looking at Roman. "You should go through them with me. We could take this downstairs in the lobby."

"No. I'll just lie down and listen." Kendra stood and went to the sofa bed, stretching out onto her back with her head on the pillow he'd slept on last night. She closed her eyes and moments later, fell asleep.

"Well, she doesn't have any trouble sleeping at night," Cal said.

"Not tonight." He went to the table with Cal and

settled in for a few more hours of work. It took him a while. He kept looking over at her, sound asleep and looking so sweet all he wanted to do was lie next to her and put his arm over her.

"You find it hard to maintain relationships in your line of work?"

Roman looked at Cal, who had clearly been watching him. Roman couldn't stop himself from looking at Kendra most of the time. She was not only a beautiful redhead, she had somehow worked her way into his heart.

"I don't meet women that way." The women he encountered through work were either family of victims or other cops. He had never met anyone who had attracted him that way.

"I make it a policy not to. I was involved with one woman." He dipped his head to indicate Kendra. "She was a stunner like her." He turned back to Roman with rueful eyes. "It didn't last, and then we had to work together."

"I take it you ended it?"

"Only after I found out she was seeing another guy."

"Nice."

"She wasn't the worst. I knew we weren't right for each other. I could have thanked her for making the cutoff so decisive."

Roman grunted, reminded of his own past relationships that ended on a sour note. No woman had ever two-timed him, but they had told him they were interested in someone else.

"It happened. If it isn't right, it isn't right."

"It would take an exceptional woman for me to want to get serious."

Cal was younger than Roman and had more time for patience. Strange, how he hadn't thought this way before meeting Kendra. Now all of a sudden, he thought in terms of ticking clocks and running out of time. He didn't think it mattered all that much to him to have a companion. He liked being alone. He liked the freedom. Kendra was the same way, though. She definitely liked her freedom.

"Tolerant of the hours you work for sure," Roman said.

"Amen to that. Why are women so demanding about schedules? I don't have a lot of time to give, and if I made it available, a lot of dangerous reprobates would go free."

Roman scanned through a page he had open on the laptop screen. It was rare when he connected with someone who could relate to the difficulties of being a homicide detective. "The dead deserve justice. I spend more time with them than I do women." He chuckled a little and Cal joined him briefly.

"That's why I *see* them but don't *date* them, that's my policy." Cal looked at his own laptop screen.

Something must have happened to make him so rigid. Roman didn't ask. He hadn't really ever had his heart broken, but he could imagine how something like that would alter a man's view on love. A woman's, as well. Take Kendra as an example.

"My only policy is it has to be real," he said. "That's the only way you know if it's love."

Cal looked up, and then back at the computer screen, mulling that over awhile and then asked, "What about her?"

"Kendra?" What about her? "I guess you could say I'm seeing her."

"Is it love?" Although Cal seemed to be reading whatever he had up on his screen, he'd asked in a curious way.

"I can't tell yet." Kendra clouded his senses with desire most of the time.

"She seems different than some women I've known. Not clingy."

"No." Roman grunted his derision. "She's anything but clingy. Independent to a fault, I'd say."

"I've had women say that to me."

Roman spent time with his women. He did run into issues when he worked nights, though, and he worked a lot of nights. He doubted Cal's baggage stemmed from clingy women. He'd bet whoever had broken his heart had been independent like Kendra.

"Do you think Kendra could turn into something good?" Cal asked.

"We're pretty different. She's creative and I don't have a creative molecule in my body." Which he'd always found strange, given that his dad was a popular writer. He must have taken after his mother. "She also holds back a lot."

"You mean her feelings? You *want* a woman to express her feelings?" Cal's eyebrows rose as he glanced up from the computer.

"Just enough to let me know she's on the same level."

"You're on a level with Kendra?"

He gave up trying to concentrate on the page glowing on his computer screen. "At first, I thought she was too sheltered, but then I got to know her. She isn't where she is in life because she needs to be sheltered.

She's where she is because she's a survivor. Her adolescence makes her guarded."

"And if she let go, what then?"

"I'm afraid to speculate." He looked over at Cal, his newest friend, a genuine one.

"Because then you'd fall hard for her, huh?"

Roman didn't respond, but he didn't have to. Cal understood, except for one thing. He avoided women who'd make him fall hard for them. Roman waited patiently for a woman like that. He just didn't believe they existed. Kendra could change all that. What if she was the one he'd been waiting for that he didn't think would ever show up?

Kendra woke warm and snuggled under blankets— and something else.

She opened her eyes and grew aware of Roman lying next to her on his side, with his arm draped over her waist. She'd fallen asleep on top of the covers and he must have covered her. She was still fully clothed. Roman had slept in his jeans. His consideration warmed her even more. He made no assumption based on their previous encounter in her office.

She looked up at his face so close to hers, his eyes closed, breath falling even on her face. No bad morning breath for him. She studied him at her leisure, every slope and pore.

As though sensing her attentiveness, his eyes began to open. Focusing on her, he rose up onto his elbow and pressed a sleepy kiss to her mouth.

"You fell asleep on my bed." His gruff and groggy tone tickled her senses.

"Sorry." She sounded gruff herself.

"I'm not."

Lying like this with him, even clothed, became too intimate. Smiling, she eased away and climbed off the bed.

Roman's cell phone rang or maybe he would have tried to stop her.

Cal was in the lobby and would meet them for breakfast. He had news on Kaelyn's car and the rock.

Kendra always took care in getting herself ready for the day. She applied minimal makeup, just enough to accentuate her eyes and lips. She dried her hair with a side part so her long bangs would drape and the wavy red strands were smooth and shiny. She'd chosen a blue-and-white-striped trapeze dress. The uneven horizontal lines popped out to the eye. She didn't own many jeans. She wore mostly dresses and slacks. Maybe that was the artist in her, the creative part. Lately, however, getting ready for her day held a little more zing. Once again, she felt as though she were dressing for Roman. Or maybe she was more aware of how she looked with him around.

Why was that so important? She'd never felt this way with a man. She had never felt the need to look her best.

Leaving the bathroom, she saw him sitting on the end of the bed in his underwear, towel beside him. He'd waited for her to finish before taking his own shower.

He looked up at her and then his gaze moved down her body, slow and not missing a single detail. He stared where the dress ended at her knees before lifting his eyes. He made her tingle when he looked at her like that.

"Sorry I took so long," she said.

"It was worth the wait." He stood and walked toward her.

When he neared, she stepped out of his way, but he stopped her with his hands on her arms.

"You're beautiful."

Her face began to flush and not from embarrassment. He heated her up.

As he noticed, he grinned and lowered his head, putting his face right above hers. "Did you do that for me?"

Had any of her previous boyfriends told her she was beautiful? Hot, maybe. They'd been sexual, selfish creatures, not the warm, loving one standing before her now. His honorable traits, along with a keenly intelligent mind, made him stronger than any man she'd ever met. She didn't have to compare him physically. Her previous boyfriends had all been fit, but none had the formidable presence Roman carried.

She didn't answer, just closed the distance between their mouths and kissed him. As his eyes flared in answer, she moved back.

"I think I'll go do some crossword puzzles while I wait for you."

His hand slid off her arm as she stepped farther away. She smiled coyly at him before she turned and went into the living room where she'd left her Kindle.

Listening to him run the shower, she tried not to imagine his trim, muscular body naked in there. She found a puzzle and soon she distracted herself until he finished in the shower.

In light, soft blue jeans that fit his crotch not too loose and not too tight, she soaked in the sight of him in a short-sleeved textured gray shirt. His gray eyes glowed with warmth that hadn't cooled with his shower.

He put his hand on her lower back and guided her toward the door as though forcing himself to do so, lest they wind up in bed. Her heart beat deeply as she walked with him down the hall to the elevator. His fresh scent fed her arousal. In the elevator, she stood on one side and he the other, meeting her gaze.

When the elevator doors opened, she didn't move, tempted to press their floor and ride back up to the room. A couple appeared at the entrance and waited for them to exit.

Thankful the choice had been taken from her, she left the elevator ahead of Roman and led him to the hotel restaurant. Cal had already gotten a booth. He sipped some coffee as he saw them.

Roman let her in first and sat beside her. She grew uncomfortable as he sat close enough for her to feel the side of his thigh against hers. All she wanted to do was go upstairs.

She glanced at him and saw he'd refocused on the business at hand.

"What have you got?" he asked Cal.

"Kaelyn didn't have another email account, for one," he said.

"I didn't think that was going to lead anywhere."

"The forensics confirm Kaelyn's body was in the trunk of her car, though," he said. "Her body was likely placed on something like a sheet or a rug. There were traces of hair and bloodstains that were cleaned. The killer probably used what he found at Kaelyn's house to try and cover up the evidence. The rock didn't produce much, other than it may have come from a landscaping bed in someone's yard. The paper fastened to the rock is typical of that from a common notebook. No prints. No DNA. I sent you an email with the report."

"The rock is out," Roman said. "But great news on the car."

Kaelyn had driven to Chesterville and at some point intercepted her killer, who put her body in the trunk of her car and drove her back to her house. How had the killer gotten back to Chesterville?

"We should go look at landscaping in Glenn's yard," Kendra said. "Hudson's, too."

"Let's get some warrants."

Kendra saw Roman's intent expression. He became absorbed in his cases. She doubted the gore of crime scenes bothered him the way it would others not close to the investigation. He didn't see gore. He saw evidence. He also saw a person whose life had been cut short, robbed from him or her.

He glanced at her and caught her admiration.

Cal's cell phone rang and spared them from an awkward moment in front of Cal.

"Yeah," Cal said into his phone.

She and Roman watched him listen to the caller.

Then Cal's gaze shot to Roman's. "We'll be right there." He disconnected. "Deidra's body has been stolen. A couple of teenage witnesses reported seeing a white, windowless van driving away from the site late last night."

The teenagers couldn't provide a description of the driver of the van but said they thought they saw two people and the driver was a man in a hooded sweatshirt. Cal had people checking for white vans registered in this and surrounding counties. They also would use the media asking for anyone with information on a white van seen late last night.

"What now?" Kendra asked.

"We wait." Roman caught sight of a parked car one lane over from the dug-up grave site. Recognizing Glenn Franklin, he started to walk over. To his surprise, Glenn didn't try to race off.

Roman stopped at his driver's side window and Kendra stopped beside him.

Glenn slid down his window. "So, you really did exhume her body."

Roman cocked his head. "We didn't exhume it. In fact, we were wondering if you knew what happened to her body."

"Me?" Glenn's head flinched backward a little. "What do you mean?"

"Deidra's body was dug up last night and taken."

"Dug…" Glenn looked toward the grave site and then back up at Roman. "I didn't dig up her body."

"Any idea of who else would have?"

"Why would anyone dig up my first wife's body?" He shook his head. "I don't believe this."

"Well, you better," Kendra said. "Someone stole her body and we're confident the reason why is she was murdered. Someone doesn't want us finding out how she really died."

Glenn ran his hand down his face. "This is out of control."

"What is out of control?" Roman asked. Glenn seemed honestly agitated, but not because he was shocked that someone had stolen Deidra's body. He had to know something.

He seemed to gather himself, and then said, "Kaelyn being murdered and now this."

"You could help us if you tell us everything you know," Roman said.

Glenn met his eyes. "I can't help you if I don't know any more than you do."

"Now, see, that's where you lose me, Glenn. I think you *can* help us."

Glenn jerked his car in gear. "I don't have to take this from you. I've done nothing wrong. You need to find the killer. If you want to talk to me again, you'll have to go through my attorney."

"What are you afraid of?" Kendra asked.

"Wouldn't you be afraid?" he said. "If your first spouse was killed and then your lover?"

"Depends on how you're involved," Roman said.

Glenn drove off down the lane with an angry scowl.

"He's afraid of being caught," Kendra said.

"Or afraid of what we'll find out."

Cal approached from the grassy area. His steps were long and hurried.

When he reached them, he said, "We got a tip on the location of the van."

Excitement surged up in Roman. He often felt this way when something was about to break in a case. He felt it, sensed its emergence. It was exhilarating.

Cal handed him a small piece of paper and Roman saw an address written there. He took the paper.

"Someone said they saw a white, windowless van drive up to the property next to theirs," Cal said. "It's in the mountains. And—you won't believe this—that address is a cabin owned by Melody and Hudson Franklin. Police are on the way there now."

There it was, the break. If they found the van and caught whoever had taken it, they'd have their killer.

"You head there," Cal said. "I have to stay here a little longer."

Maybe he'd find some evidence. There were tire tracks that the forensics team were making molds of, but Roman hoped they'd find some fibers or hairs or anything that would link the grave robbery to the perpetrators.

"I'll call you when we get there." Roman took Kendra's hand. "Let's go."

He held her hand all the way to his rental, the warmth they generated mixing with his excitement. What would he find when they arrived at the cabin?

After driving to the Franklin cabin, Roman saw all the law enforcement vehicles up by the cabin and stopped where two officers guarded the driveway. He showed his identification.

"Cal said you'd be coming. Go on up." The officers stepped away from the car and let them pass.

Roman got out and walked with Kendra to the front door. A detective stood just inside the doorway.

"Anything yet?" Roman asked.

"Nothing. Shed's clean, too."

No sign of the body. Roman inwardly cursed. Then he looked outside.

"We did find the van, though."

Roman turned back to the man. Why hadn't he said that right away? His excitement revved into overdrive.

"It was abandoned up the highway. Stolen. We're taking it in for processing."

"Good." Seeing all the officers inside the cabin, he decided there were enough people searching in here. "We'll have a look around outside. How much property is there?"

"About twenty acres. Goes from the road to the fence of the next property."

"Thanks."

Kendra stepped down the porch ahead of him and walked toward the back of the cabin. She must have seen the narrow dirt road at the same time he did. None of the officers had ventured there yet. They were searching the surrounding trees and the shed.

At midday, it was getting warm. Birds chirped and insects buzzed. Clouds were building in the west.

"Nice day for a walk," he said.

"On the way to look for a dead body."

He saw her smile and grinned.

"I'd much rather be picnicking" she said.

"Not me." He'd rather be right here with her.

She angled her head when she glanced at him. "You'd rather be solving murder cases?"

"That, too."

Seeing she'd caught on, her smile returned. "I thought you weren't happy with what you did for a living."

He eyed her legs in that dress. She had on low-heeled sandals and her balance was remarkable over the uneven surface of the road. "I'm happy with it."

"Then why do you feel like you followed your dad's footsteps?"

He walked without answering for a while. He didn't think he had followed his dad's footsteps. His dad may have led him into homicide investigations, but he'd been interested. His parents had always told him he could do whatever he wanted in life. They had never pressured him into going to college. They'd believed a young man should find his own way, with a little encouragement from his parents.

"I love what I do." He surprised himself when he said it. He hadn't thought he felt that passionate about what he did, but now he really thought about it. He got excited when leads came through, as Kaelyn's case had shown him. And nothing could describe the gratification he felt when he caught killers. Cases like Kaelyn's were perfect examples. If Kendra hadn't insisted he look into her death, no one would have ever solved her murder. She would have gone into eternity with everyone thinking she'd committed suicide. That he could—and would—solve her case gave him the deepest satisfaction.

"I can see you do."

Seeing her smile again—this time more from triumph for being right about him—he realized how much showed on his face.

"Why are you at such odds with your parents then?"

"I'm not." But even as he said those words, something in him denied the truth in them. "I don't know. I suppose I always felt I'd never accomplish more than they have. But I should have looked at what I enjoy doing, and that's solving murders, putting killers in prison, keeping people safe."

"I think what you do is just as sensational as what they do."

"That's not what you said before."

"I meant from a popularity standpoint. You're a renowned detective. People seek out your services. It's sensational in its own way."

"Thanks…I think."

"You should be proud of what you do. Your parents are proud of you. They love you. I saw that when I met them."

She was right. He'd avoided them for no good reason. "They still live a charmed life."

"Just because they don't have a survival kit in the event of an apocalypse doesn't make them ignorant of the world's threats."

"I don't have a survival kit." He chuckled. "I'm not that extreme, am I?"

"You were. Frankly I'm shocked you don't have a survival kit."

"I could survive with my *bare hands*." He held out his palms for emphasis.

She laughed. "I'm so relieved."

"That I could survive with my bare hands?"

"No, that you aren't as extreme as I thought. I might have a chance with you after all."

Although she joked, he heard purpose in her tone.

"Do you want a chance with me?" he asked.

Her smile vanished and she looked straight ahead as she walked beside him.

"Apparently not," he said. "Where I use reality as a crutch, you don't trust anyone."

"I trust people." Her brow lowered with mild insult.

"Who?" He'd like for her to name one person.

"My sister."

"She doesn't count anymore. And I'm talking about men."

"I trusted blindly when I was younger. I won't do that again."

"That's a good policy to have but not to the point where it stops you from testing out love." Did he sound soft? He didn't think he'd ever talked with a woman like this before, as though he were contemplating the possibility of love with her.

"You want me to test that out with you?"

"I don't think you're capable. You shut yourself off too much."

She walked without responding for a while. Then said, "I wouldn't if it was right."

"Would you know if it was?"

When she said no more, he sensed her blocking the emotion that must be trying to break through her wall. Did she worry what she felt was too right? Too in sync? Would she try to stop herself from falling in love? The problem this posed for him was he had the same concern, that he felt this thing between them was too right and maybe he wasn't ready for that.

Roman searched the property. "There's nothing here. The grave robbers must have switched vehicles where they left the van."

She turned and headed back to the cabin, still not talking.

Roman told himself it was better this way. He'd stand firm to his conviction that a serious relationship wasn't worth a penny if it wasn't real, and Kendra had just shown him she either wasn't ready or was incapable of entering into anything like that. Ironic that he should find a woman he'd like to get to know more intimately and she was everything he thought he'd never want. Ambitious, successful. Not sheltered. He supposed that's what made her different.

Figured. Oh well. He had a case to solve, and then he'd go back to Wyoming.

Chapter 16

Glenn was understandably quite unhappy to see them the following day. More casual than usual in jeans and a polo shirt, his dark blond hair was still neatly combed and blue eyes just as chilly as always. Kendra entered his big and fancy house behind Roman and several officers, including Cal, who held the search warrant.

"You can't come in here!" Glenn roared at Cal.

Cal handed him the search warrant.

Glenn took it as his wife appeared at the top of an open, curving staircase, looking like she'd just woken up. In a flowing white nightgown and robe, she folded her arms in front of her. Her shoulder-length blond hair stuck out in places and her trophy-wife blue eyes looked tired.

"What's going on?" she asked sleepily.

Kendra checked her phone for the time. It was well past eleven. Why was Vikki still in bed?

"What do you think you're going to find here?" Glenn shouted.

Cal just gave the go-ahead to the team with a twirl of his forefinger.

Kendra followed Roman into the living room, where officers had begun searching through shelves and drawers. Other agents went into the kitchen and library and den. She and Roman headed for the stairs.

"Are you feeling all right?" Kendra asked Vikki when they reached the top.

"I'm just a little under the weather. Flu bug." She rubbed her stomach.

Kendra glanced at Roman, dark, wavy short hair slightly windblown and light gray eyes meeting hers with mutual curiosity. He wore a black short-sleeved golf shirt with light blue jeans just as he had the day she'd met him, the shirt covered by his leather jacket.

The officers already had orders to take samples of all the food and anything granular or liquid that could be mixed in drinks or food.

"How long have you been feeling bad?" Roman asked.

"Just a couple of days. I'm feeling better today."

That might be good. Maybe she wasn't being poisoned.

They found nothing of significance in any of the bedrooms or bathrooms. The master bedroom was messy, indicating this was where Vikki had spent the last two days and also that she still slept with her husband. Good relationship? No reason to off her?

Kendra went back downstairs. Officers carried Glenn's computer out to a waiting van despite his belligerent protests. He wouldn't be able to work from home.

She walked out onto the back patio. The yard was

full of blooming flowers and artfully planned beds. A few decorative rocks had been placed here and there.

"Melody did all that."

Kendra turned and saw Vikki with a glass of iced tea in her hand, hugging her midsection with one arm and drinking with the other.

"Melody?"

"Glenn's mom. She loves to flower garden. You should see her house."

"We probably will," Kendra said, not meaning to sound mocking.

"She doesn't work, but she stays busy with volunteer work and her hobbies. When it's cold, she does jewelry and candles. She'd probably love your store if she could lower herself enough to go there."

"Lower herself?" Kendra thought she got along well with Melody. It seemed Melody got along well with both of Glenn's wives.

"She only goes to high-end places."

Kendra considered her shop high-end, but she supposed she didn't always carry the loftiest name brands. She wanted everyone to be able to afford her items. "She looks like she spends a lot of time in a salon. And boutique shops." Kendra didn't say she considered her shop boutique, also.

"It used to intimidate me when I first met her."

"Really? Melody intimidated you?"

"She has a way of making you feel like you don't measure up. But for some reason, she liked me and we became friends."

Deidra and Melody were close, too. "So, even though she's materialistic, she's a nice person?"

"She'd be the first to admit she's materialistic. What

I like about her is she's so family-oriented. She *adores* Glenn. And when Deidra died, she was here all the time taking care of him."

"He was upset over her death?"

"Yes. He still talks about her sometimes. He was devastated when he lost her. Sometimes I think he still loves her and can never love another woman more."

Wow, that was news. Kendra glanced back into the house for Roman. He stood talking to Cal.

"His mother would do anything for him, but the one thing she couldn't do was bring his wife back to life."

That didn't sound like the reaction of a man who'd murdered his wife. Had he duped Vikki into believing that?

"I told Glenn that Kaelyn called me before she died."

Kendra went utterly still.

"He was stunned at first…more like confused. He asked why and I told her she wanted to warn me about him. He sort of laughed and said, *Me?*"

"Like he found that ridiculous?"

"Yeah. But I told him Kaelyn must have had something to warn me about and asked him if he knew what that might be."

Kendra waited with anxious excitement.

"He said no, and he had no idea why Kaelyn felt she had to warn me about him. He said she must have been jealous or somehow sensed or found out that he was going to break it off with her and devote himself to his marriage. He said that's what he wanted with Deidra, and the reason he went to Kaelyn was because he felt lost and needed to find himself. Being shown the wrongness of having an affair made him realize marriage was important to him and he loved me."

And she'd fallen for that sappy story? Maybe Kendra was too distrusting, but if a man ever told her he slept with another woman to *find himself* she'd laugh, and then tell him to go get lost again.

"So, you really think you have nothing to fear from Glenn?"

"Not anymore. We've been married long enough for us to know each other very well. I can tell when he's telling me the truth and when he's being sincere. He didn't kill Deidra. He had nothing to do with Kaelyn's death. And he certainly wouldn't hurt me." She paused and seemed to mull something over, fret over it. "He did say after you presented him with Kaelyn's murder he thought maybe his dad had something to do with it, and if so maybe Deidra, too. You know, because of the whole scandal with the mayor. I asked Melody about that at our last lunch and she was standoffish. She doesn't like talking about it."

"Hudson has done more than grease the law for the mayor's son," Kendra said. "He takes bribes on a regular basis."

"That's what Glenn thinks, too. But he spoke with his father and said he believed him when he denied he could murder anyone. I'm not so sure. Glenn was angry when I said I thought if anyone would want to kill, it would be his father. He's very protective of his dad."

Roman appeared in the patio doorway holding a receipt he showed to Vikki. "Do you recognize this?"

Vikki took the receipt. "Oh, that's the general store near our beach house."

"You have a beach house?"

"We share it with Glenn's parents. The cabin is the same. It's shared. I'll give you the address if you need it."

"We'd like to search that, as well, so if you could let us in, that would be helpful."

"Sure. I'll give you a key. If Glenn isn't happy about that, then he can go with you."

He sure could. Vikki was being awfully accommodating while her husband resisted at every turn. Did he have something to feel guilty about?

Glenn wasn't happy to learn they intended to search the beach house. He'd snapped at Vikki for giving them a key. Cal had to get another search warrant, but that only took an hour. Then Roman had a DAI plane fly him and Kendra to North Carolina. Now approaching nighttime, a team of police swarmed the beach house property.

It didn't take long before one of the officers found a body in the freezer. Someone had dug a fresh fire pit in the backyard, as well. Even though Kendra was no detective, she didn't need it spelled out for her that someone had planned to burn Deidra's body as soon as they felt safe.

"Someone had weekend plans," Roman said.

Luckily, they'd arrived before someone could destroy crucial evidence. They stood on the back patio to give everyone plenty of room to search the house. Local authorities had joined them and helped get the warrant.

Cal appeared in the dining area and came through the open sliding door. "We're wrapped up here. They'll make arrangements with local authorities to have the body transported back to Chesterville. Once I have the coroner's report, I'll give you a call."

"Thanks." Roman glanced around, and then turned

to Kendra. "It's getting late. Do you want to fly back tonight or stay somewhere here?"

She listened to waves wash ashore, lights from the house fading at the sandy edge of the beach. No point in making the pilot lose sleep.

"Might as well find a place here."

"There's an inn not far from here," one of the local policemen said as he approached from the side of the yard. A few officers searched outside, as well, and took samples from the fire pit.

"It's on the beach," the officer added. "White Pelican Inn."

"I could use a good night's sleep," Kendra said, thinking, *and a long walk on the beach.*

The innkeeper yawned as she waved good-night. The tall, thin woman ran the place by herself, her husband having passed a few years ago. She'd been generous to take them in after ten. Now with a passcode to get back inside, Kendra walked past the stairs where the innkeeper had instructed them to go, then first door on the right.

"Kendra?"

Roman had stopped at the stairs.

She turned. "I'm going for a walk on the beach."

"Now?" He sounded incredulous.

"Yes. I've never been to the beach before."

He walked to her. "Never?"

"No. I've taken trips to Europe and Canada, but never anywhere there was a beach. A real beach, with white sand and no metropolitan areas."

"I'll go with you." His tone had softened and she wasn't sure of his motive.

"In case we were followed," he added.

Or was that a cover? They'd been so busy chasing Deidra's body that they'd barely had a moment alone. Kendra had told herself that was for the best, but now she felt a need to just be with him.

Ignoring the caution pricking her, she started for the door again. "Okay."

Outside, the smell of salt water hit her and sparked excitement. This wasn't a vacation but for now, she could pretend.

Away from the glow of house lights, moonlight reflected on choppy waves in the distance. Her feet sank into the sand. She stopped and removed one sandal then the other, dangling them from her fingers.

Beside her, Roman walked in his loafers until sand must have gotten inside. She smiled as he stopped and did the same as her.

Then they walked together, looking out at the water, listening to the ebb and flow of the tide. No one else was on the beach even though the shore was lined with houses. If she lived here, she'd never get tired of the beach.

"If you like the ocean so much, why not move closer?" Roman asked.

He'd noticed that much about her?

"I've never been to the beach. I didn't know I loved it so much." Photos. Books about them, yes, but to live on the beach? She imagined opening a Christmas shop in a small community like this one. The population was only about fifteen hundred, but it was surrounded by other cities and towns.

"Chesterville isn't that far from here."

True. She could drive here whenever she wanted.

With Kaelyn dying, she hadn't even thought about doing anything like that. "It's been ages since I went on a vacation."

"Not since you lost Kaelyn?"

She shook her head.

"We might have to change that when we catch her killer."

She studied his profile and saw a relaxed brow and slight upward curve to his mouth. What did he mean? Did he even know what he'd just said? He talked as though they'd still be together after the investigation closed.

She did like how he sounded so certain, though. She doubted Roman had any uncertainties once he made up his mind. Well, save for one. He was getting over that, though. At least, she sensed he was. Even so, he needed to feel he was in a real relationship, and Kendra didn't think she could give him that, not for a long, long time. For her to trust a man, to really trust him and open her heart to him, she needed time, probably more than he could give. It might be years before she could truly let down her guard with a man, to trust that he was all she thought he was with no surprises lurking in the future.

Just then, he stopped her with his hand on her arm, pointing up to the sky. She looked in time to see a shooting star fade into space.

"Make a wish," he said.

"You, Mr. Must Have It Real, believe in that sort of thing?"

"You ruined your chance for a wish," he said, facing her and pulling her to face him. "But that's okay. I made a wish for both of us."

What was he doing? Had he lost his mind? What happened to thinking she lived in a cushy bubble of nonreality?

"You aren't supposed to tell, are you?" She tried to make light of this moment but the onset of passion kept building.

"No." He slid his hand to her lower back and released her hand to hold her closer.

The warm, romantic feelings he stirred kept her from withdrawing. That and wonder over what he'd wished for. Roman didn't strike her as the sentimental type. Something about them as a couple had compelled him, something she didn't think he would have done had he had time to think it over.

Lulled, she tipped her head back and met his kiss. Endless and soft, the joining went on for several seconds, until she slid her hands up his chest and pressed for more. He answered with more heat, stoking the mystical fire they generated. With the ocean waves rolling and gliding back of the sandy shore, with the moonlight and stars and distant, faint lights from widely spaced houses, she gave over to pure sensation.

At last, he parted from her and she looked up into eyes that mirrored what she felt, a deep, driving need.

Without saying anything, he took her hand and walked with her back up the beach toward the inn.

Kendra quietly opened the patio door and entered, Roman closing it and locking them in. With the kiss still going through her mind and body, she didn't question the rightness of climbing the stairs to their room. Besides, this didn't have to last. She didn't have to commit to anything. They didn't know each other that well yet.

In the room, she went to the window. The inn was far enough back and on a high enough hill that she could see the beach from here. She watched the waves crest white and smooth and then climb up onto the beach. The tall grass in the foreground danced in a shadowy sway. The view helped rekindle what had begun on the beach.

Hearing no sound behind her, she turned. Roman stood near the bed, watching and waiting. He wouldn't make a move until she gave him a sign.

She'd been bold with boyfriends before, but was never this into it. Slowly, she lifted the hem of her sundress over her head and walked toward him. The dress required no bra, so after she kicked off her sandals, all she wore was her underwear.

That should be enough of a sign for him.

With eyes burning hotter, Roman lifted his shirt off, muscles rippling, and kicked off his own shoes. By the time she reached him, he had unfastened his pants.

"Are you sure about this?"

"If I wasn't I wouldn't be doing it."

"Yeah, but…" He pushed down his pants and stepped out of them.

She touched his stomach and chest. "We're both adults. We don't have to expect anything from each other just because we enjoy each other."

His mouth turned up in a one-sided grin. "You might want more than you think after this."

She chose not to listen to him anymore. But she did want to know one thing. "Do you want more than this?" She curved her arm around his shoulder and pressed her bare breasts to him.

He sank his hands into her hair and pulled her head

back more. "It might not be enough. I might need to do this a few more times."

That heated her up even more. He hadn't said he required a commitment, which relaxed her guard. She let go all the way, taking his mouth for a soul-deep kiss and forgetting all else but the magic they created.

Chapter 17

Raelyn hadn't gone through her mother's things since she went to the house to pick out the things she wanted to take with her. Late at night, she couldn't sleep for thinking about her. She couldn't explain why, but she had to be among her mother's things right now. Be with her in any way she could.

Her dad had been a total ass the whole time she'd packed her mother's personal belongings, trying to direct her and tell her what she could and couldn't take. Raelyn had taken everything. All her mother's clothes, all her jewelry and her computer. She still couldn't bear to try on any of her clothes or jewelry. The clothes smelled like her and the jewelry would just make her sad. But ever since Kendra had weaved her way into her life, she'd been worried someday she'd forget what her mother looked like. She could forget memories that were special when they'd actually been made. Traits. Her mother's personality.

When it was just the two of them and her mom felt safe, she was funny and bright and cheery. She was sarcastic but not in a mean way. Raelyn would laugh and see how her mother enjoyed that, making her laugh. That was the girl her aunt once knew, the twin she'd grown up with until they'd been separated. Her mother wasn't the cowering, terrified woman Dad turned her into. The silent woman. The one who had to agree with every stupid thing her dad ever said, especially when he was drinking. How she must have felt suffocated, being forced to be an idiot's version of what a wife should be—always in his putrid shadow.

Raelyn hated her father. Always would. About the only memory she had of him was how easy it was to set him off. Even the most insignificant things—dinner, a movie or just correcting him when he was clearly wrong about some trivial fact—would turn him into a monster. And once he was in his rage, nothing could be said or done to stop him. He'd have his rant and his physical violence and everyone would have to just live through it—or pray to.

Hated him. Hated him with every molecule in her body and mind.

She'd let him know, too. She'd sent him a letter when she found out he'd been sent to prison. She told him he was where he belonged and she was a happier person knowing he'd never be able to see her again. And if he ever was released from prison, then she'd be armed. And if he ever dared come near her again, she'd kill him on sight.

Now, she hoped she'd never have to do that, but

damn if she wouldn't, especially now that her mother's death had not been suicide. Her father had stolen years of happiness from her mother.

No way would she let her father ruin this moment. No more thoughts of him. Only her mother. She missed her mother so much.

Raelyn sat down with the laptop, her mother's laptop, and opened her pictures folder. Her mother had loved to take pictures, mostly of Raelyn, but also of nature. Their low-income backyard had turned into artful masterpieces when her mother would isolate a flower or part of a fence. A picture of the entire yard would reveal the truth, but her mother had an eye for all things beautiful. Aunt Kendra was wrong if she thought she was the only artistic one.

Raelyn went through photo after photo, seeing herself grow up in the eyes of her mother, one picture at a time until she reached the last one taken. It had been her the summer before her senior year in high school. She'd died shortly thereafter. Raelyn ran her finger down the laptop screen when she came to a photo of the two of them. Her mother had taken a selfie of them.

When she saw more pictures were in this file, she clicked to view them. She hadn't known these were here.

"That's odd." Raelyn angled her head, trying to figure out why her mother would take a picture of a rock. It looked like it was in a flower bed, and nothing this fancy was at their house.

She clicked to see the next. This time the rock had been rolled away to expose the wormy ground. The next photo was a hole and the top of a can could be seen.

"Where is this?" And *what* is this?

The next photo was of the back of a nice, big house,

one she didn't recognize. The last photo was of the front of the same house, and something eerie and cryptic was captioned beneath.

It's still there.

Chapter 18

Roman woke to a ringing phone. His cell phone. He blinked open his eyes. Lying flat on his back with one arm folded above his head, he grew aware of someone next to him—the warm, even breaths, the tickle of hair. The night came rushing back. Kendra lay on her stomach with one leg bent, a slender thigh sticking out from tangled covers. He enjoyed the view until his phone rang for the fourth time.

Reluctantly, he turned from the sight and memory, and reached for his phone.

"Cooper."

Kendra stirred, a soft moan distracting him and making him wish the morning hadn't been interrupted.

"Roman. Cal. You and Kendra need to get to the Chesterville Hospital as soon as possible. Vikki was taken here late last night. I'm making sure the doctors check her for poison."

He sat up on the bed. Beside him, Kendra lifted her tousled, red-haired head and sleepily looked up at him, momentarily arresting his senses.

"Did you hear me?" Cal asked.

Roman swung his feet over the side of the bed. "Yeah. Just woke up, that's all."

"It's noon."

He stood from the bed, careful not to look at the sexy thing in the bed. "We'll fly back as soon as we get ready."

"Why did you sleep so late? Were you up with that long-legged beauty all night?"

Not just bold and direct, Cal was incredibly intuitive. "Cal, I'm sure you and I are going to be friends for a long time, but we aren't that close yet."

Just before Roman disconnected, he heard Cal's deep chuckle and, "Lucky man."

Kendra got off the bed and captured his senses again as she walked naked to the bathroom.

Hearing the shower run, he went in. She'd left the door open. Was that an invitation or was it more a surrender to the inevitable? They'd already made love. Why be modest now?

He climbed into the shower behind her. With her back to him as she rinsed herself, he took the opportunity to soak in the sight of her. Then she turned around, tipping her head back to slick back her hair. She presented an erotic vision.

Opening her eyes, she moved out of the spray. "Your turn." Although she smiled, Roman picked up on her stiffness right away.

He went under the spray and rinsed off, eyeing her when he didn't have to close his eyes to water. She

shampooed her hair with occasional glances at him.
She didn't look at him with passion. She seemed to
have withdrawn. Back to not trusting. She must be
going over last night and feeling too vulnerable. This
morning she protected herself and Roman would get
only what she felt comfortable showing him.

He'd been thrilled to see her let go the way she had
last night. He'd thought maybe he'd finally found that
special woman. But now…

"Come on. I want to talk to Vikki before she decides
not to say anything," Roman snapped as he walked
briskly toward the hospital entrance. She'd barely spoken to him and the shower had felt invasive.

"I'm coming. Slow down. A few seconds won't matter." She trotted to keep up with him.

Roman didn't mean to be surly but finding out Kendra had put her wall back up disappointed too much.
She let go during sex but at no other time. She reminded him of the CEO he'd dated. Except Kendra
was completely different and he hadn't felt this irritated
with the prospect of not being with the CEO.

All the way back to Chesterville, he'd avoided talking to her at all. That hadn't been difficult since she
hadn't said much, either. Thankfully, it was a short
flight.

He let her push through the door first, glancing
around to make sure they weren't followed. The sun
was low in the sky and shadows were getting long.

Maybe he felt this way because he wanted Kendra
to be the woman he craved and couldn't shake the instinct that she wouldn't reciprocate. Her barriers were
too cemented into place for her to allow him in. He

didn't like being wrong about people and he strongly suspected he'd been wrong about Kendra and his first impression had been accurate. He should never forget how good he was at reading people. That was partly what made him such a good detective. He picked up on undercurrents in people. Kendra's may as well flash in bright red neon letters: Stay back.

She must be one of those people—no, she *was* one of those people—who avoided attachments.

In the elevator, he sensed her watching him. She turned her head slightly every once in a while, just enough to get a glimpse of him. Her eyes would go all over his black shirt tucked in tan slacks, and then steal a look at his face. If she wondered why he was in such a testy mood, she didn't ask to find out why, which told him she already knew and probably didn't want it out in the open, freely communicated. That only served to irritate him more, and for the umpteenth time, he wished he could light up a cigarette. It didn't help that she wore another figure-flattering sundress, this one blue and white with a slit that allowed her knees to peek out when she moved. She'd also left her hair down and he didn't like how much he enjoyed its smooth waving as she walked.

On the floor where Vikki was staying, he walked with long strides down the hall. Cal had left already and the local cops had probably already spoken with her.

He entered the hospital room and saw Vikki watching television.

She saw them and Roman instantly recognized her fear.

"Hello, Vikki, how are you feeling?"

"Not well, but I'm improving. I already answered questions. I don't know anything."

That told him she did know something. Why else would someone try to kill her? Of course, they had no proof yet, but Roman was certain the test results wouldn't surprise him.

"We don't want to bother you long."

Kendra's phone rang and she took it out in the hall. Roman briefly wondered why she had to leave the room. In case whoever called asked her about him?

"Do you think your husband is poisoning you?" Roman asked.

"No."

She sounded sure. "Who, then?"

"I don't know." She averted her face.

"You can tell me, Vikki. I can make sure no one hurts you."

"No, you can't."

In other words, she knew someone was trying to kill her and she knew why.

"What will you do if the tests confirm poisoning?" he asked.

"When I get out of the hospital, I'm going to stay with my mother in Florida," she said.

That was probably wise, at least until they caught the killer.

"Then you are afraid of Glenn?"

She shook her head. "I don't trust anyone right now."

"You must suspect someone, or you wouldn't have made plans to go to Florida."

"Look, I appreciate all you and the local police are doing, but there's nothing more I can do for you."

Kendra entered the room again with rounder eyes than when she'd left. "That was Raelyn."

The way she looked at him said that's all she'd say in front of anyone else. With Vikki not talking, who knew whose side she was on?

"We'll leave you be."

"Thanks for stopping by."

Roman left the room and stopped with Kendra outside the door.

"She said she found some photos her mother took of a house she didn't recognize. She took a cell phone picture of them and sent them to me." Kendra showed him her phone.

He thumbed through each photo.

"That's Glenn and Vikki's backyard," she said.

It was. He looked at Kendra as the significance rang through, then handed back her phone.

"Good. You're both finally here."

Roman saw Cal rushing down the hall.

"It's just been confirmed," Cal said. "Vikki was poisoned with ethylene glycol."

A doctor passed them on the way into Vikki's room, likely to go inform her. Roman followed him, staying just out of sight but within earshot.

"We received your test results," the doctor said. "The reason you've been feeling so sick is because there was a toxic amount of ethylene glycol in your system. Ethylene glycol is found in antifreeze."

After a few seconds, Vikki said, "Y-you mean… I…I was poisoned?"

"I'm sorry to say, yes. Who do you think would have done this to you?"

"I…I…I don't know. I…I need to call my mother. She's supposed to come and get me."

Roman didn't need to hear any more. Vikki wasn't ready to talk.

"We're bringing Glenn in for more questioning." Why don't you two follow me to the station?"

"You might want to get another warrant first." Kendra handed him her phone and he looked at the photos.

"That's Glenn and Vikki's backyard."

Cal looked up at Roman, and then walked into the hospital room.

Roman followed with Kendra.

The doctor finished up with his patient and left them after acknowledging Cal and then Roman and Kendra. He seemed to know Cal from talking to him about the case.

"Not you again," Vikki said. "I need some time alone."

"What's your favorite thing to drink?" Cal asked.

"I like lots of things. Coffee. Tea. Juice. But I suppose if I had to choose I'd say sweet tea. I have a glass every day."

"Where do you get your tea?" Roman asked.

"I order it online most of the time."

"Has anyone ever given you tea for any special occasion?"

"Why, yes. Glenn and his parents almost always do."

Cal had the police wait to bring Glenn back in for questioning and arranged for another search warrant at his house. Glenn had gone to work that day and didn't stop by the hospital on his way home. Kendra found that peculiar. Didn't he want to see how his wife was doing?

This time when police approached him, he looked scared rather than defensive. And he was accommodating with the team who would be searching his house.

"Come in," he'd said when Cal handed him the warrant.

Police went straight to the backyard, though, and Kendra watched how Glenn went a little paler and stuffed his hands in his pockets. He trailed behind the team of criminal investigators.

Kendra followed Glenn, Cal and Roman onto the back patio.

Two team members checked the photo Kendra had given to Cal and found the location of the rock.

When one of them rolled the rock over and took a shovel handed to him, Glenn asked, "Why are they digging in the flower bed?"

Was he pretending? Did he actually know the answer?

"We have reason to believe someone buried evidence here," Cal said.

"Evidence of what?" He seemed genuinely perplexed.

Roman moved to stand right in front of Glenn. "Your wife was poisoned, Mr. Franklin. We just received confirmation from the hospital."

Glenn's mouth opened a fraction, and then he closed his mouth as though recovering from some revelation. His eyes drooped in defeat.

"Is that why you haven't been by to visit your wife?" Kendra asked.

Glenn shot an insulted look her way. "You aren't a cop. Stop asking me questions."

There was the belligerent Glenn Franklin, aka Bear. Is that how he'd gotten his nickname?

"Speaking of questions," Cal said, standing to

Glenn's left. "We'd like you to come to the station to give us your statement."

"As soon as I contact my attorney, I'll stop by."

Kendra resumed watching the investigators dig in the flower bed. She moved to the edge of the patio, leaving Roman and Cal to deal with Glenn. They'd get nothing out of him with an attorney present. They'd have to prove who killed Kaelyn and Deidra the hard way.

The investigator digging put the shovel aside and went to his knees to dig with his hands.

"We've got something." The investigator standing near him said, looking down into the hole.

The kneeling investigator stood with a can in hand. It was an old-fashioned can that once held coffee. It could have been a valuable piece of art had it been preserved.

Cal and Roman put on gloves and approached the two.

Kendra watched Glenn. His brow had creased as though confused over what they'd found.

Cal took the can and inspected it. He opened the lid.

"There's a white powder filling this to about a quarter of the way," Cal said, then he looked over at Glenn. "Ethylene glycol?"

"I don't know what that is. I didn't bury it."

Kendra would have to say she believed him. He seemed not to understand why anyone would want to dig up his flower bed.

Cal put the can into a bag and handed it back to the investigator.

"We're going to have that tested, Mr. Franklin," Roman said as he walked back to the patio.

"I'm telling you, I didn't bury that."

"Did you buy the powder?" Roman asked.

"No," Glenn answered defensively. "And I didn't put it into the can and bury it, either."

Roman took his time before he said, "You could make this a lot easier on yourself if you talk to us."

Glenn just glowered at him.

"If you're convicted of murder and attempted murder, you could get a harsher sentence than you would if you cooperate with us," Cal added. "We can't work any deals unless you cooperate. Do you understand?"

"I understand, Detective, but I didn't kill anyone, least of all my first wife and I'd never try to kill Vikki. We might have our issues but I'd never kill her over them."

"What issues?"

"My affair with Kaelyn," he said.

"We'll talk to you soon." Cal nodded to Roman, signaling them to follow him.

Outside on the front porch, he faced them.

"The coroner found calcium oxalate crystals in Deidra's tissues. That's ample evidence she was poisoned with ethylene glycol."

Kendra leaned her head back in relief. "That's great news." But what about Kaelyn? How would they identify her killer?

Roman waited with Kendra for detectives to bring Hudson Franklin into the interview room. The detectives had just finished with Glenn, and not much had been gained. All they'd established was that Deidra had also drunk tea on a regular basis, as well as powdered lemonade. Cal and his team were poring through all of Glenn's financials to try and link him to a purchase of the poison. They were also examining his computer and other electronic devices.

When asked about his father's bribery practices, Glenn had denied knowing anything about it. He conceded he'd heard about the affair with the mayor's wife but couldn't say whether it was true or not.

Next was his father. They'd see how much he corroborated.

Cal remained standing in the room when Hudson was brought in. To Roman's surprise, he hadn't asked for an attorney. Glenn had been brought in separately and no one told Hudson he was being questioned, as well.

Call began with small talk as Hudson sat and someone brought him a bottle of water.

"Would you mind telling me why I'm here today? I know it's about Deidra, but how do you think I can help?"

Moving closer to the table, Cal leaned on his hands as he faced the man. "We know you took bribes and can prove it in court, Mr. Franklin. If you cooperate with us now, we might be able to make some kind of deal with you."

"Bribery? What are you talking about?"

Cal straightened. "There's no point in denying it. We have proof you accepted gifts and money, which all coincide with cases you prosecuted that could not have coincidentally gone so well otherwise. The mayor's son? I can name others."

After a long while where Hudson stared up at Cal, he asked, "What kind of deal?"

"That depends on how much you can tell us." Cal walked around the table to the other end.

"What do you need to know?"

"Let's start with the murders." Cal folded his arms, palms flat against his rib cage. "Did your son kill his first wife Deidra and attempt to do the same with Vikki?"

Hudson's head lowered as he seemed to think things over gravely. Finally he lifted his head. "No."

"What about Kaelyn Johnston?" Cal asked.

"I believed her death was suicide."

"Did you?" Cal challenged.

Hudson sighed long and deep, head lowered again. This time, he answered without lifting his head.

"I suspected it would come to this. I almost came in to talk to you before detectives came to my door and asked me to come here this afternoon."

Cal didn't move, nor did he say anything. Hudson had reached a point where he'd decided to stop running, to stop hiding, and maybe even stop protecting his son.

"The day Kaelyn died, I was at work all day," Hudson said. "My wife called late morning and asked me to meet her in Chicago so we could fly to New York."

Kendra gripped Roman's forearm. This was an enormous revelation. Kendra would finally know what happened to her twin sister.

To a detective standing in the room with them, Roman said, "Get Melody Hudson's phone records. See if we can place her near Chesterville, along the highway where Kaelyn was last known to have been."

The detective nodded once and left the room.

"I asked her what she was doing in Chicago, and she told me she flew there to shop."

"You believed her?" Cal asked.

Hudson shook his head. "I did at first, but I always

thought it was strange. We had already planned to go to New York, so I flew to Chicago and picked her up, and then we did go to New York."

"She called you late morning?" Cal asked.

"Yes, at around eleven thirty. It may have been later. I don't recall."

That would coincide with Kaelyn's time of death. Melody must have killed her, and then phoned her husband to cover her tracks for the rest of the day. All she would have had to do is drive Kaelyn's car back to where she planned to stage the suicide, then get to Chicago to meet Hudson. Kaelyn wasn't heavy. Melody would have struggled, but she could have carried out her plan.

"Did you ask her why Chicago?"

Hudson lifted his head. "Yes. More than once. But she wouldn't talk to me about it."

"And you didn't think that was strange?" Cal asked.

"I did, but I hardly would have thought my wife capable of murder. I did wonder if she had started having an affair, but she adamantly denied that and I believed her. Melody is many things, but she isn't unfaithful. I provided her everything she wanted or needed in life."

So he'd let it go all these years. Melody indeed wanted and needed things in life, expensive things. So much that she'd kill to preserve the lifestyle.

Cal asked if they had a driver and he answered they did and he was the same driver they'd had for nearly a decade. Cal got his name and Roman made a note of it. Melody had likely had her driver take her somewhere she knew she'd intercept Kaelyn. Maybe she'd even arranged to meet Kaelyn. Had she called her when she was on her way and manipulated her into meeting? Maybe she'd lied and said she had information on Glenn and they had to meet somewhere private.

"Did you ever have any reason to believe your wife may have poisoned Deidra?" Cal asked.

Hudson shook his head. "Or Glenn's second wife. I had no reason at all to believe she'd do something like that."

She was the diamond-glittering beauty on his arm and that's all he cared about. He cared about status and reputation. Money.

Cal studied him awhile as though contemplating all Hudson had said. "Why are you telling us all of this? And with no attorney? Your son insisted on having an attorney."

"You questioned my son?"

"We just finished with him before we brought you in."

"My son is innocent."

"We found an old tin of powdered ethylene glycol buried in his backyard. Do you know anything about that?"

"In his…" Hudson looked confused. "Melody must have buried it there, not Glenn."

"Are you sure? Wouldn't Glenn bury evidence implicating his mother? And you. You are his parents."

"I would hope Glenn would do what I'm doing right now."

"What are you doing?"

Hudson leaned back against his chair. "Melody withdrew a large amount of money from our account."

"When?"

"Today."

"Where is she now?"

"I'm afraid I don't know, but I can't support her if she's going around committing murder."

"You supported her when she staged a suicide."

"I told you, I believed it was a suicide and I believed my wife went shopping in Chicago."

"But you suspected your wife might have had something to do with her death."

"I asked her why she went to Chicago. She liked shopping in different cities. While it came up rather suddenly, I didn't think it that odd at the time."

But he had thought it odd.

"Did she show you what she bought?"

"No, and I didn't think to ask."

Roman made another note to check for charges either to their credit cards or debit cards.

Cal walked behind the chair to Hudson's other side. "You're facing charges yourself, Mr. Franklin. Bribery."

"For that, I do require an attorney."

They were finished for today. Hudson would be convicted of bribery and most likely sent to jail for a period of time, but nowhere near the length Melody would serve.

Kendra should have felt elated that she finally had closure to her sister's death. Instead, she just felt empty, and full of more questions.

They waited in a conference room with Cal, who had his laptop open and periodically checked his email for the files on Melody's calls and purchase record for the day of Kaelyn's murder.

At last, he swung his feet off the table and faced the screen directly. "Here it is."

Kendra moved to the chair on one side of him and Roman the other. Then they leaned in to read the files.

Melody had made a call from her cell phone at the time Hudson had said she had called him. The triangulation performed placed her on the highway just outside of Chesterville at a truck stop.

"The email is from the detective I sent to question Hudson and Melody's driver," Cal said. "He kept a log of everywhere he drove them and confirmed he dropped her off at the truck stop with no instructions on picking her up. He'd remembered because he'd thought it was so strange that a lady like her would want to be dropped off at a truck stop."

Kendra read through the bank transactions the day of Kaelyn's death. "There are no purchases from a mall or anything resembling items bought while shopping."

"Only fuel," Roman said.

Kendra found the fuel purchases. There were only two. One near Chesterville and another near her house. "She left us a tidy trail."

"I doubt she ever thought she'd get caught," Cal said. "The fiber forensics came in today. I bet we'll find a match to Melody somewhere in their house or car."

"We've got her." Roman looked over at Kendra and she saw and felt his deep satisfaction that not only had he solved a tough case, he also did it for her.

She smiled softly back at him, letting go for just a moment or two to let him know how grateful she was.

Cal turned his head from one to the other. "Enough

ogling. We have to find her first. By now, she's probably aware we're about to make an arrest."

That made her dangerous, even more now than before. Knowing she was about to be caught, what would she do?

Chapter 19

Raelyn gathered her laundry into a basket and left her apartment, a tiny one-bedroom she could barely afford working at the gas station. It was getting late to make a run to the Laundromat, but she was out of socks. Someday she'd have a nice house like her aunt that had its own laundry room.

She thought about Aunt Kendra on her way down to the parking lot.

She couldn't believe the photos she had found had helped with Roman's case. She'd spoken with Kendra an hour ago and the cops were bringing Glenn and Hudson in for questioning. Had Glenn killed her mother? So far, Aunt Kendra said they had no evidence implicating him. Wouldn't it be rotten if they never did? Her mother's murder would go unsolved.

Her only hope was in Roman. Kendra said he was

one of the best detectives out there. Raelyn sure hoped she was right.

So far, all they had were some bribery violations against Glenn's dad. Was Glenn protecting his dad?

She'd have to wait to find out. Aunt Kendra said she'd call after the interviews.

Her phone rang. Maybe that was her.

She dumped her basket into the back of her car and pulled the cell out of her back jean pocket. The caller ID said it was Adam, which disappointed her. He hadn't taken the breakup very well. He still thought they were perfect for each other. Aunt Kendra had shown her how wrong he was.

She put her phone back in her pocket without answering.

Aunt Kendra made her feel she was worth something more. Raelyn couldn't say why or how her aunt did it. Maybe it was the pep talks. Maybe it was the candor about her mother. Maybe it was the way she cared about her. Or maybe it was a combination of everything.

Kendra was awesome. She'd had a rough adolescence, too, but she'd dug herself out of it and made a decent living for herself. Raelyn wondered if she'd let her work full-time at her shop. She could learn management that way.

Shutting the back hatch, she headed for the driver's side when a car drove up beside her. A nice car. A sleek black Mercedes. She paused with her hand on the door handle of her car when she noticed Melody Franklin get out of the driver's side.

The woman stood and faced her from the other side of the vehicle, her blond hair combed smooth in a shoulder-length bob, revealing glimpses of dangling diamond earrings. "Well, hello, Raelyn."

Something weird struck her about a woman like the prosecutor's wife being in the parking lot of a low-rent apartment complex. "What are you doing here?"

Melody walked around the back of her car, heels clicking on the pavement. As she rounded the rear, Raelyn saw her hand was inside her blue-and-black-patterned purse, which looked like it had been custom made for her dress, a blue fitted business suit. The heels were about three inches and the shoes black. She wore a diamond necklace and watch. The woman liked her accessories.

But it was her hand that Raelyn watched the closest.

Just as a tingle of apprehension trickled up the skin of her neck, Melody produced a gun.

"Get in my car, dear."

Raelyn glanced around for anyone who might be able to help.

"We're alone," Melody said, stepping forward with the gun. "Get in."

When Raelyn still didn't move, Melody raised the gun to aim for her head. "I don't have to take you alive."

Believing she had no choice, Raelyn went with her gut and got into the car.

Melody bent over. "Get into the driver's seat."

Raelyn looked down at the gun aimed at her and complied.

Melody got in and shut the passenger door. "Drive. I'll tell you where to go but for now, get to the highway and head for the mountains."

Raelyn backed out of the parking space and drove

out of the lot, looking in the rearview mirror at her disappearing apartment building. Would her life end this
way? She hadn't even begun to live. Would this crazy
woman cut it short?

Not if she could stop her. What would Kendra do in
this situation? Play it cool until she saw a safer opportunity to escape? Try to get information out of Melody?

The mountains were a good distance away. Melody
wouldn't be able to watch her closely the entire way.
Maybe she could wreck the car or something.

"Why are you doing this?" Raelyn asked. "Why me?"

"Because you're important to your aunt," Melody
answered in a lofty tone, calm and composed. "She
should have left well enough alone."

"What do you want from her?"

"This is all her fault. I wouldn't have to resort to
this if not for her. The police know too much and now
I can't stay. I have to get away, and you're my ticket."

"Why not just go to the bank and make a withdrawal?" She and her husband had to have enough
money.

"There's not enough in our accounts for me to live
on. I already took everything I could."

But she needed more. Raelyn eyed her impeccable
attire. Even her purse made a statement. Her husband
must have had to spend a lot on a house and everything
in it on top of all the other material things a woman
like her needed. *Wanted* was a better word.

"And you think my aunt has that kind of money?"

"No, but the detective she hired will be able to
get what she needs. Fitting end for them, don't you
think? They're the ones who caused all of this, so now

they're going to pay." Melody's red lipstick slathered lips curved upward devilishly.

"I hate to break it to you, lady, but you're the one who has to pay."

The smile vanished. "Shut up and drive. I don't have to talk to you."

Raelyn watched the road, keeping an eye out for a place to turn to get help. Would this insane woman try to shoot her in front of a crowd of people? She had to assume yes. She had reached the edge of her desperation to silence anyone who caught on to her evil.

"You killed my mother because she found out about Deidra?" Raelyn asked.

"I said shut up."

"What does Vikki know?"

"She and I had lunch one day. I wanted to find out what she knew about my son's affair with your mother. Turns out she knew everything. She even talked with Glenn about it." Melody's face contorted in disgust. "They even agreed to go to marriage counseling."

"That's why you tried to poison her?"

"She asked Glenn about Deidra's death. She asked me about it, too. She was getting suspicious, and Glenn came to me and assured me Vikki knew nothing, but I could see he was only trying to protect her. Sooner or later, she'd become too much of a risk. I had to get rid of her."

"Like you got rid of my mother?"

Melody scoffed. "Your mother." She shook her head incredulously, mockingly so. "Your mother actually thought she could have a man like Glenn, that he'd leave his wife for her."

"What makes you so special?"

"I come from a good family. When Hudson proposed, my father had to approve. Of course, he did. My family has money."

"Then why don't you ask them to pay you off?"

Melody turned her head and between focusing her attention on the road and glancing at the woman, Raelyn saw condescension. "You're just like your mother, you know. You think feistiness will overrule heritage."

"My mother didn't need heritage to be a good person."

"Do good women have affairs with married men?"

Raelyn couldn't argue that hadn't been wrong. "My mother was in an abusive marriage. She was trying to leave my dad when she was—when you killed her."

"Women without family wealth get themselves into situations like that. She had no choice other than to marry a substandard man."

"He didn't present himself as substandard before she married him. He had a drinking problem. You don't know a thing about my mother. She was strong and full of love. She was a happy, ambitious person until my dad beat that out of her. You killed a good, decent human being. Doesn't that matter to you?" She knew without asking that a woman like Melody—one capable of heartlessly killing—would not care.

"What matters to me…" Melody hesitated. Raelyn imagined the pampered woman now faced the reality of her new circumstances. "What mattered to me was protecting Hudson's career." She looked over at Raelyn as though beseeching her to understand. "If he's ruined, then I'm ruined. I couldn't have that."

"And so now that you've failed in that endeavor, you'll do what…go make a new life for yourself in Mexico?"

"My plans are not your concern. Now, if you don't shut up, I will shoot you."

Raelyn didn't tell her she'd never get the money, and even if she did, she'd never make it on the run, not a woman like her. She needed a sheltered life, one her rich husband provided.

"Roman won't negotiate with you. A detective like that, one with the kind of backing he has, will come in shooting. You should listen to me, Melody. This will go badly for you if you go through with this."

"This will go exactly as I say, or you die."

Raelyn drove down the highway, the lights of Chesterville fading in her rearview mirror. The cover of darkness would help her, but the isolation might not.

She stayed silent for a while, until she noticed Melody losing some of her edge. She no longer watched her so intently. Slowly, Raelyn moved her arm to her side, then eased her hand up and into her back pocket. Slipping her phone out, she placed it beside her on the car seat.

Going still, she waited until Melody looked over at her and then straight ahead before using her thumb to press the main button. Her recent calls were still up on the screen.

She pressed Call.

Chapter 20

Later that night, Kendra sat in Roman's hotel room as he prepared something microwavable to eat. Her stomach was empty, but she had no appetite. Raelyn still hadn't answered her phone and she'd called twice. But just then, her cell rang and she saw it was Raelyn.

"Hey. Where have you been?"

No one responded on the other end. Kendra heard a funny background noise, like Raelyn was driving in a car and had accidentally dialed her.

"Raelyn?" she said in a louder voice. That got Roman's attention. He turned from the microwave to watch her.

"Raelyn?"

"Where are we going?" she heard Raelyn ask.

"What?" Kendra asked.

"Shut up and keep driving. I'll tell you when to turn off the highway."

Kendra gasped as blood left her head and she felt cold and shaky with apprehension. She put the phone down and pressed the speaker button.

"Melody has Raelyn. They're in a car driving on a highway."

Roman came to the table as Raelyn spoke again.

"This highway goes to Snowshoe. Are you going to your cabin?"

Kendra stared at Roman. The seconds felt like torturous minutes.

"What are you going to do when we get there?"

"If you don't shut up, I swear I'll—"

"All right, all right." Raelyn said no more but she kept the line open.

Roman had already gone into action mode. He made a call to Cal and gathered his gun and ammunition.

Kendra grabbed her purse and held on to her phone as they left the building. They had to reach Raelyn in time.

On the way to meet Cal and his team, Kendra still had Raelyn on the line. Roman heard Melody direct her to turn at the driveway to the cabin. A few minutes later, the car stopped.

"Get out," Melody said.

Roman listened to Raelyn get out.

"What's that in your hand?"

"Nothing."

The sound of a scuffle followed. Melody must have gotten out of the car and Raelyn must be trying to hide her phone.

Roman saw Kendra grip her hands together in frightened apprehension.

"Who did you call?" Now Melody must have held the phone to her ear. "Hello?"

Roman put his finger to his mouth, indicating to Kendra not to say a word. She'd already muted her phone so Melody wouldn't hear anything.

"Kendra? I know it's you, you meddling bitch. If you interfere again, I'll kill your precious niece. You don't want that, do you? You've already lost your parents *and* your stupid sister. Do you really want to lose the last person you have?"

If she put one finger on her niece, Kendra would rip the lady's heart out with her own hands. "Tell me we're going to get her."

"We'll get her." Roman reached over from the driver's side and took her hand. "Don't unmute the phone."

He knew her enough already that he'd predicted she'd say something hostile.

"It doesn't matter that you know where I am. That was part of my plan," Melody said. "You need to know where I am so Hudson can deliver the money."

"What money?" Kendra asked even though Melody couldn't hear her.

"I've already called Hudson. He'll tell you what has to be done if you want Raelyn alive."

The line went dead.

Now all Kendra could do was imagine what Raelyn must be experiencing. She'd been through enough with her father. She didn't need to be tortured by a madwoman.

"She needs Raelyn alive," Roman said. "If she's dead, she won't get any money and she knows that."

"Drive faster."

* * *

After meeting Cal at the rendezvous point, Kendra rode with Roman toward Snowshoe, a town near the Franklins' cabin. They and Cal's team formed a caravan of speeding vehicles, Cal's leading the way with lights flashing. Roman had a radio in his lap, waiting for word that Hudson had made contact with Melody.

The radio finally crackled to life and Cal's voice came over the airwaves. "Cal here, over."

"Roger, over."

"Hudson said she wants a million dollars in exchange for Raelyn. He told her he doesn't have that kind of money because she drained their accounts, but she said he better find a way and to try the agency Kendra hired."

"Tell her DAI will cover the ransom. Let's stall her for as long as possible to give us time to free Raelyn. Make her think we're going along with her demands. We don't want her scared. We need her confident she's going to escape. If she's confident, she won't harm Raelyn."

"Roger that."

Kendra reached for the radio from Roman, who handed it to her.

She pressed the Talk lever. "Cal, when will she let Raelyn go?"

She released the lever and the radio crackled as Cal was about to speak. "She didn't say. She wants the money ready first then she'll tell us where the exchange will take place."

Roman took the radio from her and pressed the lever. "It doesn't matter anyway."

No, because he would get Raelyn back before Melody got away.

The radio crackled again. "She'll do anything to maintain her lifestyle as she's morbidly demonstrated, but she's messing up now."

"Taking on law enforcement with a hostage? Yeah."

"See you in five."

They were almost at the cabin, which no doubt Melody expected.

Roman used his cell phone to make another call. "I need a bag of money. You know the drill."

Who had he called? Someone he had already lined up before heading out to the cabin?

Reaching the driveway, Roman parked in front of Cal and two sheriff's department vans. Officers got out of the last van and dispersed into the trees. They'd surround the cabin. The other van had all the comms.

Cal got out of his car and Hudson from the other side. Roman and Kendra met them on the dirt and gravel driveway. Hudson's face sagged with gravity.

"Hold your fire until I give the order," Cal said into the radio he still held. Then to the two of them said, "I had Hudson tell her he was getting the money from DAI."

"My drop guy should be here any moment."

"Did you really get all that money?"

"Most of it isn't real," Roman said. "We have bags like that on hand for situations like this."

Cal breathed a laugh. "The more I hear about that company of yours, the more I like them."

The conversation led to mundane things like the weather and good food, anything to ease some of the tension. All the while, Hudson remained silent, glancing up the road that curved through the trees. The cabin wasn't visible from here.

A few minutes later, a car drove to a stop in front of them. Roman walked to the driver's side. A man got out. Almost as tall as Roman, he had a dark, mercenary look to him. Opening the back door, he leaned in and retrieved a black duffel bag and handed it to Roman.

"You stationed somewhere near here?" Kendra barely heard Roman asked the man.

"DC. Kadin asked me to be ready to deliver this to you. I used it in another case." The man, who didn't appear to have much humor in him, pitched his head westward. "I found a place about twenty miles from Chesterville. Been vacationing until I got your call."

"Sorry to interrupt." Roman grinned.

"It's the way these things go, isn't it? You never know when work is going to take you for another ride."

Roman nodded, still with a grin. "Isn't that the truth."

"As long as I'm here, I might as well help. You have a hostage situation going on?"

"We've got it covered." Roman glanced over at Cal.

Kendra followed his gaze. Cal continued to watch, strength and confidence radiating.

"All right. I'm going to go do some fishing."

"Thanks for coming out here."

"No problem." He got into the car and made a U-turn on the highway, giving a salute with two fingers as he passed.

Kendra had the feeling that all three of these men had no girlfriends. She knew Roman didn't. But all three, and probably many more detectives who worked for the renowned Dark Alley Investigations agency, devoted their lives to justice and vengeance for victims and their families.

Did Melody know DAI could pull off anything and that's why she'd planned to force them to come up with money? Maybe she wasn't as incompetent as everyone here seemed to think.

One look at Hudson only convinced her more. He was afraid of his own wife.

Roman returned to the group with the bag in hand.

"Go ahead and call her now," Cal said to Hudson.

Hudson took his phone out and dialed Melody's cell number. "I have it."

"She wants me to bring it to the cabin."

"Tell her Raelyn goes out of the cabin first," Roman said.

Hudson relayed the order, then looked up at Roman. "She said no. She wants to be on her way out of here before she lets Raelyn go."

Roman glanced at Kendra. She could see he knew she didn't like that plan. It would be risky rushing the cabin with a desperate woman armed and determined to flee. Letting her take Raelyn *with* the money wasn't a good plan, either.

Roman shook his head. "Cal, you and I are going to get a look inside that cabin. I want to make sure Raelyn is all right."

"Roger that."

"If there's a way in, we'll do it. Hudson, you're going to be the deterrent. You distract Melody while we go in from the back. Try to get Raelyn as close to the back door as you can."

Hudson nodded.

"Can we trust him?" Kendra asked. "Melody is his wife and he's taken bribes from criminals. What if he's been playing us this whole time?"

"I'm not," Hudson said. "So I took a few bribes. No one really got hurt. I'd never kill anyone. I did it for her." He looked to the winding road. "I'm not going down for her. She made the decision to kill people, not me. I'm no killer."

Roman turned to Kendra. "This is our best option."

Either they trusted Hudson or they rushed in without offering any money. Raelyn's life would be in much more danger. But if Melody had her hands on the bagful of money, she'd feel as though she were on her way to a rich life somewhere, a life much different than the one she had with Hudson, but one with the money she craved above all else.

Kendra met Roman's eyes and grew warm with the realization that he awaited her go-ahead.

After a few seconds, she nodded twice.

"That's my girl." He hooked an arm around her shoulders and leaned in to kiss her forehead. Moving back, he said, "You two wait here for now."

Cal handed her a radio.

Roman led Cal into the trees toward the cabin, slowing as lighted windows came into view. Hudson and Melody's cabin. He ran with Cal toward the side of the cabin, out of sight of the front windows. Approaching from the side, he moved along the log siding of the cabin to the first window. It was a bedroom. No one inside. He moved farther along. The next window was the living area. He bobbed his head quickly and spotted Raelyn tied to a chair. Melody paced from the kitchen to the living area holding a pistol in one hand and a glass of wine in the other.

"Raelyn is all right," he whispered into the radio, letting Kendra know.

"What's Melody doing?" Cal asked.

"Drinking wine."

Cal's head jerked back in disbelief and a few of the other officers chuckled over the airwaves.

"Heading back to the trees," Roman said. "Send Hudson up."

Moments later, Kendra and Hudson appeared on the road. Kendra walked to Roman and Cal, and Roman signaled Hudson to go to the cabin. He'd been wired so they could all hear him.

"I'm going in," Hudson said. "Can you hear me?"

"You're good," Roman said. "We'll be close by."

A few moments later, Hudson appeared on the dirt driveway, walking toward the cabin with the bag of money. He looked around as though trying to find them, and then focused on the cabin. When he reached the door, it opened. Melody stepped outside.

"What are you doing, Melody?" Hudson asked.

"Give me the money, Hudson."

He handed her the bag. She took it and dropped it onto the small front porch. Unzipping the top, she reached inside and brought out a bundle and inspected it.

Roman held his breath. Anyone who knew counterfeit money would be able to recognize the bills beneath the top few were fake.

Melody dropped the bundle back into the bag without looking closer.

"Come inside," she said to Hudson, standing with the bag in hand. He followed her into the cabin.

"Melody, it's not too late to stop this," Hudson said.

"Shut up, Hudson. If it weren't for you, none of this would have happened."

"You killed your son's first wife."

"She would have ruined you. You should be thanking me."

"You tried to kill his second wife."

Melody said nothing for a few seconds. "You can go with me. We can start a new life somewhere else."

"I was wrong for taking bribes, Melody. I should have stopped after helping the mayor's son."

"Since when are you so conscientious? You liked our life as much as I did. You aren't fooling me." The sound of Melody walking across the room came through the radio in Roman's ear. "Where are they?"

"Who?"

"The detectives. I know they're out there."

"You won't get away with this," Raelyn said.

"Be quiet or I'll shut you up myself."

"You have the money. Let the girl go, Melody."

"Not yet. We're going to go for a ride. If I'm not allowed to get away from here, then I'll kill her."

"We can't let her get in the car with Raelyn," Roman said.

"I don't have a clear shot," the sniper on the team said.

'I'm going in," Roman replied.

"I'll go with you. We'll go in the back."

"Let's move." Roman left the shelter of the trees, staying out of the line of sight from the front windows of the cabin. Cal followed, jogging to the back of the cabin.

Roman drew his gun and tested the back doorknob. He could see inside through the top half of the door, which was a French-trimmed window.

"Get up," Melody ordered.

"I'm not going anywhere with you," Roman heard Raelyn answer.

"Get up or I'll shoot you right now."

Using a rock, Roman smashed one of the small square pieces of glass and reached in to unlock the door.

"Move, move, move!" He heard a team leader say.

As soon as Roman entered, he saw that Raelyn must have gotten free of her ties. She lunged at Melody, grabbing her gun hand. Raelyn forced the gun above their heads. Melody's eyes all but glowed red with determined rage. Sheer will empowered her. She shoved Raelyn, who lost her grip on the weapon as she stumbled back.

"I said *get-in-the-car!*"

Roman charged for Melody, who turned to see him just as he reached her. He knocked her gun hand and swiped his foot behind her ankles, sending the gun flying and her dropping to the cabin floor.

He checked on Raelyn, seeing her regain her balance and stand at the other side of the room and Cal going to her to make sure she was all right.

Melody rolled to her hands and knees and climbed

to her feet before stumbling toward the door. Roman headed for her as Hudson moved in her way.

"Melody, stop. It's over," Hudson said, taking hold of her shoulders.

With an inhuman growl, she shoved him out of her way, grabbed the bag of money and resumed her rush for the door. "I am not going to jail."

Roman chased after her. Through the front door, he saw Melody making a run for the car parked in front of the porch. He didn't want to shoot her. As he approached the vehicle, he saw her toss the bag onto the passenger seat and then get in. She leaned over and retrieved something. When she rose up, he saw it was another gun.

He ducked as she shot through the passenger window, shattering the glass.

Roman shot out the front tire and then the rear. Melody tried to drive off anyway. He shot out the other rear tire and she lost control. The car rammed into a tree.

Melody tried to restart the car. Roman reached the rear.

"Get out with your hands up," he yelled.

Melody twisted in the seat and fired her gun with poor aim. She fired twice more, and then opened the door. With better aim that had him crouching behind the car, she fired again and again until she ran out of bullets.

Then she made a run for it, abandoning the bag of money in her mad dash for freedom.

Kendra emerged from the cover of trees and intercepted the woman, her slender body swooping low and long legs swinging out to catch Melody's ankle. A shoe went flying as Melody went airborne, arms out and landing facedown on the grassy earth.

Roman pointed his pistol at Melody, who rolled onto her back and stared up at him with crazed eyes.

"Nice job," he said to Kendra.

"You better not have hurt my niece," she said to Melody.

Cal appeared from the cabin with Raelyn and Kendra ran to her. Cal walked to Melody with handcuffs as the two women embraced, laughing and crying at the same time. Both of them talking, breathy and fast and unintelligible.

Cal helped Melody to her feet and cuffed her as he read her rights to her.

Hudson stood on the front porch, a couple of officers joining him to make sure he didn't decide to make his own run for freedom. Roman didn't think he would. He'd accepted his fate.

Roman walked with Cal, who guided Melody toward the driveway, where officers had driven a van. They stopped before the gathering crowd of officers, Hudson and the two officers from the porch also meeting there.

Hudson approached his wife, face drawn and grave. "Melody...why?" He didn't seem able to understand.

"Why do you *think*?" Melody spat.

Hudson looked at her as though seeing a stranger. "You were going to ransom a woman for money and leave? You were going to leave me?"

"As if *you* would have ever done something to protect us. I had to be the one."

"No, Melody, you didn't."

"If it weren't for me, you'd already be in jail!"

He said nothing, seeing his wife with new eyes, disbelieving eyes.

"Doesn't that matter to you?"

"I never asked you to do any of this."

Melody gaped at him, and then grew incensed. Cal handed her over to a waiting officer, who opened the van and put her in the back.

Chapter 21

Roman walked along the street toward Kendra's shop. He hadn't slept much the last two nights. After he, Kendra and Cal had talked awhile the night before last, Kendra had decided to go home and take Raelyn with her. He hadn't heard from her since, and he hadn't tried to call. She no longer had to worry about a killer on the loose so there was no longer any need for her to stay with him. There was no longer any need for him to stay in Chesterville, but here he was, still in Chesterville.

The way Kendra had looked at him as they were about to disperse and go their own ways stayed on his mind. That's what had kept him from sleeping. Had that look been an indication that she would withdraw and turn him away, or had she been disappointed that she wouldn't be seeing him every day anymore? He'd have to go home now.

Funny how Wyoming didn't feel like home anymore. Chesterville was his home. Always had been. After college, he hadn't returned except to see his parents. Reflecting back, he didn't feel like the same man who'd arrived. He'd come here solely to check into Kaelyn's death. He'd come to do a job. He'd come to dispel the need for an investigation and had been ambitious to solve his other active case. No matter, when he'd arrived, he'd been all about work, but from the first moment he'd met Kendra in person he'd been drawn to her.

He hadn't coerced her to go to that pub and play pool with him for the sake of his work. He'd coerced her because he had been drawn to her—on a personal level. From then on, she'd challenged the core beliefs that he lived by.

He hadn't avoided his parents because he compared himself to them or felt they didn't approve of his choices. He'd avoided them because, until now, he hadn't thought he had made the right choices for himself. He always felt he'd followed in their footsteps—or tried to. The truth was, he hadn't done either of those things. He'd always been interested in crime, mysteries. As he grew older, that transitioned to a desire to seek justice for victims of crimes. Maybe his father had introduced him to that line of work. It didn't matter what led him there; what mattered is he got where he was because his heart had led him the entire way. Not his parents. Not anyone. Only himself.

Roman was doing what he'd been called to this earth to do. He wouldn't be happy doing anything else. As long as he worked to avenge victims, dead or alive, he would be fulfilled.

Kendra had done the same thing, only her journey

had been different. She'd had to be smart and tough to overcome the tragedy of losing her parents and the fallout from that. From that experience, she'd developed a shell. Add a couple of boyfriends who betrayed her trust and what did you have? A woman who might not be able to overcome her internal obstacles the way Roman just realized he had overcome his.

All this time, he'd told himself he was looking for a woman who didn't surround herself with delusions of security, and he'd been the delusional one. Except for one thing. He had never been delusional about wanting a real woman. Kendra had such a thick protective layer, he didn't have much confidence she'd be able or even want to break it down to let him in all the way.

He could, and probably would, suggest they see each other awhile. It would have to be a long-distance relationship at first. He wouldn't pack up his life and move it to Chesterville for a woman he wasn't sure about.

He argued with himself that he could move back home to be closer to his parents, but he was afraid that was more of an excuse. Kadin Tandy was open to his investigators working remotely. The nature of the business didn't limit anyone to Wyoming. DAI did nationwide investigations. His job wouldn't stop him from going wherever he wanted. Kendra would, however.

His ringing phone stopped him just before he reached Kendra's shop. It was Cal. He was going to follow up with Melody's driver. With Hudson cooperating, they didn't need to talk to any of those who bribed him. For his help in apprehending his wife, he'd get a reduced sentence, possibly even probation. He'd have to step down as prosecutor, but he'd at least have a chance to live out the rest of his life in dignity. That was a lot more than his wife would get.

"Still in town?" Cal asked when he answered the phone.

"I don't have to be back in Wyoming for a while." Kadin had talked of a new case but no contract had been signed yet.

"I bet something else is keeping you here. Aren't you going to open a field office here?"

He'd forgotten about that. With the reminder, he began thinking on it more seriously. If he opened a field office, he didn't have to leave Chesterville. He could stay here, where Kendra lived.

"Did you talk to that driver?" Roman asked.

Cal chuckled. "I sure am glad I don't have your problem right now."

Roman wouldn't call Kendra a problem. Well, unless she shut him out.

"When we threatened accessory to a crime charges, he told us who Melody hired to take care of you and Kendra. We apprehended him and he finally confessed."

"Looks like the case is officially closed."

"It always baffles me how criminals like Melody Franklin think killing a detective and his client will make all their troubles go away. And how in the world did she think she'd get away with poisoning her son's second wife?"

"Don't try to get in the minds of someone capable of killing," Roman said. "Just outsmart them. Killers like Melody are the easy ones. Their vanity gets them in the end."

"Yeah, suppose so."

"It's always bothered me how Melody intercepted Kaelyn." He'd finished going through all the phone records last night. "One of the numbers in Kaelyn's phone matches the driver's. Melody must have used it to lure Kendra to the truck stop."

"Except she must have gotten into her car before they went inside. No one could place Kaelyn inside the truck stop."

"That's what I think, too."

"I'll add that to the evidence."

Not that they needed it. Melody would be convicted of murder and attempted murder. She'd never see the outside of a prison fence.

"Hey. Think over opening that field office."

Cal wanted to go to work for DAI. "You can open it. I'll talk to Kadin and get you in touch with him."

"Naw. You open the office. You know you're going to end up moving here anyway, don't you?"

He didn't.

"I've seen you with her. I may not be big on love, but I know it when I see it and you have it bad for that woman. You might as well give in."

"Thanks for the brotherly advice."

With another chuckle, he said, "Talk to you later," and they ended the call.

Looking ahead, he saw Kendra through her shop window, looking as angelic as the first day he saw her. He walked toward the door, seeing her turn and go deeper in the shop.

Roman entered, leaving the bright and sunny day behind to step into another bright and cheery environment. Christmas trees glowed in multiple colors, each with a new theme added, some to reflect the season.

Midafternoon on a Wednesday, there were no customers.

He heard Kendra talking to Raelyn in the back. He found them at the computer in Kendra's office.

They both looked up, so obviously related with their pretty green eyes and red hair. Kendra was in a yellow dress with a short-sleeved white knit summer jacket and Raelyn wore a soft green spaghetti-strap dress. They both smiled as they looked up, but the smiles had already been there before he'd arrived.

"Kendra's going to teach me the financials," Raelyn said.

"And she's catching on quick despite her joking around." Kendra elbowed her niece. Behind them, he noticed a framed picture of Kaelyn. She sat on a bench holding a single white rose to her nose. She looked up at the camera with smiling eyes.

"We were going over the orders for Halloween and Kendra found an error. She ordered the round-eyed ceramic pumpkin and was charged for a funny-looking, slanted-eyed pumpkin."

She and Kendra laughed anew.

It was one of those things that was funny in the moment but the later explanation failed to express the humor.

"Are you going to start working here full-time?" He hadn't come for small talk.

"Yes. Thanks to Kendra, I quit my other job."

Roman looked at Kendra. "Do you have a minute?"

Both women stopped smiling. Raelyn gave Kendra a look only the two of them likely understood, but Roman felt the young woman knew why Roman wanted to talk to her.

Kendra stood and walked from the desk. He led her outside onto the sidewalk and faced her.

"Are you heading out soon?" she asked.

Did she want him to leave? He watched how she put her hands on her hips, and then dropped them with the shift of weight from one foot to the other.

"Soon, yes." How should he broach the subject? "I've got another case."

"Yeah? What is it?"

"Someone in prison looks like he might have been falsely accused of murdering his wife. His family contacted us."

"Oh. Interesting."

"DAI gets a lot of cases like that. Most of them turn out bad for the convict. We look into them and the evidence usually confirms guilt. But we provide confirmation for everyone. Rare occasions the convict is innocent, and I think this case will end up that way."

"The prisoner is a lucky man. He has one of the best investigating." She smiled up at him, almost flirty, but he could feel her resistance to let go of what she was really feeling.

He observed her a few seconds. She did a great job concealing her emotions. She didn't trust and he didn't really expect her to yet. He just worried she'd never get to the point when she did trust, all the way. If he gave her a chance, would he be let down later? How much pain was he lining himself up for?

"I'd like to keep in touch," he said and felt lame because that only scratched the surface of what he wanted.

"Of course. You have my number," she joked, but she also looked awkward.

"No, I mean, I really want to keep in touch. See each other. Have a long-distance relationship for a while and see where things lead."

Her awkwardness faded and she sobered. "You... you want to date?"

"Yes. Talk on the phone when we're apart and plan regular trips to see each other."

He watched her mull over the logistics of carrying on that way. How often would they be able to see each other? What if the relationship worked and neither of them wanted to move closer to the other?

"Okay."

Okay? "Are you interested in seeing me again?"

Her face warmed and that flirtatiousness gushed out for a few seconds. She smiled and put her hand on his chest. "Yes."

Wow, was that genuine? She ignited him in an instant. Rather than give her too much of his affection too soon, he leaned in and kissed her mouth. Then he hovered above her face for a bit before saying, "I'll call you."

She blinked several times as he stepped back. "You're going now?"

"I fly back this afternoon." He walked backward toward his rental parked along the side of the road, loving how flustered she looked.

That would get her thinking. Come on, Kendra, wake up and shed your fears.

Kendra handed the customer a receipt, feeling as though she operated on autopilot. Roman had left a few days ago and still hadn't called. With each passing day, she grew angrier. He said he wanted a long-distance relationship. Why didn't he call her every day?

"He'll call."

Kendra turned to Raelyn, who wore a teasing look that had grown familiar. She often teased her about Roman. Kendra had told her everything about him and about them together. She had grown so close to her niece in a short period of time. It wasn't possible to spend too much time with her. Kendra could live with her and work with her, and never get tired of having her around. They had become a duo for sure, and family. Kendra went with her to her grandparents' house and had begun to get to know them. She could see why Kaelyn had been so attached to her adoptive parents.

"Yeah, whenever he damn well pleases."

"The waiting is killing you."

"What's killing me is his expectation that he's the one who decides when we talk."

"You could call him."

Kendra immediately shied away from that idea.

"You know what he's doing, don't you?" Raelyn leaned on her elbows on the checkout counter, angling her head to look up at her aunt.

"What do you mean?"

"He's giving you time to figure out how you feel about him."

How she felt about him? Kendra searched inside herself and couldn't come up with words to say. She could only feel a sting in her heart, a tingling kind of sting that warmed her entire body and jump-started her mind.

"Have you ever felt like this for anyone else?" Raelyn asked.

She sure was smart for a twenty-two-year-old. Could she see how Roman made her feel? "No."

"Well, there you go."

Kendra would wait for him to call and she would take this slow. Roman wanted her unbridled. He didn't have to tell her that for her to know. She couldn't be that way with him continuously right now. She needed time. He must have understood that or he would have suggested another kind of relationship. Roman was a man who took charge of his own destiny.

She finished her day at the shop, and they went home, Raelyn to her apartment and Kendra to her house. At the end of the month, Raelyn would move into a new apartment that had a laundry room. Kendra made sure she paid her enough to make her own way. The shop brought in sufficient income and Kendra had planned to hire another store manager this year. Why not train Raelyn?

Entering her house, she took in all the charm of the interior she'd spent hours developing in creative moments and didn't feel the warm welcome she had before Roman had come to town. Normally, her home was her castle. The entry opened to a modern living room in blues and golds accenting white furniture and trim.

She never felt lonely here. Living alone suited her. Now everything was different. She needed company.

Maybe she'd go into town for dinner. She'd be around people and be cured of this peculiar affliction.

As she went to her bedroom to change, her cell rang. She dug it out of her purse, tossing it onto the cream-colored comforter.

Roman.

With a slight, excited tremble, she answered. "I was beginning to wonder if I would have to call you."

"Miss me?"

She wouldn't answer that.

"Good. May I come in?"

Come in? "You're..." She went to the front of the house and peeked out the window.

Roman stood on the sidewalk in front of her house with his phone to his ear. Smiling, she opened the door and waited, placing her phone on the console table. He put his phone into his pocket and with a sexy grin, started toward her.

Uncertainty welled up. If she got involved with him, where would she end up months or even years later? Would he grow restless and move on to other adventures? A man like him needed constant stimulus.

He made it to the door and she let him inside. He faced her in the entry.

"Why are you here?"

"Why do you think?" His gaze ran down the front of her.

He'd come for her. Satisfaction mushroomed in her. It would be so easy to fall for him.

"You're safe with me, Kendra."

He broke down more of her defenses talking that way.

"I'm opening a field office here in Chesterville. My parents are thrilled."

She smiled. "I bet that was difficult for you."

"No. Being with you made me see how flawed my previous thinking was."

"Your previous thinking?"

"Yes. I am doing what I was called to do. My parents have nothing to do with that, other than their support growing up and being great parents. There was, however, one thing I had right." He stepped closer and lifted his hand to touch her face. "I know when something is real, and you are."

He thought the two of them together made something real. She wanted to believe that but there was no predicting the future.

"I also know you need time to give in to it."

He surprised her when he said that.

"Ever since I met you, I thought you might never let your guard down and I worried I'd lose my heart to you and go my own way broken." His thumb caressed her skin. "But then I realized as long as I'm with you, you won't run."

"Won't I?" She looped her arms around his shoulders.

He put his arms around her waist. "No. Want to know why?"

"Yes."

He lowered his mouth to hers and kissed her. "Because I plan on giving you plenty of space and time while I romance you into admitting you're falling in love with me."

Admit— "You *are* bold."

"Yes, bold enough to admit I'm falling in love with you."

She'd been so convinced he would never feel he had something real with her. Her past experiences would make her reluctant to let go completely, but he proposed giving her time, taking it slow.

"Mind if I bunk up here until I find a place of my own?" he asked.

That was taking it slow for him? He planned on

moving right in. The idea didn't upset her or make her feel closed in.

"You'll hardly know I'm there."

Was he kidding? She'd know he was there every second.

Smoke billowed up from the barbecue in Kendra's backyard. She admired Roman cooking burgers, and then watched Raelyn play in the grass with her new yellow Lab puppy they hadn't yet named. The puppy bounded toward her and then clumsily darted away, eliciting laughter from Raelyn. Her grandparents would be over soon.

Kendra reclined in a chair while Roman flipped hamburgers. She couldn't stop smiling herself. He was shirtless in the August heat, and in semibaggy shorts with no shoes. She'd seen him this casual before but not in the same light—and she didn't mean the sun. She felt relaxed with him. He turned and saw her looking at him and grinned.

She knew that grin and that glint in his eyes. Whenever she let down her guard like this, he seemed to get so inflamed. Right now, he put the spatula down. Smelling of smoke and cooking meat, he leaned over her and planted a warm, patient and lengthy kiss on her mouth.

Then he withdrew. "Keep looking at me like that."

"What if I do?" She ran her hands up his chest.

"You'll be stuck with me."

Roman hadn't left since the day he'd surprised her by showing up. She hadn't asked him to leave, either. Nor did she feel threatened. She did have moments where she experienced anxiety over the way she felt for him, but all he had to do was kiss her and she floated back into the warmth of his loving ways.

"I don't feel stuck," she said.

Grinning broadly, he kissed her again.

* * * * *

If you loved this novel, don't miss other suspenseful titles by Jennifer Morey:

RUNAWAY HEIRESS
TAMING DEPUTY HARLOW
COLD CASE RECRUIT
JUSTICE HUNTER

Available now from Harlequin Romantic Suspense!

"If I had someone to come home to, I might be more inclined not
to burn the midnight oil."

The sound of Austin's voice and her desire for the same thing
dropped on her like a ton of bricks. She glanced at him, but he
was polishing off his Danish and didn't look at her. She couldn't
read too much into those words. He was just talking.

"Jenna, I think we need to talk about this thing between us."

She set her empty cup on the tray with a thump. She stared
at him for a moment. "I know. But I don't want to pick it apart,
Austin. I feel something for you and you feel something for me."

"It's not that simple. I'm working on a case that directly
involves your family member, we have a past and if my boss
finds out I'm sleeping with you... Jesus." He ran his hand
through his hair.

"We won't tell her, Austin. It's our business. Sure, we have
a past, and we have some things we need to work through and
figure out, but I want to do that. You have a life in San Diego and
I have one in DC. We have limited time together—do we have to
be rational and serious?"

His expression changing again, he reached down and cupped her jaw, running his thumb along her bottom lip. His eyes were dark and shadowed, but she could see the hunger in them. "I'm a realist," he said, his voice gruff. He caressed her mouth again. "I understand what you want to do, but we'll have to face whatever comes. I just don't want to be blindsided, and I don't want to freaking take advantage of you."

She couldn't help but smile through this serious conversation. "Were you there this morning when I seduced you?"

He released a breath on a half laugh. "Right, and, lady, you did a thorough job of it." He caressed her cheek with his thumb. "I'm serious about this. I don't want to hurt you, and I'm not keen on getting hurt."

"I don't want that, either. But can't we just enjoy this for as long as we can? Save the big decisions for later?"

He closed his eyes and pulled her close. She slid her arm around his waist, and her eyes burned as he caught her up in a fierce hold, his face turned against hers. "All right. I'm apparently weak when it comes to you. I can't resist this…or you," he whispered.

She wanted time with him to discover exactly what had driven them apart six years ago. But a little voice whispered in her head, *You're afraid*, as the wind whipped up into a frenzy and blew hard and hot against the complex. She shivered and he drew the covers up over her shoulders.

Or maybe it was because she might discover something she couldn't live without.

Don't miss
AGENT BODYGUARD by Karen Anders,
available July 2018 wherever
Harlequin® Romantic Suspense books and ebooks are sold.

www.Harlequin.com